1972

ALSO BY MEYER LEVIN

THE FANATIC
EVA
COMPULSION: A PLAY
COMPULSION
IN SEARCH
IF I FORGET THEE
MY FATHER'S HOUSE
CITIZENS
THE OLD BUNCH
THE GOLDEN MOUNTAIN
THE NEW BRIDGE
YEHUDA
FRANKIE AND JOHNNY
   (republished as THE YOUNG
   LOVERS)
REPORTER

THE
STRONGHOLD

A NOVEL BY

MEYER LEVIN

SIMON AND SCHUSTER · NEW YORK

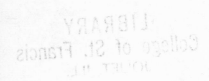

FOR GABRIEL

THE STRONGHOLD

O N HIS KNEES rested the locked steel box. Kraus
had given his driver to understand that the casket contained final orders, but from the way Gunter had of letting
him handle and carry the strongbox strictly and always by
himself, ever since they had picked their path out of the
smashed capital, Kraus knew the lad was not stupid about
the contents.

However he didn't have to worry about Gunter. Despite
the crazy senseless actions and the treachery of even the

most reliable people in these days, despite the fact that Gunter when he wanted something would not hesitate to take it, even if at times this meant knocking someone on the head, Kraus felt sure the box was safe as far as his driver was concerned. For the simplest reason of all: Gunter was his man to the end. The fellow at no time wanted to decide his own fate, his own next movement. And if the very end came, surely Gunter knew his chief would not send him off empty-handed. Besides, when a lad is with a man through all the stink and rot of his work, when he knows just how much his chief has gone through to do his job, why, he can't help having a certain respect as well as the feeling that what a man has got out of it all for himself he has a right to keep.

Behind, in the back seat of the command car, was the other treasure. The hollow decaying wraith back there had even been wrapped in a trench coat against the altitudes. At intervals Kraus, with his hand resting atop his box, half turned his head—enough to reassure himself, in his peripheral vision, of the continued existence of that article in the rear. Time and again, just as he turned his head, the old Jew would stiffen, trying to hold himself erect on the seat, trying to show nothing in his face, not his terror, not even his excitement at being out in the world again, though his hound nostrils could be seen widening to pull in the clean air, the smell of the trees, nature. Nor did the old bastard dare to show the slightest hint of the gloating that must be going on in him that here he was still alive, and the Fuehrer dead. If Kraus caught so much as a glint of this in the Jew-devil's eye . . . enough! He'd have Gunter halt the car, drag out the old carcass and make a corpse of him. He ought to do it anyway.

Yet inside Kraus a denial, like some fainter broadcast under the radio news, insisted that the announcement had been false, it was all a trick to lead the enemy off the track, and here somewhere in the heights of the last redoubt he would soon arrive to lay his final cargo, his trophy, the rarest Jew of all, at the feet of the smiling Fuehrer. The whole thing would then be like after a childish nightmare of the house burning down, when you opened your eyes and saw your papa's smiling face above you.

But also quite clear in Kraus was the knowledge that the radio news was true, and that he needed his backseat treasure even more seriously now, for that Jew-life which he had so carefully preserved within the edge of existence might somehow yet be worth his own. The Jew Premier, for Kraus!

What a sign it was of the enemy's degeneracy to have made a Jew their chief of state. To rescue those degenerates, the might of the entire world had had to be called in. And it was not over, no! It was not over. The rescuers would now turn on each other, tear each other to pieces, and thereupon like a waiting tiger the Reich would emerge from these mountains and be avenged.

Let the old hound nostrils sniff the clean fresh air. *Wet grass, my love's washed hair in the living air*—poems of Paul Vered. Kraus thought of surprising his baggage back there by suddenly spouting a quotation. That would show whether he was an uncultured lout or a man who was thorough and complete, learning everything there was to learn about each task put into his hands.

And momentarily relaxing, Kraus himself breathed in the surrounding atmosphere the way his hostage, despite his unrevealing face, must be breathing it in. The gay wooden fretwork of the *Gasthof* balconies, each wayside inn perched in its cluster of trees alongside a picturesque mountain stream that sang away under the windows. And the building walls covered with pictures of saints and madonnas painted in bright colors. It was even a desecration to have a live Jew still looking out at all this decent Christian life.

And the women glimpsed in passing, coming out, going into their houses, in white stockings and wide free-swinging dirndl skirts, in light blouses with the little tasseled tie-cords dangling between the full, gently squeezed breasts, so that you only had to give one good pull and out they would plop. And the busy children, making him hungry for the sight of his own, the whole kettle of them, his girls and boys. Like the schoolboys trudging home here, in their short *Lederhosen,* and the square-kneed little girls with yellow braids. A picture book! The war had not touched these roads, these villages; this was like driving into peacetime, and Kraus felt a great predictive sense of quietude welling up within him. Only five days from the shambles of the capital, with guns still pounding the walls down, and street pavements exploding in your face, and here was the good peaceful life. He felt a wish that he might be able to share with someone this sense of remarkable contrast. The once-poet in back of him would undoubtedly be experiencing something of the same lofty feeling, but with a clod like Gunter he could share only an occasional appreciation of a female behind.

The Jew back there ought to be jumping out of his skin for having even one day of this joy in nature. After all, for himself, Kraus had not been exactly shut off from the good things of life. This car had traversed all the conquered lands, and each time as he got away from the broken cities it had come to him anew how easily the destructions of man could be forgotten, how the war was still no more than a scratch on the globe. Forests remained standing and vast lakes lay unperturbed; in every countryside there were garden estates behind whose gates an officer might luxuriously sojourn, savoring the plums and ripe apples from the trees. Yes, all this lay on the profit side of his war, he had stored it all in, and if evil times were coming now, he must keep his account correct. For against the drearier scenes of his task there still had been so much that was lively! He had lived the high life and must not forget it when he was back home with the Sunday visits to his in-laws.

And in a great tumble through the mind of Kraus there came the glittering restaurant tables, the shining flanks of his Hungarian countess against her black satin sheets, the lifted champagne glasses in the company of the good comrades of his section, the times in one conquered city or another when a man had but to crook his finger to summon a girl from a nearby table; and also there were the visits home, with the children with their trick of climbing two on each knee, and his wife all polished up for him with her hair plastered into a fancy French style, and hardly able to wait until the children were put to bed—all this, and coming away from the war with the strongbox under his hand—why, he could not have been so stupid after all, for a fellow who had never finished high school! No, he had chosen his service well, his wife had had a good idea to push him to specialize. Even though by now he should have received his promotion to *Standartenfuehrer*, still, a lieutenant-colonelcy was not too bad, particularly with all his special privileges. Never mind, he was not so stupid. He had nothing to fear from the next phase in the world; he would find his way in the days now coming, as well. There need never arrive such a moment for him as for that rotted mummy in the back seat, when he would crawl out into a glimpse of the green world after years of imprisonment.

Why didn't the old bastard show his enjoyment? He must be scared, down to the roots of his lousy toenails. Exactly like an animal that you take from the house in your car, a mangy cat when you mean to drown it. Though even an animal would scuttle around, scratch on the windows, try to do something. A mangy cat, a hound —Kraus couldn't exactly match the animal for the old man in the back seat. A fox? Not foxy, this one. Vered was not the kind to sniff out a clever deal. Or was he perhaps so quiet because . . .

Suddenly caught by a gust of trepidation, Kraus abandoned his animal game. It came to him that his hostage back there was maybe so calm, so unexcited, because he believed he had won, and that this green world would now be his to live in. While he himself, Kraus in the same moment recognized, was in such a peculiar excitement because this could be his own last day, his last sight of natural freedom. Drinking it all in for the last time.

Smash the thought, like a glass against a wall. "Halt!" he said to his driver.

No, not to get rid of the baggage; the carcass might still be useful in some way. A turn here; he must study the map.

The jolting halt threw the ex-premier against the metal side wall of the vehicle, and brought him out of a torpor of exhaustion. Vered felt a chest pain from the sharpness of the air. But he would not permit himself speculation about his fate, or even permit himself sensation, for thought and feeling drew strength, and this might be his last bit of strength, so that he might fail to survive. What an irony, to expire now. This weary body must carry him a bit farther, to witness the denouement: either the final gesture of his assassination, or a more perfunctory, happy-end curtain —liberation. As he had always contended when a critic —why, that was in his youth! How was it that in these later years his random memory always skipped a lifetime of activity to leap back to some example in his youth

time?—but as a critic he had always contended that the
way a drama ended was not really of the greatest importance. If all a work had to say was in the fall of the curtain, why, it was an empty work. Each work of art, each
life, must be continuously saturated in meaning, and so
perhaps even these last years of inaction in the prison had
been the most meaningful for him, and what would happen to him tonight, tomorrow, could only indicate whether
that meaning would remain confined within his own spirit
or might yet be projected to the world.

But he must not think. There were trees all around him.
Why, now that the car had halted, here was birdsong. And
as had always been a failing with him, in the presence of
beauty, tears rose. Vered wanted to call attention, a companion's attention—and with this his drawn-out endless
term of loneliness reasserted itself; could there still be a
capacity in him, could a time still come if he lived, when
he would again be able to look into the eyes of another
human being without shame for all mankind?

He doubted it, doubted it with a profound bleak knowledge brought from these past years in the center of extinc-
tion. Ah, fine—the trees. It would mean something nevertheless to remain alive, for a man could be content with
the presence of green living foliage, that had no capacity
for evil.

THE CASTLE WAS EXACTLY as in the picture books. It sat across a cleft in the mountain, outlined like a cardboard cutout, with its turrets and parapets, against the rising snow peaks.

There even came into view on the other side of the castle, as the car made steep hairpin turns up a byroad, a moat with a drawbridge. And approaching the moat was a toy-model village street in which, in the peacetime fantasies that came over one in this area, one could imagine clockwork figurines of lads and shepherdesses emerging on the hour, for a mechanical pirouette.

The vehicle, pointing upward, seemed enormous, as if it must burst the toy street; but now it entered, snugly, the wheels gently rubbing the scrubbed curbs. Across the narrow sidewalks, a man could reach out his arms and touch the ruby and gold glass panes ornamentally bordering the bow windows of the shops. Sportswear was everywhere on display, white handknit sweaters and mittens, brightly patterned scarves, thick wool hose, fine hand-rubbed boots, and, in an apothecary's shop, Paris perfumes.

In a by-thought, Kraus wondered whether a Panzer

could make it through this lane. Or an American tank—was it broader?

The lane gave into a small cobblestoned plaza, ending on the far side along the moat. Two heraldic stone pillars, emblazoned with designs of a hunter and a boar, in blue and gold, flanked the approach to the drawbridge. The bridge was up.

Again the car halted, gently now, as though the driver were observing the amenities of civilian life. From the side window, Paul Vered let his eyes roam the square, recognizing not so much this particular place as all those that were its counterpart that he had visited in the beautifully illustrated fairy-tale books of his childhood, and then in the fairy tale of young manhood, hand in mittened hand with laughing girls and gay friends. He let his eyes come to rest on the blue and gold of the heraldic pillars, the enameled colors aged into perfect harmony. And this time it was not because of the inconscient beauty of natural life that his heart despaired, but the pang came even more sharply over the intolerable grace and beauty evoked by the hand of man.

Above, a cloud pattern had arranged itself, with white cumulus billows against a sky that was so present, so insistent, that it was like a too-much-repeated message. His entire being protested: No, I don't want to hear of life, I don't want to hear that the Creator exists! I don't want to hear! And the sun below them at the rim of the valley shot upward, perversely, a golden undercoating for the clouds.

The driver tore the enchantment with his car horn. Opposite them, in a deep stone archer's slit, a metal shutter snapped open. Over the sound of the horn, Kraus shouted his rank and name, in that special loudspeaker voice that was one voice, no matter which SS man it came from, and which seemed, just now, to be a mechanical continuation of the car horn.

The approach of his command car up the road and through the village could not have been unobserved; indeed the villagers had seen the car well enough in advance to clear the streets and shut themselves in. Therefore, no excuse here at the castle gate for delay.

And there was no delay. Within a moment, a proper time for assimilation of his name and rank, the reply came from the castle. It came in a correct if unmilitary voice, in the conversational tone sometimes assumed by the very highest command, though Kraus felt certain there was no one in charge here who outranked him. The voice was startlingly near, though soft, emerging from a speaker outlet in the heraldic pillar.

The *Obersturmbannfuehrer* was welcomed; in accordance with regulations, his aide would dismount and present his orders.

At the same time the drawbridge separated itself from the castle wall and swung downward, with the controlled power of an unflexing arm. There was no grinding and clanking, and the upper side of the bridge as it came into view showed beams of steel. All had been properly done here, Kraus was glad to note. In the roof turrets on both wings, behind the slits, he was sure he caught the nozzle glints of heavy machine guns, trained on his car, as was correct.

He made a side nod to Gunter, who stepped from the vehicle. The moment the drawbridge became level, a corporal emerged from a small door hinged into the huge iron-studded castle gate. The back of this door, Kraus again approvingly noted, was steel-plated.

Crossing the bridge to them, the corporal gave the *heil*, took the travel pass from Gunter, and returned with it over the moat. The door opened for him, closed behind him. In ten seconds the heavily armored castle gate swung inward, and Gunter carefully drove the command car across the bridge, which was none too wide.

In the courtyard, moss grew between the cobblestones; flower boxes were on the sills. Not a piece of military equipment was visible, nor were there bars on the windows. Indeed, the command car seemed to have blundered into a mistaken destination, and Kraus had to suppress a fleeting impulse to mumble excuses and back out.

From a carved stone doorway the Baron appeared, walking toward the car with the formal affability of a life-long host. One hardly noticed that he was in uniform. He was bareheaded; his hair, in the sunset light, shone with a silken ash-blond glow, though it was white. His walk was youthful, and his complexion had the baby-skin smooth-ness that comes sometimes to octogenarians; Kraus, mentally reviewing the Baron's file, knew he was turned seventy. His eyes were of the most pleasant boyish blue.

The Baron's salute was the briefest possible; one might

think the gesture was already something of the past. Very well, he would soon learn. Kraus returned the salute in full style, with the curt downsnap that meant business. He stepped from the car. "I have orders to take charge," he said, and presented them, in the isinglass envelope.

The Baron took a moment longer than a glance, to seem formally to inspect the orders, handing back the envelope with the polite carefulness of a man returning some personal document, perhaps a family snapshot, in which he has had to evince interest. "Very good, *Herr Obersturmbannfuehrer*," he said cheerfully. "I trust you will find everything in order."

"I have brought one more prisoner," Kraus announced, with his characteristic side inclination of the head, indicating the rear of the car.

The Baron hesitated as though to understand the borders of his new subordinate role, then stepped to the car, looking in. It was clear that he recognized the enemy's ex-premier, but also there was the barest, fleeting expression of shock on his baby-smooth face. His hand went automatically to the door handle, but he checked his gesture and withdrew, leaving Gunter to open the car door.

Two soldiers, Kraus noted, satisfied, had meanwhile appeared from a barracks in a corner of the courtyard.

Vered did not want to have to be helped out. Summoning energy, he raised himself from the corner of the vehicle and placed one leg outside the door, pulling himself with his arms to secure his balance. He tottered; the Baron watched, even with a slight emanation of encouragement, like a surgeon watching a patient's first postoperative efforts to rise from bed.

The premier succeeded, but did not look at them nor at the soldiers as he steadied himself. In the last few days and nights, from camp to camp, he had managed; let this only be the final place, and he would have measured his energy exactly, like a bowl of soup to the last drop, for there was no more.

How many effectives were on duty here? Kraus demanded. Already, he saw himself in the tower with his loyal men, holding off a great onslaught, filling the ravine with smashed enemy armor.

The normal complement was fifty-two, the Baron said. But in the last few days . . .

"It has been increased?"

Why, no. Indeed, on the contrary—the Baron dropped his voice in an accent of regret—due to the situation, some of the men seemed to be slipping away.

"How many have gone?"

He would have to check, as a number of the guards were quartered in the village.

"I want to see your roster. And a roster of the prisoners." Who knew? This old clown might even have been allowing the prisoners to slip away!

"If you please." The Baron indicated the entrance.

Taking his strongbox from the front seat, Kraus strode into the castle. A deep, lofty hall, spanned by elaborately

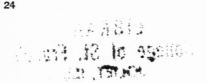

carved beams. Life-size portraits of ancestors, in gilt frames, and larger than life, a portrait of the Fuehrer, facing them from the great stair landing at the far end. Against the side wall was a massive stone fireplace, high enough for a man to stand in, with a spit on chains, large enough to roast a boar.

Kraus had half expected the prisoners to be lined up for him in the hall, as in some British film when the servants of the manor await the new master. He knew the list in his mind, a dozen of them, the Marshal of the Armies, two more prime ministers, a handful of Cabinet members, a troublesome priest of some kind, and there was an unofficial item as well, a woman prisoner who had come voluntarily, the mistress of one of the ex-premiers. Some other time he might have been more interested. But he had not come here to be a prison keeper, nor had he come here simply to turn them over. His orders were open: Take command. In this place, he felt in his bones, he was going at last to fight his war.

In the doorway, the strength of that old carrion he'd carried up here had finally given out; Vered's spindly legs dissolved under him, and but for a guard catching his arm, the relic of a Jew premier would have made a heap of bones on the floor.

Momentarily, Kraus had a sense of misgiving, a feeling that he had brought with him the root for some dreadful error that was yet to take place. Indeed, the Baron's collection of bigwig prisoners here would have been quite enough for a trading stock. Why had he gone to so much

25

trouble to drag this specimen all the way into the redoubt when it would have been enough to leave him in some still-uncaptured camp along the way? Or even finish him off. Who could have known how it came about? Natural death, air attack, anything—if anyone were ever still to ask. No, it was out of principle, Kraus told himself, out of his principle to do a job correctly and completely to the end that he had not let go of Vered. Never mind, the old Jew could still prove to be a trump card.

Meanwhile the carcass had to be put somewhere; the upper rooms were all occupied, the Baron said, but there was a small maid's room under the stairs that might do for the time being. The maid herself, said the old goat, hardly ever slept in it.

Vered was carried to the room. Half aware, he yet knew he had reached a real bed, that he was deposited on a high, old-fashioned feather quilt. As his body melted into the down, he vaguely felt himself melting into eternity and was not sure—and harbored no sorrow—that he would take form again.

FROM THE TIME it had turned off the main road below, the progress of the command car had been excitedly followed from several windows in the prisoners' wing of the castle. But would the Allies appear to rescue them in this singular fashion, with a lone vehicle penetrating the area?

"Yes, why not! German resistance has collapsed, completely!" This was the optimist, Senator Joras, who ran bulkily from window to window to glimpse the car on the turns.

Then Marshal Philippe, using his binoculars—which the Baron as a matter of *noblesse oblige* had permitted him to keep and which had until now served only for bird-watching—was able to determine that the lone military vehicle was still after all a German one.

The little group crowding around him at his window had greeted the news with chagrin. A lone German vehicle, on this last day? "What could they want with us now?" The binoculars passed from hand to hand, and as the vehicle twisted its way up the mountainside the distinguished prisoners swarmed back and forth across the corridor, to watch from whichever room gave the best momentary

view. Could the car be bringing orders for a transfer, so
that their freedom was still to be snatched from them?

"Maybe they want us to negotiate the peace!" the ir-
repressible Joras declared. Why not? Were they not the
last official members of the government, and certain to be
the leaders of the new regime? Perhaps a trade was about
to be attempted by leaders of the Reich?

From the marshal's window they swarmed to Frère
Luc's window, then even to the end room occupied by the
former Foreign Minister, Richard Delorme, who had always been reserved about asking people into his quarters.
Delorme greeted them with formality; his valises stood just
inside the door, all packed.

As the car became visible to the naked eye the swarm
broke up, a few prisoners watching from their own windows, a few returning to Frère Luc's room to listen for a
spark of news from the radio.

In the last weeks, after the Allied crossing of the Rhine,
they had ceased to make any show of clandestine caution
in using the radio. True, the monk's door was usually kept
closed and the instrument was turned low—no higher than
their own voices, which could engulf the broadcast in a
general hum. The military map which Marshal Philippe
had prepared, with its pinpoints, was kept in a drawer
except for coordination during broadcasts, but this dis-
simulation now had an accent of modesty instead of caution, as though it was intended to avoid making more
painful, to the Baron and his entourage, the total collapse
of their army and their nation. The BBC listenings them-

selves however were no longer held in the conspiratorial guise of a study group or with any other transparent excuse. A dozen times a day, at broadcast hours, the flock assembled, and indeed various individuals were continually darting in and out of Luc's "radio room." Even the withdrawn old banker, Barnhard Schall, who had dismissed the world and immersed himself entirely in the painting of miniatures, appeared from time to time, to stand silently listening to the news, and depart.

The excitement of the final advance, the imminent rending of the curtain of space that separated them from the Allies, had brought a curious unity into the castle, so that most of the servants and many of the guards, with wry, almost grinning expressions, would halt one or another of the notable prisoners on a stairway or in the courtyard with the universal question, "Where are they now?" —almost the way adherents of opposing sides in a big sports event will ask each other the score.

In a way there had been more of a relaxation of barriers between the Germans and their prisoners than between the two groups among the prisoners themselves. While the two groups could not precisely be arranged in opposing camps, while through these years of enforced contact there had been a certain fluidity between them, and while a few individuals like the embittered Richard Delorme and the rural leader Auguste Rieber, who had his own set of ideas, had kept themselves apart from either faction, there still remained the two circles, grouped around the two ex-premiers, Remy and Dortolot.

If anything, each man's views had deepened during the imprisonment into that profound well of self-justification that seems to reach to the fundamental source of all urges in humankind. To prove that he was right, right the whole time in everything he did, a man will kill, starve, lie, betray, sacrifice his family, his fortune, and himself. Of these two chiefs of government, neither could be categorized as leftist or rightist in everything he had done, but Remy was thought of as to the left and Dortolot as the conservative. Each had taken part in the government of the other, during the desperate efforts at national unity, just as both had taken part in the government of Paul Vered.

Though Remy and Dortolot had by temperament a rather natural dislike for each other, there existed a degree of grudging sympathy between them, as in two men who had had a great failure together. Too civilized to allow themselves outbursts of personal blame and recrimination, each gave the impression of holding in deep reserve some final knowledge of the other's failings which had brought down the nation. Each was certain he must return to power, when it would at last be seen that he had always been right.

In Dortolot's camp first of all came Marshal Philippe, with his brave wounded air of a man who has been thoroughly misunderstood, a man who has had to bear the blame for the mistakes of others. Together, the marshal and Dortolot maintained toward Remy the air of men who had to deal with a mutual, unconscionable in-law who should never have been admitted to the family. There was between them also a certain masculine camaraderie. They passed a good deal of their time in each other's company, playing chess; they shared their tobacco; and Dortolot was the only person to whom the marshal had shown the memoirs he was writing.

A third who had recently settled into their circle, as though for his final choice before re-entry into home politics, was the ebullient Emile Joras, several times president of the Senate, who in his long career had at one time or another belonged to every political party from the Communists to the Royalists.

As for Remy, his closest ally was the labor leader, Vincent Maasi. Hulking, moody, a man who bore the imprisonment with enormous discomfort, Maasi seemed somehow to suffer more than the others from the same conditions, so that a number of them were impatient with him while a few felt rather sorry for poor morose Vincent. He hung about Remy, according to Joras, not so much because of their vaunted shared radicalism but because of Marianne; poor, fat Maasi was obviously enamored of her, though he tried to disguise this even to himself by moaning constantly for his wife.

Actually Maasi was drawn to Remy and Marianne by a craving for domestic warmth. And perhaps out of the nearness of Marianne, perhaps out of true loyalty to his wife, perhaps in solidarity with all the men in real prison camps who were deprived of women, Maasi would not allow himself the easy contact that a number of the other men had made with the Polish girls who were slaveys around the castle, or with the German women who came in from the village for various household tasks. The most accommodating of these girls and women were always being pointed out and recommended to him by another of Remy's adherents, the knobby-headed press lord, Michaelis, who liked to have it remarked that he was exceptionally vigorous and potent at sixty-six.

Undoubtedly Remy's was the livelier, more human group because of the presence of the woman. Marianne had made an effort to minimize any provocative effect in her appearance; she wore loose sweaters, and virtually no cosmetics, though the German women offered to provide the best from France.

By inclination, Frère Luc belonged in Remy's circle, although he maintained an air of neutrality. Raw-skinned, energetically gaunt, the "social action priest" had before the war become an electrifying symbol of rejuvenation in the Church, and he had been speedily arrested after the conquest lest he become a symbol of resistance. Luc's mission was to the moderns, the godless, the freethinkers; he shook them with the appeal of the equalitarian and the communal in early Christianity. That Vincent Maasi as a Laborite had little use for Church politics, though he had welcomed Frère Luc's help in the great strikes of the thirties, that Remy himself was an agnostic who had had his children baptized only for his wife's sake, did not alienate the priest. Though Luc tried intellectually to bring himself to disregard the circumstance that Remy and Marianne were living in adultery only a few doors from his room, though he told himself that theirs was obviously a sincere and profound union, still the fact of their sin, the proximity of it and the open naturalness of it, pierced to the core of dogma that remained like a live coal within his breast. But beyond everything Frère Luc saw himself as a servant of Christ through the living Church, and therefore his work was with all.

So his room had become common territory. It was there a few days ago in the midst of a BBC broadcast that everyone had heard the first full description of the newly liberated concentration camps, Buchenwald, Dachau, Bergen Belsen, Mauthausen. Nightmarish, incredible descriptions of specially constructed gas chambers in which used-up slaves and masses of Jews were put to death, and of a bank of ovens for burning the bodies.

Among statistics of incomprehensible magnitude, reports of millions of human beings annihilated in the gas chambers, there had been names of important personages. At each name—a member of Dortolot's cabinet, Remy's director of mines, a senator who had sat next to Joras—some special little sound had escaped from one or another of the listeners, almost of guilt at their own safe and comfortable incarceration.

Then came names of important survivors. And suddenly Marianne gripped Remy's hand. "Missing, however, is former Premier Paul Vered, who was known to have been in Buchenwald until recently, and is believed to have been moved to another place of detention."

The name had resounded among them. Vered, alive! At least until a few days ago.

Surely, Remy comforted Marianne, they would not hurt Paul now. They would be careful to preserve him as a most valuable hostage.

Others too repeated this opinion, like an incantation. Dortolot had declared, "It makes one feel the nation has survived," showing that bitter as had been their differences, he was able to rise above them in homage to a figure as revered as Vered.

Even Auguste Rieber, the dark-browed farmer, wouldn't have wanted Vered to die in that way, he told himself. Often when Vered had been in power, Rieber had wished him dead. But after all, no matter what could be said about the Jew, Vered was a patriot. Still, if Vered had not been killed, wasn't it proof that all these tales about their gassing all the Jews were false, or at least heavily exaggerated? It was not the moment, Rieber felt, to make a point of it. There were many things he was storing up in himself as ammunition to be used after the return home.

"How old would Paul be now?" This came from Joras, who at once answered himself: "He was sixty-four when his government fell—"

"Sixty-five," Marshal Philippe corrected, as a man a few years younger, who will not be cheated of the difference.

"That would make him seventy-one." Joras, himself only approaching sixty, gazed around the entire group as a man who had made his point. For with Paul Vered alive, a good many calculations for the return might have to be recast. Joras had not given up his own ambition to become Premier; perhaps Vered would create a split that would give him his chance! But Dortolot, also in his prime for a statesman, remarked that Vered would doubtless have no thought of resuming his career, nor did he believe there would be a public call for him; it was simply good that he had survived.

In Remy's eyes Marianne had sought some private communication that had to do with what Paul Vered had been for them, for her. Yet this was one of the cold moments when Remy could be lost to her, for he too was absorbed in career speculation. "I imagine Paul will retire and write," Remy had said, satisfied.

In the tension of the last few days, with hourly rumors of the fall of Berlin, then suddenly the news of the death of Hitler, none had spoken again of the fate of Paul Vered, though in Marianne anxiety for him had never receded.

Now as the German command car was seen approaching the castle, it was for their own fate that the prisoners were concerned, and nearly all were apprehensive. In Frère Luc's room, Dortolot summed up the possibilities.

Remy had once characterized him as one of those leaders who believe that by dividing a problem into a, b, c, they have solved it.

Optimum possibility, said Dortolot, an exchange. Second, transfer to the interior of the redoubt. Third, the battle was indeed to begin, here.

They watched as the drawbridge was let down and the car entered the courtyard. An officer emerged. Then came a civilian.

"Please—please"—Marianne waited for the marshal to pass the binoculars. Something, a fugitive impulse of recognition, had come to her but she dared not voice it. Only for an instant, in the bearing of that figure in the formless trench coat . . .

Her heart had leaped, but it was impossible really to tell—and then the group had moved inside the castle.

Hurrying toward the central stairway, Marianne saw only their backs as they disappeared into the Baron's wing. She returned to the others; at this moment it seemed necessary for everyone to stay together, waiting.

THE HEAVY OAKEN DOOR, Kraus noticed, swung slowly as befitted life in a manor where doors could not be slammed. The walls of the Baron's office, off the great hall, were hung with mounted heads of animals. There was a broad desk of black mahogany, its legs rising from the backs of small carved lions; behind the desk was an imposing tall chair.

The Baron seemed to hesitate to take his place there, and Kraus for the moment did not want to supplant him. But as one taking possession, he deposited his strongbox on the desk. Motioning the old aristocrat to a gilt sofa, he himself remained standing.

"They think it is over." He jerked his head, indicating the prisoners somewhere in the castle. "No doubt they are packing their suitcases." Kraus glared directly at the Baron. *"You* think it is over. The enemy is only thirty miles away," he mocked. Then Kraus swung his arm to the window, to the snow peaks. "Here, thirty miles could as well be thirty thousand."

With the air of a commander forgiving his subordinate a moment of ignorance and weakness, he opened his map case on the elegant desk. Did the Baron realize just where he was situated? "You are at the mouth of the redoubt. A new war begins here." This was the word he had brought from Berlin. "Three months, three months is all we need, and we will turn them upside down."

Kraus had spoken more quickly than was his habit, and even passionately, for it was himself that he had to convince. Then, from the Baron's indulgent look, he realized that the fellow must of course already know all this, being right in the middle of it. And so he slowed his speech to the matter-of-fact tone of a commander passing on the latest necessary information to a member of his staff.

Behind them, in the high area, important installations had recently been built. Ultra-secret of course, but now that the operation was about to begin he had been briefed on certain items, in Berlin. There were vast cave hangars for the new propellerless planes. Doubtless the Baron was aware that these planes had already been tested in combat a few weeks ago over the Rhineland, taking the enemy by total surprise and driving him from the sky. These new planes were invincible. They were twice as fast as the propeller planes; everything else in the air was now obsolete.

In the mountain fastness, mass-production factories for these jet planes were now ready, and in one month's time the super-fighters would be rolling off the production lines. The enemy had nothing to oppose to them; the enemy was two years behind when it came to reaction motors. Once the new fleet was in the air, enemy bombers and fighters would not even dare venture forth.

Secondly, rocket-bomb installations. London was already half destroyed by the V2, and had barely been saved when the first launching sites had been overrun. But new sites had been built in these mountains, for super-rockets that could reach every enemy capital in Europe. As soon as the redoubt was sealed off from attack, so that their positions could be safeguarded, these rocket launchers would begin firing. Terror would grip the enemy populations, and the Allies would beg for peace.

As if this was not enough, there was a great arsenal of new weapons emerging from secret laboratories in the redoubt. The Baron was probably unaware of it but a stone's throw from here, in another castle, was an experimental laboratory where a new kind of bomb was being perfected. It was whispered that this bomb was of a chemical nature unknown until now. The experimental stage was finished. An entirely new era in warfare would be opened by this explosive, a thousand times more powerful than dynamite. One such bomb, attached to a V2 rocket, could annihilate an entire city, an entire army.

Here at this point—Kraus's finger traced a road line on the map, and at last the mummified Baron was showing some excitement, for he had come to the desk and was bending his head with Kraus's over the area plan—here, heavy armor was on the way to seal off the pass. Vast stores of ammunition and food supplies had long ago been sent to the region. Last Monday the air marshal had left Berlin to shift his command to the secret headquarters in the redoubt. The war would take a new turn. Victory, in the memory of the Fuehrer!

Kraus straightened up.

Like an uncertain pupil who does not know whether he is permitted a comment, the Baron raised his head from the map and remarked, Had the *Obersturmbannfuehrer* listened this morning to the news from the other side?

"Only ours!"

"This close to the enemy lines, one cannot avoid the enemy's powerful broadcasts. The report was that the air marshal had surrendered to the enemy at eight this morning, at a Tyrolean inn. Just here—" the Baron touched the map with his small, jeweled finger—"down here at a crossroad."

"Propaganda!"

"I believe it was authentic. They have recorded his

voice. It was unmistakable."

"*Scheiss!*" Kraus exploded.

Softly, with a tone of some perplexity, the Baron remarked that he did a good deal of hunting in the area: The security sections mentioned by Kraus, he was bound to observe, had not yet been closed off, though a few trains of goods, it was true, had arrived at a nearby station. He was familiar with the sanatorium, farther up, and a number of scientists had in fact arrived in February but they complained that they were lacking in laboratory equipment, and had been spending their time skiing. Doubtless many of the hidden factories and air installations, having been built under absolute and successful secrecy, could be ready for action, but . . .

His limpid eyes gazed directly, innocently, into the lieutenant colonel's.

While the Baron spoke, Kraus's mind wandered; it was as though all this had been inwardly known to him. And all this had been prepared for too. A man must always have alternative plans. The second plan was now being brought as by some automatic conveyor to the front of his mind. It was a plan whose existence he had only half acknowledged to himself on his way here. Yet why, already in Berlin, with an open directive, had he chosen precisely this place with its selection of top-level prisoners for his headquarters in the redoubt?

"There is still the question of the prisoners," Kraus remarked matter-of-factly, an officer brought back from grand strategy to the items of daily routine. Where was the Baron's list?

The Baron slipped behind the desk, opened a drawer, and supplied him with a folder. As Kraus lifted out the sheet of names, he had a curiously disheartening sensation; the entire armored wall that had existed up until a moment ago, an impregnable timeless wall between himself and the enemy, himself and his fate, suddenly dissolved into this single sheet of paper.

And in his mind's eye he saw, as though it were on the reverse of this sheet, another list of prisoners. The air marshal, surrendered this morning. The commander of Stalingrad, long ago, the first. The name of the SS chief, Himmler's own name, seemed to be forming on the list, and far, far down, after other great names, was there even the name of Kraus? Where would he figure? Did the enemy know of his real importance? And two impulses battled, shifting his name high and low.

Among the few dozen most important? Why not? Had he not carried out, virtually unaided, and with the smallest force, a few score men, the key mission of the conflict, destroying the greatest number of the enemy? The number-one enemy designated by the Fuehrer himself?

Yet in another view his name slid far down, virtually off the list, for what was he but an obscure minor officer in a sub-administration? Not even a full colonel. And tomorrow or the day after tomorrow—prisoner Kraus.

Would it be such a deluxe prison as this? Doubtless not!

Not here, he saw himself, but in some mass encampment with thousands of anonymous soldiers, behind barbed wire. That would indeed be best. But then came the echo of gruesome jokes at the headquarters in Berlin: "They have got us on a list, Kraus, have you heard? We are War Criminals. They have all our names, they say, and they are going to pop us right into our own ovens!"

Gangster revenge! Why, here in this very castle was proof that all of the enemy's higher-ups had been treated according to the honorable rules of warfare. Even kept in luxury. Even permitted to bring along their mistresses! It wasn't their wives they had wanted, those degenerates, but their mistresses. And suddenly, distractingly, a parade of his own war females moved across Kraus's vision; which one would he have chosen?

Meanwhile he had scanned the Baron's sheet. A dozen names. "The list is complete? Don't you have one more here? A woman?"

Ah, the Baron said, as though to smooth over a natural social error on the part of a commoner, "the list is complete as to prisoners. One of the gentlemen has a lady, but she is in voluntary detention here. A companion."

"A prison whorehouse!" Kraus snorted. He ought to take the whole gang out and slaughter them and be done. "Assemble them all! I want to see them!"

Just now—before dinner? They would all naturally appear at dinner.

At dinner! Did this baboon eat with them? "I'll see them now. At once!" March them out into the courtyard and mow them down, just to watch the look on the mummy's face.

Like a distinguished hotel manager obeying the whim of a nabob, the Baron said a word to a long-nosed old servant in the corridor, a civilian, who paddled off on his errand.

Meanwhile, the Baron remarked, the colonel must have had a tiring journey; would he care for a schnapps?

As the Baron produced the liquor, Kraus said, "I came through without a stop today. There were stretches where no one knew if the road was still open." He accepted the glass. "My troops are on the way, not far behind me." There was no toast; what was there to toast any more? "My orders are to hold the pass as long as possible. Those are my primary orders . . ."

The Baron caught the opening, all right, for he held his own drink in midair, waiting to hear what the secondary orders might be. No, clearly, from the little worried expression around his eyes, the aristocrat didn't care to have a last-ditch stand made here in his toy castle.

"Secondly, to utilize the prisoners for exchange."

The worried look changed to one of civilized understanding, of complicity. The Baron sipped.

"Or else"—Kraus smashed him with it—"at my discretion, to execute the lot of them."

At least the mummy didn't come out with any nonsense about the legal treatment of prisoners of war. "Is that what you want to tell them?" the Baron asked.

"I want a good look at them."

It was Julka, the lively, easy Polish girl who always came hurrying to Marianne with the latest kitchen gossip, who passed in the corridor now, laughing, to tell Marianne the latest joke on herself. They had put a man in her bed, but an old one! Sick, too. What good was that!

"Is he one of ours?" Marianne asked breathlessly. Julka did not know. He was already asleep. Very tired, very old.

Half afraid of her intuition, Marianne hurried down with the girl, to look at him.

And it was Paul Vered. So frail, his mouth fallen open, his labored breath even in sleep seeming to hover each time on the verge of cessation, his face, with the colorless skin, like some inanimate mask of himself, not so much aged as given its final form, eternalized. She stepped soundlessly to his bedside and touched her palm to his forehead. The peak of her anxiety passed; there was no fever. Then she bent down; she must not wake him, but with all the blessing that was in her being Marianne let her lips hover against the back of his hand.

The girl watched her. "You know him?"

"Yes." In the years in this place it was with this girl alone that Marianne had been able to communicate without that automatic adjustment a woman must always make in talking to a man, even to a loved one with whom she is in total accord. "Julka, he is very dear to me. Watch carefully over him." And she hurried back to tell Remy.

The men were just then coming down the stairs, summoned. At Remy's side, Marianne whispered, "It's Paul they brought!"

His look was joyous. Maasi's, too. Indeed, everyone's, as the word spread in their own little group, and even the others showed gladness. Even among those who had brought him down, there was a look of relief at knowing Vered was alive, and here. His presence was like a sign— they were complete. It was really over.

They were standing, a collection of civilians grouped in twos and threes, small inconsequential people under the baronial portraits. Some wore sweaters, even carpet slippers; only one or two wore neckties—a vacation resort! Kraus had half a mind to snap them into an attention line and treat them like any lousy bunch of deportees. What did they look so pleased about? The woman was there too—he let his eyes sweep past, to come back to her later. An ordinary sweater and skirt, a blonde, younger than he had imagined, not bad, but the kind that you had to look at twice to see if she was anything special. The man next to her, yes, Kraus recognized him from newsreels before the war, the one who was the last premier.

What a collection! They had had too easy a time here. The marshal, in uniform, at least was standing straight, a soldier. He looked the tallest, although that slouched-over bear, the fat one, was probably bigger if he would straighten up. Who was he? The labor leader, the Baron informed Kraus. Vincent Maasi. And there was another premier Kraus recognized, the one in the pressed suit with the striped tie, all ready to step back into office, the famous Robert Dortolot.

Perhaps that would be the one to deal with? For now as he looked them over, an idea, a purpose, came to Kraus, as though it was something he had intended all along. It could even be the reason that had made him bring along the extra one, the Jew. He scanned the notables carefully, while telling himself, Yes, he had every right. If the air marshal had surrendered, surely only after making some kind of deal, why, he too had every right to protect himself. But the approach would have to be made carefully; he must choose the right one.

"Prisoners!" he called out.

Some of them half jumped out of their skins. They stared at him and then glanced at each other as if to make sure they had heard right. Then they turned their eyes questioningly to the Baron.

"We have a new commander," the Baron announced. "*Obersturmbannfuehrer* Kraus has been sent to take charge here."

They turned their faces to him again; all were casting for a meaning. Why? He could see the wheels of all these great brains whirling around: Why, when the war was practically over, why this? And he saw the realization dawn from face to face that the war was not over. And a man could be killed no matter who he was, even on the last day of the war.

Good. Now they knew.

He began to call their names, so as to identify those he could not recognize. What a common lot they were. Not that this was a new experience to him; he had seen the greatest, the most famous, the most powerful pass through the mill—groveling nothings. And it was as though he saw this group too, naked, stumpy, potbellied nothings, no better than a bunch of Jews. There flashed in his mind the arrival lineup on the siding at Auschwitz. And then one time when he had used the peephole to the chamber. It had been a mixed lot in there, men, women, and even kids clutching onto their mothers' thighs where the skirts would be—a regular horror sight. Why did it come to him now? That was another job entirely, not his. But he could see this very lot, their clothes dropped off, the knobs and rolls and lumps of their civilian bodies, the stupid astonishment in their eyes as all their clever ideas, all the ambitions and schemes of their lives, and all their importance came to an end.

The men had answered to their names. "The armies are approaching," Kraus announced. "This will become a scene of battle. Strict discipline will be observed." He let them stand a moment and then snapped, "Dismissed."

The quickness of it really awoke their fear.

They looked to the Baron in dismay, in shock. Conversations were beginning among them: What did all this mean? Who was this officer? What was to become of them under fire?

"Return to quarters!" he shouted.

And with startled looks, half hesitations, murmurings

among themselves—oh, they didn't look so pleased any more—the great men began to mount the stairs.

Motioning to the Baron to follow him, Kraus strode to the little office which he already considered his command post.

But suddenly, inexplicably, his sense of power left him; he felt undermined. He had done something wrong, he had made some mistake. He knew he had made some stupid blunder, and yet he could not think what. He stood stockstill but could think of nothing.

It was as though the finger of tomorrow were reaching to collar him, to whirl him around and place him instead of them on the prisoner line. It was as though all those premiers and ministers and marshals, mounting the stairs, were looking back from tomorrow and mocking at him, as though he had been unmasked, blockhead Bruno Kraus, the tinsmith's son, who couldn't even pass his high-school examination. What was he doing here, giving orders to men who tomorrow would again be heads of their government while he was a prisoner of war? And who was he to crook his finger for a Baron to follow him?

Against this feeling Kraus threw all the power of the last years. What was this puny castle alongside the Rothschild palace which he had made his headquarters? The Baron trotting after him at his command—that was real. The millions of bodies climbing into boxcars at his order, that was real. These ministers and generals, scurrying upstairs at one word from him—that was no play-acting. The Hungarian countess, she had been real to the inside of her insides; no, that was no countess taking her pleasure from the village tinsmith's son, that was a female under the complete rule of her lord. And defiantly, Kraus marched into his command post and took his place this time behind the desk, on the Baron's chair. Defiantly, as though it were no frightened subterfuge but a clever way to circumvent the enemy and preserve themselves for the new struggle in the future, Kraus brought up the idea that had just come to his mind, the idea that he had carried submerged within him on the long journey to the redoubt.

As he talked he knew that it was this thought that had been ruling him from beneath, all the while. Yes, he had come here to fight, certainly he would fight to the last. But all the while, like that Jew-baggage in the back of the car, he had carried this other thought with him.

The Baron knew—did he not?—that the enemy had made a list of what they called war criminals, and had shamelessly announced their intention of hanging these officers and men who had done no more than carry out their military duty.

"Shameful!" the Baron agreed. A reversion to the age of savages. And for some reason half whispering, he reminded Kraus how the Fuehrer himself had believed they would exhibit him in a cage, and therefore had put himself out of their reach. Perhaps that was the best course for anyone on the enemy list? As a matter of honor? And the Baron opened his baby-blue eyes a little wider.

Was the senile bastard mocking him? Oh, Kraus knew what the old toad was thinking; for himself the Baron felt perfectly safe, with the model rest house he had operated here, playing host in his elegant castle! All his guests were fat and prime; why, he had even provided one of them with his mistress, and doubtless supplied a brothel of local *Maedchen* for the rest. No, the conquerors would leave the Baron his honor and his castle, and probably these same high-flown guests would return for summer holidays.

All at once Kraus knew exactly how to use the Baron. The plan came whole. He nearly laughed at the beauty of it. The idea was no longer a shadowy thought but a detailed plan of action, all complete and foolproof in the forefront of his mind. "Some of these prisoners of yours will certainly again be high in their government, even at the top," Kraus said. "Now, I am sure they would be glad to sign a declaration for you that they have been well treated here, to absolve us of any possible accusation of war crimes."

The Baron opened his mouth; the word "us!" was about to pop out. Why, this blood-smeared *Kerl* who had carried out the rottenest job in the Reich—"us!" Did he imagine it was so difficult to understand who he was, coming here with that last Jew under his arm?

"Do you really think any such testimonial is necessary?" he asked blandly.

"It could be useful. With these bloodthirsty gangsters you never know what mistakes can be made," Kraus said. "They have gone crazy with this war-criminals idea."

"And if my charges," the Baron said, "should refuse to sign for us?"

"In that case they must be informed I have orders to execute them." Kraus stared him down.

No doubt he was capable of it, the Baron told himself. With the Fuehrer's death, the movement had died, and this was the degradation. He temporized. "What if none of them comes to power?"

"It has to be one of them, at least for the start," Kraus replied. "The honor of their country will demand that they put things back the way they were. Besides, what other leaders have they got? They will not put a military man in power, they're afraid of it, and their allies won't like it either. It's bound to be one of these we've got right here."

"And do you believe they wouldn't repudiate such a declaration?"

"Once they sign for us, they will be ashamed as their first action to dishonor their word."

The Baron continued to stare, as a man trying to absorb an idea that he himself would never have thought of.

"What I want from you," Kraus went on, "as you have observed them for a long time, is some simple information. Who is the leader among them?"

"Ah." The Baron allowed himself a twinkle. "Their leader. That has always been their trouble, they can't agree on anything. Twenty political parties. Complete instability. They quarrel from morning to night here like a bunch of cockerels."

The word hooked onto a little notion, in Kraus. One was indeed cock of the walk—the one who had a woman.

"Of course they don't quarrel in front of me," the

Baron chuckled. "Ah no. A united patriotic front. If there is some little thing to regulate, they send a spokesman."

"The one with the woman?" Kraus offered his guess. "Remy?"

Usually a committee, the Baron said, but the colonel was right: Remy was generally at the head.

And with him came the other premier, in the striped suit, and the marshal?

Correct. After only one glimpse he had picked them all. Though occasionally the priest replaced the marshal.

This time it must be the marshal, Kraus snorted, so that the pledge should have military weight. Let them be summoned. . . . Or, he wondered, would it be better to make the offer before the entire group? No, before a group there was always danger of heroics.

Very true, the Baron agreed; the colonel understood human nature.

Yes, Kraus felt, he had learned much in the war; he was using well his experience in Slovakia, in Hungary, in Greece, in France. In Poland he had not yet learned so well, but later he had evolved his infallible system: always get the leaders to work for you, to persuade their people for you. Make the committee believe they are helping to save what can be saved. How well this had succeeded! With a few squads of men he had manipulated millions. Perhaps indeed if he got free he would find a way to use all this experience in business or in politics. He could use the high connections he had made, too; he would never have to return to the measly cattle-fodder commerce of his father-in-law, counting off bales of hay. And after a few years the time would come to put the movement together again and he would come into his own!

"Call them!" Kraus commanded. "Bring the committee here."

S TILL IN PART SLEEP, there came to Vered, over the slate-clean country-washed odor of the sheets, the somehow recognized aura of a young woman. The presence brought him a euphoric sense of freshness and renewal, and he let himself float in a fantasy of childhood; this was his mother reaching her face down to him, and in her hand was a glass, all white, his bedtime milk on a saucer, and beside the glass on the saucer was something smelling warm and delicious.

"Drink this, Papaul," the voice said.

For the moment he could not let himself believe in the clarity of his recognition; the echo of the childhood endearment, Papaul, belonged with mother fantasy. He would not yet confirm to himself that this was Marianne, who had in that other world to which he was surely not yet returned, the world of the Residence, called him by the nickname he had given himself in childhood when going to bed, when he would play to himself that he was not himself but Papa, and Mother would come with the milk to say good night, and call him Papa Paul.

It was indeed milk, warm, fresh, with a surface of foam, milk only now from the udder. Though he felt quite sure he had not yet crossed the border into freedom, it seemed he had returned to the world of mankind, where the more docile animals of nature had been domesticated, where good husbandmen and good farmers' wives drew milk from cows, made butter, where grain from the fields became warm bread.

Placing his two hands around the glass, like an infant, Vered drank, knowing he would soon be fully awake, soon understand where he was and how Marianne came to be here. And then she seemed even to enter into his fantasy of childhood—a womanly presence whose garments flutter in and out of a sickroom when one is not really sick any more but only self-indulging. She fed him now with her hand, putting a soft *Apfel* cake to his lips as he paused in sipping his milk.

The goodness, undreamed of ever to be savored again, the fresh apple taste with the melting and dissolving butter crust, the cinnamon aroma, and the milk that flowed the delicacy into his mouth and into his being, was so heavenly that his eyes teared. In these years when he had so skillfully been kept on the edge of starvation, his body seemed to have returned to some simpler stage seen in infants, when food without intervention turned directly into strength. In the same way, with the slightest respose and comfort—he had seen it happen in the camps—the body seemed to regain itself from exhaustion.

Marianne saw how his eyes became washed over as he looked up at her, and then his gray pupils became quite clear. She reached her face down closer and placed her cheek to his. Paul's skin was warm, fragile, dry. He smiled, and breathed a soft "Thank you, my dear," and in his voice there was that exquisite warmth that addressed itself to you alone, and yet never imposed on you. He was himself.

Several of the men had been hovering in the doorway, and now Remy came into the room crying, "Paul! Paul! Thank heaven!" And behind him Vincent Maasi hunched forward, filling the remaining space, his voice the voice of an anxious comrade of many years, asking, "Old man, are you all right?"

Remy bent over the bed. "Paul, they haven't treated you too badly?"

"Not quite like the nobility here," Vered managed, and his words passed back to the others in the corridor; Vered's irony had survived, he was intact!

"We heard only at the beginning, that you were in Dachau," Remy said with a touch of apology for their own luxurious incarceration. "It could not have been very gay."

"No. But it was worse for others."

"And your wife? She went there with you." But at once

Remy wanted to withdraw his words. Marianne felt Paul's fingers pressing her hand to reassure her that the question could be borne.

"She was in the camp for a year," he stated. "For a time they even allowed us to stay together in the special section. Then they separated us. Then when the final solution of the Jews was put under way I learned they took her to the gas chamber. I was apparently classified as still of potential value to them."

He had ended. His statement was complete.

"Then it is all true, what we heard on BBC of the gassing?"

"It has not been told before?"

"Only rumors. It seemed too enormous to believe, even of them. And even now they claim it was all atrocity propaganda."

"It is true," the old man said impersonally, as one might affirm a mathematical truth.

They stood gazing at him, and there became almost palpable a sense of shame, of horror, that extended over the entire human race and even included themselves.

In this moment of heavy silence, an orderly appeared with the message for Remy, Dortolot and the marshal to present themselves at once to the new commander.

Kraus had them stand before him. At least it was no longer Jews that he had to deal with, and he no longer felt the anger and the impatience, the dirt of contact that had crisped his nerves all these years when he had had to listen to their conniving offers, their pleading, the shameless weeping of grown men, when he had had to be on the lookout for all of their tricks, when he had had at times to pretend to make them silly promises in order to keep things moving without disorder. Now he spoke as to worthy representatives of a worthy enemy.

Doubtless they had formed some idea as to the military situation, though certain highly essential facts could not be known to them. Despite propaganda in the news, the war was not yet decided and surprises were coming. As to the immediate local situation, as he had already told them, there would be fighting here—that was why he had come. Fighting on an important scale. "Gentlemen, I am not a prison warden, I am a combat officer, and I would prefer not to be burdened with the protection of prisoners of war. I prefer to evacuate you. I am prepared to send your group down with my own transport, tomorrow, and to release you within a short distance of your own lines."

Kraus paused to allow the good news to settle into them. They kept their dignity however; he was not dealing with small fry. Though permitting themselves raised brows and smiles, they did not burst out with gratitude. Two premiers and the marshal. They were indeed behaving correctly, he would concede.

One condition had to be put on their release, he now added, with a slight shrug so as to belittle its importance. He glanced at the Baron, who stood half withdrawn behind him, and said, "There has been much talk from your allies of punishment. Honest soldiers are being labeled war criminals. We all understand that in war there is propaganda and that these threats are not to be taken too seriously." But still, in the atmosphere that had been created, mistakes could be made in the field by excited underlings. Surely no honorable modern nation would indulge in such vindictiveness, ruled out in warfare since the times of primitive tribes. But simply for the record and to prevent mistakes he asked from them, as high personalities who had been well treated, a statement in behalf of the Baron and himself, a declaration that would prevent any such accusations.

Kraus waited a moment. Their faces were blank. In a light tone he added that under the Baron's hospitality he was certain there were no complaints, and as for himself, he would be responsible for their release.

There. He had played his card. Why did he feel as though he had made a fool of himself? He should have been more clever, should have had the Baron ask for the bit of paper, casually, as a matter of course, with his own name included as an afterthought. The persistent sense of some blunder, something he had neglected or forgotten, welled up again. His mind raced over his entire line of retreat. How could anyone here know who he was? Even the Baron didn't know. He had always kept out of sight, away from the camps. Even on his occasional inspection tours, only the commandants could know him. If the Allies would get him on their damned list it could only be through high-ups.

Damn them all, why was he worried? He was just an ordinary colonel to them, and after all they were still his prisoners!

The marshal tried not to look pleased. But still this was a moment of surrender. For all his bluster, this little lieutenant colonel admitted it was all over; he was scurrying for cover. How scared he was! Why not sign some sort of paper? It was virtually a required courtesy to the Baron. As for war criminals—that could apply only to the very top rank of the Nazi rulers; what a world it would be if a soldier, for carrying out his duty, could be accused of war crimes!

Marshal Philippe turned to Dortolot with an air of assent.

Absorbed in the great sense of release—a car to drive them down to the Allied lines—Dortolot had not yet come to the tacked-on condition. This was the first return into their own hands of destiny, not only personal destiny but the fate of others, their comrades upstairs. He was coming into his own again, a responsible leader. "Obviously we cannot speak for our colleagues until we have consulted them," he said, in the tone of a man who is accustomed to have his colleagues follow his word.

Only, as Dortolot paused, Remy interjected, "Exactly. We cannot even speak for ourselves until we have consulted the others."

The harshness of Remy's tone startled them all—even

himself. Something within him had signaled that there was a complication.

And on his side, irritated by Remy's tone, and by that continuing sense of having forgotten something, the *Obersturmbannfuehrer* burst out as he stood up, "You must be aware, gentlemen, that I came here with alternative orders. I am in no circumstances to be burdened with the protection of prisoners during the final battle for the redoubt."

The three men looked at each other. What could he mean? That he would move them all elsewhere? To the last innermost recess of the mountains, where it would still be a long time before they could find freedom? Then, in each of them, an impossible, a forbidden thought arose; their eyes became opaque. The "alternative order" could not possibly mean execution!

It was Remy who finally spoke. "What is the nature of the alternative?"

"The order is secret," Kraus snapped. "But I advise you to accept."

The nature of the alternative was on his face. "I must have your answer tonight. By eight o'clock," he decreed.

Already, Kraus knew he should not have made that threat. The accursed Jews, it was with them that he had got into the habit of shouting finalities. Still, why should these men choose to risk their lives? They would sign his document; they might try to repudiate it later, but for now he would have his safe-conduct; he would have time to work something out.

As they retreated from the room, Remy broke out at once with the conviction that had been augmenting in him until it was like a loudspeaker shouting: "Why should our signatures on such a paper be so important to this Kraus unless he committed war crimes!"

"Oh, come, Remy!" The marshal strode ahead to impart the great news—liberation! "He's a little lieutenant colonel, nervous over his great responsibility for the battle here. Naturally he wants us out of the way."

"And he wants a little insurance!" Dortolot was jovial. "Remy, can't you see things at their face value for once! We will simply write out a little recommendation. After all, he did bring out your dear friend Vered." With sudden youthful vigor, Dortolot was leaping up the stairs two at a time; he probably already saw himself riding into the capital, waving at the throngs.

Let the two of them take credit for the great news. Remy turned toward the room where Vered had been put.

Marianne alone had remained with him. As Remy opened the door, she raised her eyes; they were luminous. Now she had them both again, like father and husband, even though neither was exactly the case.

For an instant that joy in her eyes carried Remy away, even from the question of Kraus. And Remy had an odd prefiguration. He saw her too riding into the capital, and Marianne was with Vered.

Why not with himself? The image was brought, Remy knew, by a ferretlike aspect in his mind that he was sometimes ashamed of, but that nevertheless had pointed him in his rise. For Remy too had had the vision of the return, of riding back to the hailing crowds, and where would his car halt? It had to be at the very door from which he had left, the Residence. And would Marianne be at his side?

Until now it had been so. It was the only honest way. Even now he exorcized the ferret thought; he himself would return with Marianne, openly, and all the problems concerning Carmela and the children would have to solve themselves at last. With a war in between, one did not come back to find such problems unchanged.

He checked himself. All this was sheer euphoria. It was not so certain that any of them would be going back at all. "Paul," Remy asked, "this officer Kraus that brought you here—do you know anything about him?"

Vered knew. During the whole of the war, Kraus's particular task had been to administer the Final Solution of the Jewish question. It was Kraus who had devised the entire system of the extermination camps, the gas chambers, the ovens.

Behind the marshal's closed door the room bubbled, a busy headquarters. Unlike the others, the marshal had refrained from adorning his room with family pictures or personal items; indeed he had had all the decorative matter removed—pictures, bric-a-brac—and had sternly confined himself to a bed, a desk, a few chairs.

In one corner Michaelis, his bald dome beaded in concentration, was trying to formulate, with Dortolot, a statement of good treatment that would come within the commander's request while remaining essentially meaningless. At home, in his editorials, Michaelis had been a master at this sort of thing. Meanwhile the marshal, standing before his desk, was expounding the situation in that flat voice of his, with his characteristically long-winded definitions of the obvious. It was true that if the Germans made a resistance here, the geographical conformation was highly in their favor and a delay of weeks or perhaps even months could result; therefore if a proper formulation could be found . . .

"Ah, here's Remy." Michaelis started reading a phrase for his approval. " 'At considerable risk, undertaken in the interest of saving the life of former Premier Paul Vered, the aforementioned Colonel Kraus—' "

"I can now tell you about Kraus," Remy said. It was even a relief from the bleak, leaden disgust that had taken possession of him, to bring them down to his own reality, to watch their toy freedom drop from their hands.

It was Kraus, he told them, who had measured with a stopwatch how many moments it took for three hundred men, women, and children jammed into a sealed room to die from cyanide gas. It was he who had calculated the quantity of gas needed and taken bids from chemical concerns to find the cheapest mixture. It was Kraus who had timed how long it took to clear the gas chamber of bodies, and calculated how many batches could therefore be put through in twenty-four hours of constant operation, and how many ovens were needed to keep pace with the gas

chambers and burn all the bodies. It was this little lieutenant colonel who had reasoned that the cost of a bullet in
the back of the neck was higher than the cost of a shared
gas pellet, and argued that mass extermination at central
death camps was the method of choice. This was the man
who was attempting to extract from them a statement he
hoped would absolve him of war crimes.

As Remy spoke, their effervescence congealed. Until
this moment, what they had heard on the radio and even
what they had heard a while ago from Vered had not
come home to them. The image of that ordinary officer
downstairs in this house, who had done these things, over-
whelmed even the image of the armies of liberation coming to their rescue, for from all this that had already been
done, mankind could never be rescued. To a few of the
men, Frère Luc, Maasi, it seemed now a travesty even to
try to rescue themselves.

And by the same token, it became clear that Kraus's
ambiguous remark about an alternative, should they refuse
to sign for him, did not mean transfer to a remote area of
the redoubt. It meant slaughter.

Michaelis dropped the sheet of paper on which he had
been writing. The marshal sat down. His neck had turned
red.

Vincent Maasi's eyes stopped floating and remained
fixed on Remy's eyes, as if to ask for a final confirmation
about Kraus, and then Vincent shambled from the room,
looking so bleak that Frère Luc hurried after him.

But it did not take long for their revulsion and despair

to turn. Du Caux, in his febrile, clipped manner, snapped at Remy, aside, "Really, Remy, wouldn't it have been better for you at this moment to have kept all this to yourself?"

And Auguste Rieber came out with it bluntly, his words tumbling over each other in the thickness of tongue that affected him when excited. Why had Vered come here to bring his Jewish curse on them! Could they help those who were already dead? Tomorrow morning they would have been free! They would have signed in good faith, and afterward if anything came out about Kraus the question would have been up to the Allied courts!

Generally no one paid any attention to Rieber's ranted outbursts. But now even his anti-Semitic allusion was swallowed, in their stupor and fear.

Michaelis, with his journalistic bounce, was the first to recover. Very well, now that they knew who Kraus was, they had all the more reason to outwit him. Use him. Against such a man all means were legitimate. Give him the document he asked for, and the moment they were free, repudiate it and bring about the capture of this monster.

Joras vigorously agreed. A statement signed under the threat of massacre was like a confession signed under duress! Michaelis began to rework his document, and something in Remy revolted. Why was this humbug grouped with him! Michaelis could always be counted on to voice the easy way, the way that had inwardly to be refused. His glib, amoral mind was Remy's anticonscience. And automatically the pain came, whose existence Remy wished to deny in himself, that dullish throbbing pain in his upper arm. Dismissing it as tension, he yet knew it was a signal of some profound, final incompatibility between what he was and what he wanted and pretended to be. Shuddering, Remy commanded himself to face the real problem in this room. He would have to be the one to speak out against this devious form of self-rescue, this national rebirth in chicanery. But what could he offer instead? Mass martyrdom? Who could counsel others, between a lie and death? Or even for himself? Was he such a moral hero?

He was posturing. The simple, plain necessity was to find a more honest way to rescue themselves. He spoke. "We in this room represent the national leadership. Our return, no matter what happens afterward, represents the return of the government. Can we return under such a subterfuge?"

"Have you another suggestion, my dear Remy?" Dortolot asked bitingly.

Remy as yet had nothing to offer, but surely this was no time for competitiveness. "Among all of us—we are not stupid—we must be a match for this one Nazi. We must find a way."

They turned from him; then he saw that Paul Vered had come into the room, leaning on Marianne.

It was only a moment after he had identified Kraus to Remy that Paul Vered realized he had placed everyone in a fatal dilemma. The shock had brought back a measure of strength; he had to go to them.

They all turned to Vered, Remy saw, as the moral arbiter. So it would still be at home. It would be to old Vered that the populace would automatically turn, as the pure one, the one who had suffered.

He had not wanted to put them in an impossible position, Vered said. Where he had been, a different view came of life and death. One existed as within death, and so while the instinct of life preservation held to the end and beyond the end—for in the camps there existed a kind of walking dead whose spirit and awareness had already deserted them but whose starved bodies functioned on, not knowing how to cease—from the viewpoint of a death camp, death had no meaning. And in a parallel way, morality had no meaning. For some, morality retained an existence in itself, as their bodies existed in themselves. Therefore decisions were made on a more elemental level. Unthinkingly, he had placed before them the most difficult of moral decisions.

Auguste Rieber glared at him with a density that seemed actually palpable, as though it might force Vered's presence away from them and restore the situation to what it had been without him. Within himself Rieber fought to maintain his Christian humanity, to be shocked by what those devils on earth had done to Vered's people, but against this was the automatic tightening up of all his senses that had always, even in the days before the war, come upon him at the mere sight of this man, at the sound of his voice. He didn't have to hear the words. The same high-sounding words that always meant in the end that you couldn't do what you wanted to do. But Vered's presence withstood the glare, the presence would not go away, and Rieber turned his eyes to du Caux. Though he hated the aristocrat too, there were times at least when du Caux seemed to think as he did. But not now. That damned snob was listening to Vered with a look of agreement.

There were things you did and things you did not do, without any measuring of the consequences, Vered was saying; and to this du Caux in his mind agreed.

A moral absolute, Dortolot thought. Vered had closed the way. In his same old style of moral reference he made compromise on some questions impossible. Then what? Tears? Resignation not from office but from life?

"But he means to shoot us!" Michaelis shouted.

Remy heard himself saying, "No! He means to frighten us. He didn't even dare make it a clear ultimatum." Why assume that Kraus would carry things to the extreme? "The whole thing is a bluff!"

How far back his words echoed. How many times, in crisis after crisis before the war, had he not uttered these same words? Wasn't it ever possible to learn? "Follow through his possible actions," Remy said. "If he harms us he is finished for certain, a confirmed criminal on his own initiative. He will doubtless claim he had orders, but even so, such an act would be too much. If on the other hand he can show that he refused to carry out those orders, and saved us, then he can claim some consideration for himself for the past."

Marianne's eyes had darkened. He knew that look. It had come on the word consideration.

"But you can't mean, Remy," she said, impersonally, simply as another voice at the meeting, "you can't mean that this man would be spared for sparing us, the few of us here—are you counting our lives as equivalent for the millions he exterminated in the camps?"

"No, no!" How she could at times completely misunderstand him. Remy turned to the men, to Vered. Vered knew, they all knew, he could have not the remotest thought of letting such a monster escape. He had only been presenting a tactic, a possible argument to use on Kraus right now, in this immediate danger. "We must use what *he* thinks, not what we think." They must sway the rat with the rat's own reasoning. Doubtless Kraus would argue that he had never been responsible for the mass killings, that he was only a colonel, not even a full colonel but a lieutenant colonel, a lower officer who carried out orders, a cog in the machine. Hence he could be persuaded that if he today acted on his own initiative and released this group without any promise on their part, he could come before a war crimes commission and prove that at the first possibility of acting on his own he had defied his orders. Yes, using his own amoral mentality, this was the argument to present to him.

She was following him with her intense, probing look.

The others appeared skeptical of his psychological maneuver. Vered, who he had felt would back him, look preoccupied, as though he had lost interest, even contact. And Marshal Philippe now suddenly proposed another solution —to fight. Next, Frère Luc would propose that they pray! Remy burned to fight, to strike out at last, but how could they, a dozen elderly men without a weapon among them, stand against the tough fully armed guards?

"Wait!" It was all a question of strategy, Dortolot declared glibly—the same glib Dortolot who with his strategy had planned at the very outset to get the Nazis to attack Communist Russia and leave the West alone. That had worked fine, in reverse.

He was persuasive, as ever. What was the situation? he began. A new commander, this Kraus, had arrived, declaring this would be the scene of a heavy battle. Did the local guards want such a battle? They had had an easy time here, a quiet war, and were glad to be coming to the end safe and sound. Indeed a number had already, in the last few days, slipped away. Why should the troops here suddenly risk themselves in a hopeless battle, and die in the last days of a lost war?

"Kraus says he has his own troops coming," Remy pointed out.

"A lie!" Joras jumped into the argument. "He came here alone, with one man, his driver. And a hostage. It has every appearance of a desperate lone flight." He turned to Vered. "Paul, have you seen any troops following Kraus?"

What had he seen? What stood before Vered's eyes was

a circle of bodies fallen just within the gates of the camp. The prisoners lay in a geometric pattern, accentuated by the stripes of their garb. And in his ears there remained the rhythmic hammer strokes of the pistols, as he had often heard them during the years in his bunker, the same hammer strokes that had accented those endless days in the camp, each stroke representing a shot in someone's neck, from behind. So long had he himself waited in expectation of that bullet, so long had he been adjusted to its coming, that to be released alive was the harder, now, to comprehend. He could more readily envision everyone here led out in file into the courtyard or onto the parapet, and the file dispatched one by one as the liberators approached.

To place himself here in a discussion of resistance, of strategy, of the exercise of their own choice and will, still required a laborious turning of the mind. He was assimilating the first stage—he was no longer in an endlessly protracted loneliness and silence, but in a room with people of his own life. He was again in the nearness, close to the touch of this young woman who was one of the dear ones, the so few dear ones in a man's lifetime, Marianne, who had sustained him in that empty time long ago between his two marriages, sustained him with the same compassionate energy that came to him from her now.

Troops? they asked.

He must evoke the entire confusing time of the emergence from the camp. There had been lines of prisoners, marched off on the road. He had heard shouts, commands, the loud hard whistles, and the occasional short gun bursts. Guards from the camp, motorcycles, what else? Troops, squads marching, but under some other command. In the car, then, with Kraus. They had passed armored forces on the road. They had stopped overnight in other camps, he hardly knew where or how many nights. And always and again in the car, behind Kraus. There had been halts, changes, times of waiting; he had seen smashed vehicles, tanks, huge guns, all pushed to the side of the roadway, overturned, abandoned. But their own car had gone on. There had been a railroad yard and a train, and Kraus shouting and running back and forth while he had remained in the car. But of troops belonging to Kraus, in the command of Kraus, he did not know. Still, he had to remind them that it might be very true that troops were on the way, for it could not be doubted that some sort of plan existed for the redoubt, curtailed and torn as it might have become.

"Conclusion," snapped Joras, "a bluff. Kraus has no men of his own. This Kraus is an administrator, from what he says. He has never commanded any combat troops. He is alone with his driver."

"He has taken charge of the force here," Remy reminded him, dubiously.

"That is exactly the point, my dear Remy." Dortolot was patronizing in his exposition. "We have only to persuade the Baron to resume command of his own men, who are in no mood to fight." And now, even though it was his opponent who had thought of the plan, Remy saw its possibility. For what Dortolot and Marshal Philippe intended was as usual not to fight. The marshal was scarcely proposing a bare-handed assault on their executioners as they were marched to the wall. No, they must simply turn the Baron against Kraus.

This should not prove difficult. Until now the Baron had had a perfect record to present to the Allies. Only by becoming involved with this mass murderer did he risk being branded as a war criminal. "If the Baron permits any harm to come to us," Dortolot sawed on, "even if he is commanded by a superior officer, he jeopardizes himself. If on the contrary he joins us and even helps to capture a war criminal like Kraus, a war criminal who is certainly high on the list, why, then he is in a most favorable position." He smiled as though by this exposition the deed was already accomplished.

"That's right!" Rieber agreed. "Kraus is alone. All the Baron has to do is throw him out!"

"Then the Baron surrenders his garrison to us!" Joras cried. A new euphoria seemed to have seized them all as they vied with each other to give examples of guards who in the last weeks had begun to curry their favor, to speak of the folly of the war, even to make remarks indicating they had never been in favor of Nazism.

There were one or two hard-core Nazis among the guards, to be sure, Marshal Philippe cautioned. And it must be kept in mind that military discipline was not exactly easily swept aside, and that the SS was a model of discipline. Men like the platoon commander, Schreiter—

"That bloodhound!" Michaelis wiped his dome with his palm. He had never stopped feeling the fellow would take a potshot at him.

"We must ask ourselves, would Schreiter follow the command of the Baron or of the new officer who is his superior?" the marshal asked.

"We might have to cut down Schreiter," Remy heard himself say. Why, he had fallen in with them. He saw himself springing at Schreiter from behind, with a knife, his left arm locking the throat. Something within him demanded risk, battle, a fight for his own liberation as the authorization for his return.

But Joras answered, "Attack Schreiter and you arouse the whole barracks against us. They'd never surrender then." And with the clacking note in his tongue that always presaged an about-face, "Suppose we reconsider. A statement given under duress—"

Frère Luc, who had quietly brought the depressed Maasi back into the room, cried, "No!"

"Frère Luc, we know that every priest has a germ of martyrdom in him," Joras began.

But the monk cut in, booming forth his own solution. Their salvation lay with the people, the villagers! The people must be alerted, warned that a great crime was in the making and that if it took place their entire town would be razed in revenge, as by the hand of God! Many of the townsfolk were devout Catholics. And many had worked in the castle. These people could influence the guards. Schreiter himself was about to marry a young war widow here. "We too have friends among them. We must seize the loudspeaker, we must let down the drawbridge and call on the townsfolk to overflow the castle and prevent this crime!"

Even if Luc's wild scheme could work, Remy felt dubious. To be rescued by the Germans—no. It was not yet the moment for this, much as he believed in an eventual entente.

Others, too, would not trust Luc's idea. "They'd come in and slaughter us themselves!" Joras sneered. And there were objections against the plan of putting their faith in the Baron, as well. Why, everyone knew that the Baron was one of the earliest financiers of the Nazi movement, the industrialist Astuque reminded them, with his air of conveying information that not everyone but indeed only the highest insiders really knew. They could well imagine that if any day in the past four years the order had come to execute them, the Baron would unblinkingly, with the most distinguished politeness, have carried out their deaths. He had been correct to them, yes, but he had never been one iota less than loyal in his adherence to his party. Though Astuque intervened rarely, it was always with the finality of a man who has lost patience with the disputes of politicians whom he himself put into office. No, the Baron could not be counted on to join them against his own commander.

"But still, the Baron might not even know who Kraus is, what he has done, and how much he risks in being paired with him!" Marianne cried out. "All these things were done in the greatest secrecy."

Astuque merely glanced at her without replying.

"How could he not know? He is a high Nazi," Michaelis responded for him.

"Even among them." She turned for corroboration to Vered.

Could this be possible? Could both truths be possible, that millions were put to death and that the executioners were not known?

Here he was asked once more to bring together the ends of the impossible. An opacity had grown over his sense of involvement, like some graying cataract over one's vision. Yet by their very turning to him, the opacity began to lift, and Vered felt that clarity would return. "It depends on what we mean by knowing," Vered began, and Remy shuddered inwardly, for what was the use now of another philosophical abstraction?

"Even in the camp," Vered explained, "most of us were aware, and yet we did not know, in the full sense of accepting the knowledge within ourselves, that in these buildings at the far end of the compound a massive system of death was administered. This was too much for our minds to accept as a fact of human behavior, and so we let it remain in the area of legend—it was behind a wall."

And Kraus too was therefore a legend, his function a legend. The death crews, the prisoners forced to operate the gas chambers, were themselves in their turn put through the extermination apparatus, so that there was never for more than a few weeks a living knowledge of the deed itself. The only certain knowledge could be the final knowledge, the experience of death in the chamber. And as though this knowledge, this shock at what men were capable of, grasped only in the final instant, could persist even in the corpse, the bodies were incinerated. All that remained was rumor and legend, even though the deed took place continuously only a few hundred yards away, year after year. The vastness of it was too much for the human psyche to accept.

"It will probably take twenty years for the world to accept the evidence," Vered predicted. "And even then, many will say it is all a legend. Yet in the camp some of us came to accept it. After my own wife was murdered in this way, I felt I had yet a work to do on earth. And so we found ways to learn who gave the commands."

That the death apparatus was carefully kept in obscurity could not be doubted. But as the vast operation continued over a period of three years, as a small percentage of survivors within the system were moved about from camp to camp, a slow accumulation of knowledge was transmitted. The method of command was known, and the structure of the special organization. The identity of the sub-colonel who administered the death factories had been known perhaps only to a few score men of his own department, and it was therefore possible—Vered apologized that his reply had had to be so complete—it was possible for even the Baron to have been unaware of the real function of this man, and he might therefore even now be unaware that in coupling his name with Kraus he endangered himself. "If he does know who Kraus is, then our situation is in any case unfavorable and we risk little more in approaching him. But if he should not know, we may help ourselves by telling him."

A WAY HAD TO BE FOUND for the committee to speak to the Baron, without the presence of Kraus. It was Maasi, moodily staring out the window, who saw just then that the new commander was occupied in the courtyard.

Kraus stood there talking with Schreiter while his driver and two other soldiers lifted baggage out of the car. Meanwhile, the Baron must be alone.

In the ubiquitous way he had of always seeming to be passing through the hall, or up and down the grand stairway, the Baron greeted the committee on the landing. It was a mark of his correctness that he had never invited any of them to the other side, to his own wing of the castle.

Something a touch more personal than his usual smile of host to guest was offered them today, and Remy felt certain of the Baron's next remark, and it came: Ah, now that this disagreeable episode was nearing its end, he would be resuming his life of seclusion here. Unless, he added with a worldly, resigned chuckle, it was now his turn to become a prisoner.

"That is precisely what we wish to discuss with you, if we can have a moment alone," said Dortolot.

The Baron glanced hesitantly downward toward his office, and then with a quick, understanding nod, he skipped ahead of the committee, leading them back to their own corridor. The first room was Remy's.

"Shall we go into your room?" the Baron asked. "It would not be an inconvenience for Madame?"

"Not at all, she is not here." Marianne had remained behind with Vered and the others.

The room was a large one, with the bed unobtrusive, in an alcove, and Marianne's feminine things confined to a small dressing table in a corner. Nothing more than a hairbrush, a hand mirror, a few small bottles of lotions. By the window stood Remy's desk, and backed against the desk was a small sofa which, with a few upholstered chairs, and a little table with tea things, provided, through the smallest means, a sociable atmosphere, a "woman's touch."

The marshal came at once to the point. Of the ultimatum that had been given them a while ago in the Baron's presence, the Baron surely understood there could be nothing to discuss.

The Baron's face turned blank.

For the Baron alone, of course, Dortolot put in, a recommendation would willingly be supplied.

"But I have no power to release you now," the Baron

reminded them. "The colonel has taken command."

"Baron," Remy said, "do you know who this colonel is, exactly?"

The Baron gazed at them with innocent candor. "Colonel Kraus has lately been placed in charge of all prison installations, and we come under this classification."

"But are you aware of his activity during the war?" Remy asked.

The Baron appeared mystified.

"Of his special occupation in regard to the concentration camps?"

For the slightest instant the light blue eyes were in flight. But then they became fixed in their usual nowhere. "Naturally, I am aware that there has been a great deal of atrocity propaganda about some of these camps, if that is what you are referring to."

"We are referring to mass extermination by gassing," Remy said.

The clear eyes did not waver. "Even if, though it is most difficult to believe, there proved to be some basis for these stories—"

"Baron, just now you have an eyewitness in the castle, if you care to inform yourself."

"But even so, what would this have to do with Kraus? He has only just now received command of the prisons."

"Previously, he was in charge of the extermination program," Remy said.

The Baron let his mouth fall open.

Now Dortolot put in, "You understand we could not

possibly sign any document for him. But surely, Baron, it would be unfair to you for your name to be associated with his. Now if as a consequence of our refusal he should attempt to carry out his threat against us—"

The Baron made a gesture of dismay, of helplessness.

Dortolot, in his most solemn voice, concluded, "It would be most important for you, once we were eliminated, to show that you had no part in it. We are your prisoners. You would be linked with this mass executioner."

Standing erect, Marshal Philippe, like a ghost at a future tribunal, solemnly nodded his head.

"But Kraus has assumed command!" the Baron cried. "If what you tell me is true, and I assume that your colleague Paul Vered has given you this information, then the arrival of Colonel Kraus is indeed unfortunate for me as well as for you. But how could I know of this—this activity of his?" The Baron showed a shiver of revulsion, like someone who has accidentally stepped on filth. "How could I know this was happening when even your own radio reports emphasize that it was all done in the most absolute secrecy?"

The Baron knew. Behind the unfocused eyes, he saw himself in an evening at Berchtesgaden, not too distant from here, higher up, more spectacular in view, more suited to the expression of the great, impassive surges of nature, more suited to the creation of ideas on a vast scale, and to contemplation freed from the confining effect of human contact. In the closed, private chamber for viewing films, he sat at the side of the loved one, and watched the motion picture that had been made for the eyes of only the highest, showing the process of the final solution.

Despite the moments of faulty execution and imperfection, despite the intrusion of human ugliness and disorder, there were times when the grand design stood clear in all the audacity of its conception, the way a vast work of engineering soars out of the trammel of dirt heaps and scaffolding, and the confusion of tiny, dirty bands of toiling men.

Although the code name was mysterious and foreboding too, and had made him wonder whether he was strong enough to follow into the ultimate reaches of experience already pierced by the select few, the Baron knew what was meant by the words Final Solution, and the tight little jesting phrase that went with them: "up the chimney."

For though he had preferred to spend his time, once the war was under way, in the semi-seclusion of his own mountain retreat, with his special guests as his war responsibility, he had nevertheless made occasional sallies into the victorious world, had attended triumphal celebrations and functions, and from time to time been at Berchtesgaden. What he was seeing on the private screen, he had somehow always known. He seemed to have known it as in some premonitory vision, from his very first encounters with the loved one, and finally to be seeing only the confirmation.

The arrival of the long train of boxcars, with the SS

men waiting at their correct intervals to open the sealed doors, was remarkably effective as an opening expression of the orderly carrying-out of a great planned intention. The exposition, with the clean empty chambers waiting, with the camera pausing to show the details of the false shower heads thoughtfully placed to placate fear and panic, and the handy undressing rooms with their neat rows of waiting clothing hooks, the counters where soap would be dispensed—all this had a certain purity.

For surely the overall vision itself was the vision of a genius with an artist's sense of design, an artist's lust for perfection—an artist whose material was the world. And with the complete daring of a great artist he would use this material with utter freedom, freedom from tradition, from sentiment, from preconception, shaping and forming, cutting and throwing away, creating a new structure.

Perhaps the loved one's romantic urge for a perfectly ordered society could more clearly be understood in his euthanasia program, destined to cleanse the world of the misshapen, the incomplete, the malformed and the idiot-minded, all the refuse that would have been swept away in the garbage of any well-run industry, where man was God. The larger step, to cleanse the world of an entire race, a people who really didn't fit anywhere into the plan—this was the conception that confronted the Baron now, in its final form. What he had heard until now had been in the way of sketches, ideas. Here was the work itself.

As the film progressed, the Baron had struggled to maintain the logical, objective view, struggled against a distressed, growing inner certainty that the loved one had in this area gone over the borderline into—yes, it had to be named for what it was—a streak of madness. Though he had kept repeating to himself the truism that genius and madness were interrelated, and though he had kept insisting to himself that he, a limited spirit, should not presume to set limits for a genius, there remained in the Baron an utter sadness, a fatally helpless feeling, as when one's hand encounters, under the breast of a beautiful woman, the hard nodule of cancer.

Not that the Baron had any liking or pity for the Jews. On the contrary, he had always, even when his wife with her artistic and radical pretensions had polluted the castle with writers and theater folk half of whom were Jews, and even while he had assumed the most liberal of airs, he had always retained his familial aversion for their intrusive energy; and naturally after that same wife had made off with one of her *Yupen,* an opera director, he had allowed his dislike free sway. Yet one could not permit a personal disinclination or aversion to become a ruling factor in one's thinking, in one's view of an issue that confronted the whole of mankind.

Though he had fully understood and agreed with the value of the program to cleanse Germany of the Jewish pollution, the Baron would never in his own mind have conceived of pressing the solution to what here appeared to be the logical end. Yet as the specially prepared document unrolled before them, the Baron again asked himself whether he had a right to judge the loved one, any more than a layman would have the right to judge a gifted surgeon who was about to cut out a parasitic growth from the world.

No, it was not the theory of ridding the world of Jews that upset him. It was doubtless the shock of watching the operation itself, even though it was clear that for this film an effort had been made to show it at its smoothest.

When his father, the tall brute with the mustache that flared at both ends, had first taken him hunting, he had been squeamish at the task of removing the steaming entrails of the kill, and had not wanted to eat the meat. But this was common in overcivilized man, and the aversion soon passed. On a tour of the famous stockyards in Chicago he had been told that despite the mechanization of the slaughtering process visitors tended to become vegetarians for a day or a week after their experience. The Fuehrer himself was a vegetarian out of this very compunction about killing any living thing. Therefore it was probable that when the effect of this viewing had been dissipated by an interval of time, the grotesque notion about the Fuehrer's madness would also be dissipated, and only the logic of necessity would remain.

There was nothing really gruesome in the bewildered faces of the Jews as they emerged, or even tumbled from the transports. And these scenes were relieved by humoristic touches as the camera picked out amusing types. There were the longbeards in their black coats and round fur hats, clinging fanatically to their bundles and suitcases and innumerable packages while their women and small children, all of them also loaded with possessions, hung onto their coattails. And in contrast there were the self-important Jews in more civilized attire, excellently tailored in fact, especially the ones with the finest pigskin bags, approaching the SS men as though they were porters who would carry and check the travelers' belongings!

Experience and skill were evident in the way the experts marshaled the crowd, giving out instructions and reassurances, avoiding panic, quickly establishing order and enforcing obedience. All this admirably followed the psychological axiom which the Fuehrer had propounded from the very beginning of his movement: In order to control any group, crowd, mass, one must at once give them an activity, if it be only to form ranks and march—one must keep them busy.

So here they were at once directed to pile their baggage; they were formed in rows. Then came the selection, to the right, to the left. Even though the film makers had been a little ambitious with their camera angles and their symbols in this scene, there still emerged the central theme of man himself, the superior man, creating order in his universe. Only now there had to be introduced the counterpoint of disorder, from which order is created. The breaking of ranks, the sudden surges of separated parts of families to unite themselves in one column or another, even the attempts to cheat by slipping across when guards were distracted by a commotion—all this the camera cleverly caught. And an attempt, even here, to bribe!

The howling, especially the bawling of the children, that

the Fuehrer hated so much—the Baron had the same aversion—was kept at a minimum on the sound track. Always came the quick intervention of the order makers, forcible if necessary. Here suddenly was a shout from a troublemaker, a wild-haired Communist type, then came a tangle of arms and legs, even a flash of a woman biting the leg of a guard, but almost instantly the column was cleansed of such types. All this showed the difficulty of the task, and the Fuehrer stirred and muttered.

The section of the film dealing with those led off to the right was compact and clean. There was the undressing, though the cameraman, as if he were from Hollywood, spent more time than was needed on nude women; then came the sanitary hair clipping, the enumeration on the wrists—a really clever idea to simplify record-keeping— the distribution of sterilized prison clothing, the assignment to quarters, with each group marched off by a Kapo down the long rows of barracks. Inside was shown the efficient space disposition of these workers, on three-tiered pallets.

The workers would go through the process of natural selection, the healthy and strong even achieving certain privileges, including sexual gratification for the ruling group of males, in a sanitary brothel. But in all honesty the film showed the subhuman nature of the vast bulk of this material, for once removed from their parasitical occupations in the outer world, the Jews fell to preying on one another, and could be seen haggling and trading their possessions—cleverly hidden bits of gold, stolen food, even cigarettes—with greedy, avid eyes, amid the filth of the latrine.

The weaker ones, having contributed their remaining usable energy to road labor and other constructive tasks, eventually took the path of the group that had in the first selection gone to the left, and to whom the film document now returned.

Even here it was highly difficult to achieve order with these people. As the file marched down the lane, pleasantly bordered with neatly cut grass and beds of geraniums, some sort of whispering took place and panic was spread. A few people stopped in their tracks or pulled back, though attendants from their own kind, speaking their own language, had been provided to reassure them that they were going to the showers. Children began their awful shrieking, as could be seen by their distorted mouths even though the sounds were kept inaudible. One man flung himself to the ground and had to be dragged away, his body flopping from side to side like that of a fish.

But there were gratifying touches, too, of calm faces, of a mother singing to the child in her arms, of older people quietly accepting the order of the universe. And there was a vivid scene of a long-legged longbeard hurrying forward, certainly a rabbi or a religious leader of some sort, as he had those long curls that they kept uncut to dangle in front of their ears. The curls were flying in the wind, the eyes were exalted—a perfect type of religious fanatic. The eternal Jew always rushing to get ahead of the line. Comical but effective.

Again the undressing, but a different atmosphere here, quicker. The camera did not linger on the females. And then the shower room.

A reluctance came at the door. Some held back—they didn't want to wash! At the very last moment the guards had to link arms to push the subjects inside so that the door could be closed.

As this special report had not been made to cater to morbid curiosity, views of the interior were omitted. The process resumed with the symbolic opening of the doors on the other side, and there were striking photographic compositions of the rows of oven mouths, of consuming flames, and then of an expanse of whitened ashes. A vision of purification, under a gentle breeze that blew a bridal veil across the eternal sky.

Could more thought and care have been given to devise a humane and sanitary operation? Statistics, capacities were recited in the concluding words of the commentary, with the figures extrapolated to the day when all Europe would at last be *Judenrein*. The Fuehrer nodded. The word *Judenrein* explained it all, a world cleaned of this element that had dirtied up every civilization. It was not through vengeful bloodlust, such as was pictured in enemy propaganda, nor was it through the grotesque and primitive Jew-hatred that was needed for the masses, in the filthy stuff put out by *Der Stürmer,* that this vast program had been conceived. (Even though, the Baron had to admit to himself, plain raw filth-humor from time to time was enjoyable and healthy; it had a cleansing effect in itself.) But with the loved one, he understood better than ever now, this program was simply an essential step in the remaking of the world, once and for all. A kind of perfectionism. And for the moment as they sat there together, what had seemed a streak of madness no longer appeared so irrational. Seen in reality, done, this piece of work was simply an episode that would be contained within the success of the whole great plan of the movement.

All this was beneath the Baron's unfocused look as he said, No, he had not known, and as he seemed to listen with astonishment to their explanation.

But there was something even more deeply sealed away in the Baron, quite beyond the opacity of the seemingly paper-transparent face. The Baron was in profound mourning. Since the Reich's own news had verified the death of the loved one and had told of the ceremonial self-destruction in the bunker in Berlin, the Baron had walked in mourning, in his castle, borne erect only through the substance of routine. There was not one soul to whom he could communicate his grief. This was not the bitter sorrow of the final, definite knowledge of defeat, for the nation's defeat came only as an appropriate accompaniment to the death of love.

That love had been truer in him, he was certain, than in the masses, who had caught only a spark of it. For the Baron liked to think of himself in his older, self-knowing years as a rational romantic, even a cynical romantic, and to believe that he had molded together within himself the two irreconcilable ends, the real and the wishful. Just as, in a sense, the loved one had combined in his personality the opposing characters of aristocracy and oneness with the people.

In the depths of his mourning, the Baron thought, what did it matter to him to hear of the iniquities of this Kraus? The Baron's prisoners kept telling him about this Kraus, and of the fellow himself he could almost truthfully repeat, "I had no idea." Though as soon as Kraus had popped out with that ultimatum for the prisoners he had understood that the *Kerl* must be on the enemy's list of war criminals. There were always, in every movement, overeager ambitious fellows of that kind, who never had a thought of their own, but seized on someone's idea and ran ahead of the pack with it. Doubtless Kraus had caught on to what was wanted regarding the Jews, and gone ahead and worked out the whole plan, the transports, the gas, the furnaces, just as they said. Hadn't he even heard —the Baron tried to recall—of a lieutenant, perhaps a captain, at the very outset, who had prepared the entire program on paper and had read out the plan at the main conference over the final solution, showing that the gas method was practical and not even too expensive?

Some such tale he had heard. It could very well have been this Kraus. But if Kraus planned to pass now as an innocent, why had the idiot brought with him a relic direct from the death camps—Vered?

Doubtless, the committee agreed, the Baron could not have known, could not have believed in the mass exterminations. For even in the camp itself, Vered had told them, the prisoners could not bring themselves to believe what happened behind the farthest walls. As to the part Kraus had played, the Baron must hear it directly from Vered, whom they would bring to him.

No, no, he would not trouble the poor old man to come to him; he would go to Vered.

Marianne had remained with him; he must stretch out again; he must rest, she insisted. But Paul was wakeful; it was of her own life that he wanted to know, and for her part Marianne was glad to take his thoughts away from what he had been through.

Their rapport had returned at once, or been revealed as unbroken, and now she spoke with the complete lack of withholding that she could achieve with no one else, not even with Remy.

Yes, she said to him clear-eyed, yes, she believed the relationship with Remy was a true one now, and would endure. Remy would secure his divorce no matter what the political effect—

"It will have no effect," Paul reassured her. "Remy will again be premier, I see no other possibility."

So strange, they were talking as though nothing had happened to them, as though the whole war was already relegated to an interruption. "Come in," Marianne said to the knock.

The Baron excused himself. But no, they had only been gossiping, she said.

"I see you are old friends." He had already sensed from the moment of Vered's advent something complex in their past.

"Marianne was my secretary in the Residence," Vered said.

"It was there that I met Remy," she added, with a new openness toward the Baron, as though now that the incarceration was virtually finished, they might assume human roles.

He looked from one to the other, curious, sensing something more. But he had come here ostensibly to hear about Kraus.

There was only one chair in the little room, and Marianne withdrew to leave the men to their talk.

THERE THEY WERE FACE TO FACE, two men of an age, who had twice seen such havoc in the world. And though both felt this, it did not bring any sense of communion between them.

Vered had always prided himself on the rapport he had been able to establish in all levels of society, among workers as an active socialist, and also among aristocrats, the snobbishly democratic. Emerging from an old-established family with its own high sense of worthiness, he had been enabled by his early achievement as a poet to move in "exclusive circles," though he cared little for them. But this Baron, he knew at once, belonged to those among whom he had always failed.

Though Vered rarely found a Hebrew word, or Jewish word, coming to his mind—his family had been thoroughly assimilated for more than a generation before his own—there echoed to him now, perhaps from a grandfather's lips in childhood, the word *zar*, stranger. It went beyond the now familiar word *goy*, since *goy* implied a known entity.

There was no identifiable barrier in the stranger; his pallid blue eyes were open with candor. But the whole being, with the fine lemon-white strands of hair, and the mannered considerateness of one who for centuries could decide the fates of his serfs—did this not belong to the impenetrable world of those who could say "Kill them all"? What was there to explain to this Baron? To evoke pity from him could only demean the dead.

"What is important," Vered said nonetheless, "is that what we have seen is a new capacity in man for which we have not been prepared. A capacity for total mechanical extermination, a day-to-day program continuing for years."

"Unbelievable, in all the history of mankind, unbelievable." The Baron allowed himself to punctuate Vered's recitation with small gasps of astonishment, horror of course, while his mind ran free.

"It is not only a Kraus. You must realize that thousands of men—guards, officers, engineers—and women too—accepted and participated in this principle of extermination."

Next, he would say the whole German people. Beware, here! Kraus, that vulgar lout of a sub-colonel, with his opportunistic self-importance, wasn't worth a second thought, but it was the folk itself whose fate must now be protected. The entire people would surely stand before the world's judgment, and would in some way be touched with the guilt of those like Kraus who had performed the act. It therefore must be maintained that the vast deed had been carried out by a crew utterly segregated from the nation, from the army, even from the party, an instrument used without the consent of the people and in complete secrecy by—yes, unfortunately it would now have to be claimed—a madman.

"A madman," the Baron said. "Unfortunately we could not realize it—so much that he accomplished, you must believe me, came from sheer genius. But on this tragic point there was an abnormality. He sincerely believed he fought a Jewish conspiracy to rule the world. I can tell you this was not mere propaganda in his view. He believed it. Here in this very house—in the early days he visited here —I have myself seen now haunted he was by this . . . myth of a conspiracy."

Totally a myth? Reclining on the bed before the Baron even now was a Jew who had at that very time been premier of a powerful nation. Hadn't that in itself, to a fevered mind, been proof of the plot? The chief of the enemy nation, a Jew!

The Baron tested himself. Did he feel toward Vered as a Jew? In childhood he had indeed absorbed a dislike of the Jews as Christ killers, but as a rational man he was sure he had outgrown these religious fables, only to have a certain amount of unpleasant feeling return when his wife betrayed him with a Jew. Yet this distaste for Jews, based on a justifiable personal reaction, was not a sickness with him. It certainly did not automatically reach to this man in the room with him, a Jew of highest importance. The long narrow face and the long-fingered hands recalled, if anything, the Spanish nobility as painted by El Greco. Doubtless Vered was descended from the Jews centuries ago driven from Spain by the Inquisition.

Oddly—an association arose—it had been in the crucial years of the Spanish civil war that this man had become premier. A Jew premier! To the loved one this had seemed a deliberate provocation. Here in this very castle the loved one had stormed and screamed: Was everyone blind? The real enemy was coming out into the open, taking control of nations, a Jew, a socialist in league with the Communists was premier across the border. The world plot was coming to a head. For centuries the Jews had plotted to take revenge on Spain. Now the Jew would seize Spain for Communism! Would the world sit still and wait to fall into slavery?

"If you will forgive me for saying so, even your presence as premier seemed to feed this aberration of his, this idea of a secret world conspiracy. Especially during the war in Spain."

Vered was taken aback. He had always assumed that the Fuehrer had only cunningly made use of the myth of a Jewish world conspiracy, for its propaganda effect on his followers. Why, on the contrary—

And Vered's mind leaped back to those dreadful days of decision, for he had never ceased tormenting himself with the question as to whether it had not been just there, over Spain, that he had been deflected from intervening by being a Jew. Had this been the hairsbreadth of unconscious reaction that had swayed his decision? Had not some final scruple held him from action for fear that his Jewish blood might be urging him? Should he not earlier have resigned? Would a successor have intervened, and would the great war have been averted?

In these years in the camp he had had to teach himself to halt such speculations. They could never lead to the primary cause.

The two men looked at each other now in the dim room where the Polish slave girl had affixed, beside her bed, an oleo print of the Virgin with the Child nestling against her breast. On a small shelf below the picture Julka kept a votive candle. A pink shade, which she had placed over the single light bulb in the room, gave the aged Jew's skin, and the Baron's too, something of the same artificial rosiness that shone from the cheeks of the Virgin and the Babe.

And inescapably the ultimate question, the Why of all

Jew-hatred, and of all human hatred, arose between them, each man pursuing it in his own mind in his own way, and only fragmentarily showing his thoughts to the other.

Could this image of love, Paul Vered wondered, truly be the source of so much persistent undying hatred, of a violence that periodically discharged itself in murder? Was the source really in this innocent picture of the Mother and Child—the Child destined as were all humans for sacrifice and death? But why, then, had the hatred become specifically attached to the Jews, to one people alone, and the very people to whom the Mother and Child had belonged?

Even before the Spanish Inquisition there had been the Jew-massacres of the Crusaders, passing through Germany along the Rhine and perhaps leaving the virulent germs of the massacres of today. Did Jew-hatred fundamentally go back to the charge of Christ-killing?

But the Fuehrer had himself rejected Christianity.

Even so, the hatred had already been imbedded in a boy brought up among people who never ceased vilifying the Jews. The hatred could then take any form. It could transfer itself to the myth of a Jewish conspiracy to rule the world.

Like two philosophers whose age has already given them a detached, objective view of the world they must soon leave, the high Nazi who considered that he personally was quite rational on the Jewish question, and the exalted Jew who all his life had felt only the most tenuous involvement with his origin, now probed for causes.

It was the myth of Jewish world dominion, then, that the Fuehrer had embraced. Where did it come from? Oddly, almost every people in its time had embarked on world dominion, except the Jews, and yet it was to the Jews that the myth was attached. Where had the Fuehrer's belief come from?

"Why," the Baron said, "the *Protocols*."

There stood in his mind the very first time that the loved one had visited here, and they had sat together before the great fireplace. The Baron had even sent away his favorite hound, a huge Doberman that always lay at his feet before the fire; but as the Leader had taken an aversion to the animal, the hound had been exiled for the evening.

The meeting had come about through a crony in Munich, a Heidelberg fencing comrade who had developed a money knack and even in the starvation years of the twenties had put the Baron onto some excellent mining investments. In that period, just after his wife had gone off with her Jewish opera director, the Baron had passed through a year of misanthropy, staying here at home, mostly hunting, and even reading a good deal. In the cities there were always too many nagging beggars at you. Germans, begging! Even young ex-soldiers!

A few times his Munich friend had dragged him to town, and once Kurt had said he was trying a little excitement with the brownshirts. "At least they make a noise, they stir things up." He was even giving them a bit of cash for uniforms and—with a wink, Kurt made a finger pistol—boom-boom! These boys meant business.

Their leader, Kurt said, was something of an eccentric, but then so was old General Ludendorff, who marched with them. And anyway everything else was dead; why not have a little fun with politics?

So the Baron had been drawn in. On the weekend when Kurt was to bring his new sensation to the castle, there appeared first an orderly in full military regalia, booted and belted, with a list of vegetarian dishes which might be prepared for the Leader. To the Baron this had been the first personally intriguing touch, like the finicky demands of some exotic lady who knew her worth.

This political personage, Kurt had said, was a purist, an idealist; he neither drank nor smoked, nor ate meat. As for women, he had little or no use for them though he was absolutely not a homosexual. Odd.

So they arrived. From the first step of the booted feet into his house, not at all a conquering or heavy step but the tread of a man confidently arriving in his proper place, from the first direct encounter with the perilous blue eyes, which seemed to acknowledge no barrier of privacy or self, the Baron had let himself go into this new life experience.

Even when a man was mature, with a full range of life experience and sophistication, could he choose when to love? Could he consciously select the loved one? The best that the Baron could make of this incomprehensible subject, unless he accepted a sickly Freudianism by which he would have been judged incapable of love, was to begin with the fundamental reaction of fascination. Human love was as inexplicable as the fascination of a cat for a cat, at mating time, when the partners sit for hours in front of each other, their eyes transfixed in the sexual spell.

So it had been in his own life. A young man-about-town in Vienna, under the spell of a singer, as was proper for a young blood of his time, he had married and fathered two daughters, both lost to him when his wife later made off with her Jew and migrated to America. For some years there had been no spell of fascination, only sexual adventure. And suddenly as the Leader on this day had entered the castle, the fascination had come in a long undeniable pulsation, utterly bereft of sexual feeling. The Baron had never felt drawn to homosexuals, nor did the tales of homosexuality in the movement excite him. What he felt now, he presumed, was something remotely akin to a religious experience, the love beyond animal love, a disinterested love.

Later indeed, when he was to witness the Fuehrer before a vast, limitless mass of people, and to see upon them the same effect of this love, the same fascination, he never came to feel his personal emotion shared or diminished or diffused; rather, he felt it verified. He felt as during his first love for the singer, on the occasions of her success when she held an audience enthralled and he saw their rapt faces and yet knew that it was with him that she would depart. So he knew he was among the close ones with whom the Fuehrer would leave, to sit for another hour together while the excitement of the meeting, the elation of the mass response and will, was absorbed.

More than once the loved one had come to spend a day or two in this castle, sleeping in the very room next to his own in which that loutish colonel had now chosen to install himself. Nor would that *Kerl* ever be told that it was in the same bed the Fuehrer had slept.

Always, as on his first visit, there had been a moment for him of breathing in, of uniting himself with the place, with the high free beauty of the mountain. He was home. It was here, even on that first visit, the Baron always felt, that Berchtesgaden was born.

The lofty vision of the eagle race.

At once the Baron had discovered what his coarse friend Kurt had been incapable of perceiving; the vision was not of a mundane socialism, a rule of the proletariat, but of a total elite, a *Herrenvolk*. Not a lowering of everyone to a common equality, but a raising up of the entire people to a world nobility!

What Kurt had always bragged was true—he could smell out a good investment without understanding the first thing about the product.

During dinner, after dinner, on a long walk on the estate, the young Leader had talked of nothing but his ideas, his movement, his plans, and while the Baron might have thought he would become bored with such a mono-mind, he found in this case that the personality had an undiminishing hold on him. He did not attentively listen, for he bathed in the excited aura of the young man, and yet at the same time he heard and could have repeated back every word.

The first premise he agreed with at once: the unification of the German folk. All German-speaking people were one. Austria and Germany, to begin with. This folk in the heartland of Europe, therefore the heartland of the world, was the genius folk of civilization, destined to impose order, clarity, progress on all mankind.

With what completeness of vision the young Leader had spoken! There were the detailed plans, step by step, with uncanny insights into the weaknesses of other nations, where each was cracked or rotten or tired or overconfident or afraid. One by one they must be handled, and the old shame of defeat annulled; there was no time to lose because the enemy, Jewish communism, was on the march, to combine with Jewish capitalism to rule the world.

The sudden evocation of this enemy had brought the Baron partly out of his spell. They were then seated before the fireplace, and the young Leader had reached into the pocket of his military jacket and brought out a booklet, the proof. "Do you know this?" he asked, with the tone of a man about to reveal a great secret.

It was a German copy of the *Protocols of the Elders of Zion,* the secret plan of the Jews to rule the world.

The Baron happened to know it well enough. The "secret document" had been handed around by every Russian nobleman fleeing the Revolution. They swore it was a verbatim report stolen from a mysterious conclave of world-powerful Jews conspiring to gain control of the world.

The pamphlet was of course made up. Not even made

up, but a secondhand parroting of Machiavelli. The Baron's wife, then in her period of liberalizing and Judaizing, had brought home an interesting bit of literary detective work by a London *Times* writer, showing line for line how the famous "secret protocols" had been concocted. Long ago a French lawyer had published a satire on Napoleon III in which the shade of Machiavelli gave detailed advice on how to enslave a people. This French satire had got into the hands of a Russian monk, Nilus, who had copied it out, substituting "Elders of Zion" for "Machiavelli." The effect was startling. "We shall control all the officials by getting them into debt. We shall control the police and the press. We shall seize all the gold of the goyim." And finally by setting nation against nation the Jews would seize control of the world.

The monk had even written out sections in different inks, as though a series of secretaries had actually taken down the plottings at the imaginary conclave. This document had prodded the Czar into unleashing new pogroms. And again, when the Revolution came, the "secrets" had been printed and offered to world statesmen to convince them to come to the aid of Imperial Russia against the world Jewish communist conspiracy!

The exposé of the *Protocols* was still on a shelf in the library, and the Baron had debated with himself whether to show it to the young fanatic. But the belief of the young Leader was so complete, so pure in a sense, so needed to himself—why disturb it? One encountered these passions in the most rational beings; they gave a personality a certain charm. The Baron's wife, for all her modernism, had believed absolutely in astrology. (Later, curiously, he had discovered that the Fuehrer too was a devotee.) And so, in that first meeting, the Baron had refrained from disturbing the Leader's belief that he held in his hand the absolute proof of the Jews' world plot, in their own secret words.

Afterward, as the party for its part printed millions of copies of the *Protocols* in every language, the Baron had at times wondered if he should not have shown the Fuehrer the source, if only to protect him from being made foolish by another exposé. But in the outer world the fabrication of the *Protocols* was exposed again and again without the slightest effect on what people wanted to believe.

And by then the Fuehrer had grown from the rosy-cheeked young fanatic to the care-laden loved one, tensely following the narrowing line of his intuition. To show him the truth, the Baron knew, would only be to provoke a shrieking outburst of denial, an accusation of a new Jew-trick to cover up their tracks.

And after all, Vered asked the Baron, could a single false booklet really have been the instrument with which an entire people had been sentenced to death?

No, the Baron agreed. The myth was there, and without the *Protocols* doubtless would have been embodied in some other form.

Then, Vered asked, what was the source of so ultimate a hatred and fear?

The Baron thought only of the Fuehrer. "I believe we

will never know," he said. "Nothing we know explains anything so vast." And to himself he added, That was also a part of his own fascination, his love. The sense of a helplessness, a failing, in the loved one who had power over you, the sense of a passion under which the loved one himself was enslaved as you were enslaved: and for this you loved him.

He could not say this to Vered, nor would Vered let go of his own line of reason. One man alone, even the most hypnotic of leaders, could not impose his aberration upon an entire people. It had to be accepted. They had to be his accomplices. What of those who from the beginning had burned Jewish shops and synagogues, driven Jewish children from the schools? What was the source in them? Did it not go back after all to the Christ-killer hatred? And had it not been a monk who had concocted the "secrets" by connecting this long-nurtured hatred of the Jews to the myth of world dominion?

And what of all those who had carried out the final solution, the chiefs, the technicians, the operators of the death camps? Were they all suffering from an aberration? What of a Kraus?

And so they had come to him.

The Baron felt pinned to the wall. From his own failure to show the Fuehrer the fabrication, to the activities of a Kraus, was there not the same complicity? Had he not thought, from the beginning, "Let everything he wants be done; he will lead us to conquer the world"?

Again Vered's thoughts emerged alongside his own.

"This supposed diabolic Jewish plan for world conquest," Vered said, "didn't your own Fuehrer then use it, point for point?"

The Baron had never before been struck by the parallel. The Machiavellian creation of a police state, the deliberate use of false promises, the infiltration into all enterprise, the control of officials, the absolute control of the press, the plan for world dominion by using one power to help break another and then turning on the first. True, every despot was Machiavellian, whether by instinct or imitation. But the parallel was so complete, to the plan to rule the world. Almost dreamily the Baron repeated, "The *Herrenvolk*."

And Vered found himself thinking, "The chosen people." The ancient guilt engulfed him. He had always shrunk from this conception. True, it was meant spiritually; true, every primitive people had believed itself chosen by its god; true, the Jews had never attempted to subjugate others—and yet in his horror of arrogance this was the one accusation that touched home to him.

For an instant their eyes met. For an instant the sense of the *zar*, the stranger, was gone for Vered, in what he believed was a glimpse of pain and guilt like his own.

But to the Baron that instant of shared shame had brought another meaning. "We must not be punished as they have been punished." The guilt must never touch the whole people. The loved one was dead and he had taken his sickness with him. The German people lived and must be freed from this accusation. Just so, he must at once disassociate himself from Kraus. He must in some way get rid of him.

It would have to be done at once, tonight; a way would have to be found before the Allies arrived, so that he himself could not in any way be paired with the fellow. Why had the idiot brought Vered? And it came to the Baron, nebulously, that Vered was Kraus's mark of Cain, that every man had to drag with him the witness of his own guilt. So Kraus must be thrown out to the punishers, to the self-righteous avengers who were coming, the good Christians who would now piously decry the horror of the massacre of the Jews.

Remy and the other two men were waiting for him, hovering about the stair landing, to learn the outcome of his talk with Vered. The Baron paused only for a moment, frowning a bit, telling them he would soon prepare a plan.

There was Kraus's driver moving about the hallway— already it was best not to be seen in discussion. The Baron crossed to his own side.

As for the driver, Kraus could be persuaded to let him off for a few hours so that the boys could show him where to get a drink in the village. Then there was Schreiter, the platoon leader, a soldier's soldier, a man who knew no other life than the army. He would stay for the last fight; and Kraus had already been talking with him.

Still if Kraus were simply to disappear, Schreiter could

be told that the colonel had slipped away as he was listed by the enemy as a war criminal and would be hung if captured. The driver could be told the same. And then the Baron would have his castle back in his own command; there was no need to let it be destroyed in a Götterdämmerung.

The problem was thus quite simple. He had only to close off Kraus, put him away somewhere for a day or two. And the obvious way was perhaps the best—to get the fellow drunk, to provide him with a wench.

INSTALLED IN THE GUEST ROOM adjoining the Baron's bedroom, Kraus was looking down from the window. "A little too far for a lover to climb," the Baron remarked, "and also too far to drop." He chuckled as he regaled Kraus with a few of the spicy legends about his forebears. This had been the chamber of the Baroness in times past, and as the world well knew, a female determined to deceive her husband will always find a way. Ropes of sheets had been used from this window. But a deceived husband also can find a way, for revenge, and there was a lively tale of a swain dangling from a sheet, used as a target by bowmen.

They had been so skillful that the lover had lasted a long while.

"Even with modern weapons the position is formidable, virtually impregnable," Kraus remarked. "It would take heavy guns to make a dent in these walls."

The Baron nodded, and swallowed his brandy. He didn't care just now to go into the history of sieges.

"And your defenses are excellently placed. Every approach is covered."

The Baron produced the proper modest smile.

"Schreiter is a good man, too. I have had a talk with him. There is no demoralization in that one!"

"We have done our best," the Baron said.

"I felicitate you, if I may." That "if I may" the Baron caught—a fellow who was still unsure of himself before his betters, doubtless one of the miserable unemployed who had flocked to the movement at the start, and got himself a job in one of the order-keeping squads. The rest was easy to fill in—once a stormtrooper, in his fine boots, he had married a few grades above himself.

"You'll be glad to get home," the Baron tried. "You have children?"

Out came the snapshots; two husky boys, two dimply little girls, a heavy-faced wife trying to smile. "If I ever do get home to them."

Was it the moment to suggest that he could simply take up and go? But Kraus meant to have his war here, that was clear—an armchair officer who couldn't go home to his sons until he had had his fling of combat.

"It's time your high-flown guests brought me their answer," Kraus snapped, tossing off his schnapps. At least he was a drinker.

"They've already spoken to me," the Baron said.

"Yes?" There was a bolted look of suspicion.

"They ask for a little more time, to make it unanimous. After dinner."

"They are divided? How many refuse?" The command voice did not quite cover his anxiety. Kraus stared at the Baron. "They're stalling for time! They think the Americans will arrive! I'll shoot them on the parapet, in the face of their damned liberators!"

"Only one or two are hesitating, and I'm sure the others will persuade them," the Baron said calmly. "Don't worry, Kraus," he added suddenly in his other, sharp voice. "They really have no idea who you are." And then he raised his glass and offered a smile.

Kraus slowly broke into a responding smile, clinked, and drank. He was known, then, to the Baron? he asked.

From the Fuehrer himself, who had at times been a guest here, the Baron said.

The Fuehrer. For an instant the death was gone and it was almost as though the Baron could still put in a word for Kraus's long-delayed promotion.

"You never met him?" the Baron divined.

No, not personally. As with the delay of his promotion, Kraus had always found this unaccountable, when he was carrying out the campaign closest to the Fuehrer's heart. And from the earliest days, too! From the very conception of the final solution!

"But he spoke of your work," the Baron said. "That's how I know your name."

"He spoke of me!"

"You know how he always kept track of the most amazing details, personally."

The Fuehrer's death came over them again. They sighed together, and drank. Now Kraus was sure he knew why the Fuehrer had never called him. The Fuehrer had wanted to protect him by keeping him in obscurity, in a low rank. Even while certain higher-ups had taken credit, the Fuehrer had known who did the actual work.

How many more had known?

Then suddenly Kraus struck his palm against his head. The feeling he had had all day of a blunder, of something forgotten, became illuminated as though a huge sign had flashed on: Vered. Suppose the old carcass knew who he was! At once, Kraus denied the possibility to himself. To Vered, he could only be an officer who had been instructed to pick him up and transport him. Yet why had he never until this moment considered that Vered might know? It was as though something within himself had blanked out this thought so that he would put himself in danger. No, untrue. When he had started out with Vered he had not yet thought of this plan to exact a statement from the prisoners; the plan had only come to him a while ago.

If Vered knew, it would all be spoiled. There was a

chance that Vered did know. Between the Jews there was this mysterious way, this link that existed so that somehow even through the thickest walls everything seeped through. In the last campaign in Hungary he had been careless enough to deal directly with a number of top Jews and some of them had later been sent to the camps and they might have passed on his name.

"Have the others talked to Vered?" Kraus demanded.

Why no, the Baron said. Vered had been asleep since he arrived, a sleep of exhaustion.

"I don't want them to talk to him. Vered doesn't have to sign." What a dunderhead the Baron must think him to be. And to the Baron's mildly questioning eyes he snapped, "I had to bring him to the redoubt. Orders." But the Baron perfectly well could reason that he could have dumped Vered anywhere along the way.

He could have kicked himself. To have made such a blunder! No, the hell with them all and with himself. He would stage such a last battle here as would not soon be forgotten. Kraus held out his glass.

It would have been unthinkable to have the captives of the Reich, no matter how high their former station, served by Germans, even by the peasant girls of the village. Fortunately there were the conscripted Polish girls; they took some teaching, but with a modest amount of good treatment they were fairly cheerful, and they were hard workers. The Baron used them in the fields as well; nearly every farm had taken a girl or two, to ease the labor shortage.

There could be no question of the basic workability of the *Herrenvolk* ideal.

Often enough he had taken his meals in the great hall with his prisoners, but obviously tonight it was best to have Kraus dine with him in his apartment, and the Baron had chosen Julka to serve. The girl's rump had a virtual magnetism for men's hands; when she served the guard platoon downstairs, the sound of her passing was like applause.

Julka's presence had its effect. Kraus was soon embarked on a dissertation on his wartime exploits with women. He had had probably the best opportunity of the war, he admitted, since his duty had required constant roving, with enough sojourning in each country for a thorough attachment or two.

It was the first and the last, he confided, that were at the top of his list, and he found it difficult to decide between them—the French, and the Hungarian. With a rush of narration, as though to cram the joys of the whole war into the remaining few hours, Kraus evaluated, recounted, described, relived, his hands extremely busy between his wine glass, his knife and fork, the passing rump, and also the necessary gestures, here and there, to delineate a delicious form.

His harried look of a few moments ago had vanished, and it was the face of a hearty young officer that emerged, knowing, commanding, enjoying, fooling the bitches that tried to use him—ah, what a war! The French—after all for sheer shameless excitement in sex, a Frenchwoman couldn't be beat, he still had to say it. Not that a German girl—even a good German girl, not just a whore—had any shame in it once she got started. But with them it was animal, one had to admit. In their shamelessness, their carnality, he had always found a kind of boasting; did the Baron get what he meant? The Baron blinked his understanding and encouragement. Now, when a German woman tried various positions, Kraus explained, it was as though she were bragging—look, she was naked on all fours! But a Frenchwoman, he expertized, a Frenchwoman was always natural, even in the most bizarre sexual act. And he didn't just mean any girl picked off the boulevard for a meal, but the real ones, when you got to know them, the married ones particularly—ah, when it came to their specialty—and no wonder it was called Frenching—they could float you on the edge of heaven for hours on end.

From the French, with the liveliest of intermediary examples—Czechs, Poles, Greek girls—Kraus reached the only true rivals, the Hungarian women, no doubt the most beautiful women on the Continent. And with these it was not only sex but passion. A French woman, no matter how *chéri* and *chéri* you were, you never felt but what when you went off to your duties she could have herself just as much enjoyment with the next cocko who opened her door, while with a Hungarian mistress, ah, there was passion! In a way better, in a way worse, for the Hungarian women got inside you. Now, last summer, with a certain lovely Baroness—Kraus swallowed the title with an offside apologetic glimmer to the Baron; he had not meant to sound presuming. But he charged on—until he had made love to this Hungarian he had never realized a woman can reach such pleasure. She used literally to crawl across the floor for it, on her belly.

No, no, of course he had never made use of his special situation, his war task, to get women for himself—no need!

His teeth glittered. Head thrown back, the fellow was the handsome type, the sort seen with females who wanted to be envied for whom they slept with.

It was sometimes sickening, handsome Kraus confided as man to older man, how the Jew women would find ways to get to him and offer themselves. What fun could a man have with that? It would be worse than paying for it with a prostitute. What pests those women could be! In the office corridor, in a restaurant, a hotel, they'd follow him, even to the door of the men's room. "Save my father!" "Save my husband!" Phoo! But yet, despite his particular specialty in the war . . .

Kraus gulped his wine in the promising pause of a guest who knows just what inner revelations people want to hear from him. So, holding the Polish girl firmly now with his hand under her skirt, while Julka laughed and pushed a bit and refilled his wine glass, Kraus rattled on: In spite of his special job he could say he had had his affairs with Jewish girls too, but of course without any of this save-us stupidity.

Among the elite a man could admit an occasional violation of the law against racial defilement, a rule that on the upper levels was of course meant to be honored by the breaking, if a real beauty came along. In Paris at the beginning, or even in Budapest at the end, at an officers' party anything at all might turn up. There was a captain on his staff, highest connections, a nephew of Himmler himself, and what a party thrower! Always managed to grab himself the richest Jew apartment, and there were always a few girl friends of the late occupant who just kept coming around. And it had to be said—Kraus rolled his mouth like an expert wine taster—a Jewish girl did have something a bit special. A spiciness. No, these were girls who of course knew nothing about his job. They just liked goyim. Indeed he had a theory that every Jewish bitch yearned for the uncircumcised cock; once and for all the cunts wanted to get the whole thing without a single bit missing!

Roaring at his good old joke, Kraus gave Julka a loud clear bottom-slap, and Julka laughed along with the new officer and the Baron, and Kraus continued expertly.

They were hot spice, like Christmas wine, if you really got a good one, not one of those dreary intellectuals who fornicated as though following instructions on a tonic bottle, but a good one. A Jewess could be as abandoned and inventive as a French girl, as passionate as a Hungarian. Ah, for six weeks, in Paris itself, at the very beginning of the Program, he had enjoyed a perverse little Jewish bitch who had thought he was a transport officer for foods and medical supplies. Well brought up, too, a minor branch of the Rothschilds. . . . For a moment his hand

117

rested motionless while his eyes became reflective. . . . Well, she must have been picked up at the end, after he went on to Belgium. But she could take the very marrow out of your bones, that one!

"Rothschilds too. It didn't help them," the Baron remarked appreciatively.

Some of the biggest ones got away to England and America, Kraus remarked, but that wouldn't have helped them either if the war had gone as it should. He'd have come to them in England and even in that damned America with its millions of *Yupen,* and its Jews running the government. He'd have finished his job with them, every last one!

"With more like you, we'd have done it," the Baron declared.

Kraus leaned forward intently now, to show this high-flown Baron that he was no stupid *Kerl,* that he had overcome his lack of education, grown in the party, in the movement, and that he could hold his own even in the most elevated company. "What is war?" he asked, and answered, "The reduction of the enemy. Correct?"

The Polish slavey, whom he had lifted above his knee so that he could feel her crotch with his thigh, slipped off, with an air of boredom now, and carried away the dishes. Never mind, she would return, or he'd fetch her—she had no other bed for tonight, he'd put the old Jew in her bed! —and a winey side-laughter arose in a corner of his mind at his cunning bit of foresight.

"The reduction of the enemy," he repeated. Total war —the whole of the enemy, man, woman, and child. Hadn't the American gangsters done it in their raids on Hamburg, on Dresden? Obliteration. Such were the wars of now and the future. Obliteration. Correct? And who was the first enemy of the Reich? The Jew.

Kraus let the Baron absorb this: At his table sat the officer who, though so few knew it, had carried out the most successful campaign of the war. "I flatter myself that my objective was accomplished with the minimum of means," Kraus declared. "Do you know how many men I had under my command for this task?"

The Baron could not guess. A division, at least?

"Eighty men." His face became poker-sly. "Not a man more. The enemy imagined I had thousands. With eighty men, I did it!"

Incredible, the Baron said. But how was it possible—

Ah, it had been necessary to invent a technique. Simple, once you thought of it. Make the enemy help you. Get their leaders, or appoint new leaders to do the first job of the roundup, supply you with the names and addresses. A registry. A labor registry, a registry for food rations, anything will do. Then you got the local police in each country, not your own, you didn't have any, your men were only experts, supervisors. You got the local police, French, Belgian, Dutch, Hungarian, to conduct the actual roundup. Even Jewish police, as he had done in the Polish ghettos. That had been the most brilliant stroke of all.

But in Warsaw, the Baron asked, hadn't there been some trouble? Surely it had needed more than eighty men, there?

Warsaw! That was the stupid local army commander. The job had been nearly finished, a half million of the enemy taken out of the Warsaw ghetto alone, when a handful of Zionists and Communists had started an underground sabotage. It was amazing how much money they had; the international Jews had got tons of money to them right inside the ghetto, despite the wall, enough so they could pay thousands and thousands for a few miserable pistols. If he had been on the spot he'd have smoked out the troublemakers in a hurry, but he had been busy in Greece, and the local army commander had gone in rashly, into the narrow ghetto streets with tanks, and even lost one or two Panzers because of Molotov bombs. But afterward the fellow had learned his lesson and used flame-throwers, burning the *Yupen* to cinders in their holes in the ground.

Eighty men, the Baron repeated. And how many, how many of the enemy had been destroyed? He hadn't seen any final figures. Perhaps he had missed the accounting in the rush of events of the last weeks.

"Oh no, you haven't missed the accounting," Kraus assured him, and tapped on his own forehead. "The final accounting is here and nowhere else!" He alone, not even the top men in the SS, knew the grand total from the various camps and the various local actions.

"How many would you say?"

"Five and a half, six million at least." He watched the effect.

The Baron set down his glass. "Colossal."

Kraus leaned back, for once savoring the appreciation of a close friend of the Fuehrer's.

The little Polish bitch had returned all right. She wanted it. He planted her again on his thigh and moved the knee against her sex, which was bare. The dirty bitch would stain his uniform. Never mind. She'd clean it for him tomorrow. Or—the stupid unwanted thought interfered—tomorrow he might no longer wear a uniform; he might put on someone's worn old work pants so as to melt away. A war criminal, on their list. Who would hide you? Not even the Hungarian baroness could be trusted. "There he is, the bloody Nazi!" He saw her pointing to him, for some spit-and-polish American officer, a curly-haired Jew no doubt, while he cowered like a dog, in his rags, hiding in her stable. No. A wife would hide you. Only a wife. In a forest somewhere, and she would bring him his food, and the boys would come from time to time to listen to his stories of the war. Their father, a hero in hiding. He would tell them how he had fought in the redoubt to the very last moment, to the very last man. He'd fight!

Kraus lifted his glass. "To the final battle!" He was well on, but not drunk; he knew his capacity.

"*Heil!*" The Baron raised his wine and answered the salute.

And the Polish cunt, at some permission in the old goat's eyes, lifted a glass and clinked with Kraus, laughing.

All she knew was to laugh. *"Ludern!"* She had learned that word all right. *"Herum ludern!* The whole night long," she gurgled against his ear, with a nip.

The Baron stood up, and Kraus too, spilling the bitch, who sat on the floor, laughing. They drained their glasses.

It was the Baron who led; Kraus followed, though a bit fuddled. The Baron opened the door, and there Kraus was in the adjoining bedchamber. He was walking straight, he was sure, and he walked straight to the bed. The piglet had scuttled in; she wasn't deserting him.

The old goat of a Baron stood there with his eyes screwed up, with the rosiest glow on his cheeks; he must like to watch, the old frigger, that was it! Well, Kraus had no objections; it was like those great old parties in Budapest! He gave her hardly a shove and the bitch was on the bed, her skirt fallen back, her naked legs waving in the air. The old bugger must have a regular slave harem here!

"Six million," the Baron repeated, wonderingly, admiringly.

Tomorrow the final battle! "Six million! I'll jump into my grave laughing, knowing I pushed six million *Yupen* into theirs!" Kraus cried, as he jumped onto the bed.

"Ludern!" she shrieked, and the Baron cackled.

As he plunged into her, into the dark hole of eternity, Kraus laughed with a sudden roar, six million, and presently he sensed the Baron withdrawing from the room as though he had seen all there was to see. True, there was nothing fancy to be expected from this peasant. Good solid lively beef, but no tricks. A fellow didn't have to bother to invent things, either. And his head swam away, carrying him elsewhere, now to the Hungarian baroness, now to the Jewess in Paris, even substituting for a forbidden instant his wife in this sumptuous bed, for once not worried that the kids behind their thin wall would hear them, substituting whatever female had ever lain fucking on this bed, the ancient Barons cheating their highborn wives, and a hot young Baroness cheating her impotent old baby-faced mummy with cocksman Kraus climbed up through the window. And then on this bed, dragged into this room by commanding imagination, someone else, that yellow-haired bitch here in the castle, if they wouldn't sign for him, or even if they would, a little extra demand, the premier's fuck—come on, my lady, take off your glasses and everything else, on all fours now, or I fire this pistol at his head, on all fours, that's how I like it—and unevoked, coming by itself, a sudden unwanted image of Kraus in flight up a snow peak, in torn uniform, dragging behind him, tied to a rope, a burden that kept tripping him backward and snagging itself on protruding rocks so that he had to exert his last strength to pull it loose, the formless bundle, the heap of bones in rags, the last *heftling,* some cadaverous Jew that still lived or not, he didn't know any more, but he had to drag it, a dog his bone, he was fleeing and the damned thing couldn't be let go.

MARIANNE WATCHED the beloved, unaltered face, grown only to be more deeply what it had always been; now it was in repose while he slept again. The quietest fragment of peace came over the mouth; his peacefulness drew on something within her, and Marianne let herself believe that in sleep he still sensed her presence.

So it had been in the days and nights at the Residence when, still so young, she had imagined herself an Abishag lying beside old King David to warm his bones. How was it that seven, eight years ago Paul had seemed to her an aged man, bringing to a close his long-distinguished life, while here now, after these years of the concentration camp, so thin, so fragile, he did not seem extremely aged but rather a presence that endured and could still count for a great deal? Indeed like the others and like Remy whose thoughts she so surely sensed, Marianne had felt from the instant of Vered's appearance that the entire people would respond. "Thank God that he has had the strength to survive and that he has returned to us," they would say. Though even Remy, she was sure, had almost at once put a limitation on the thought. If they chose

Vered it would be a token choice for a short while, for he was too old for the heavy tasks ahead, and after Vered had been honored, a younger man would have to be called on.

The face was at peace, as that of a man who knows in his heart that he has not given in, that he has withstood. Though they might all yet be executed tomorrow, in a last stupid flourish, this would remain for Vered: Whatever could be accomplished by truth to himself, he had done.

It was no more the self-tormented face that she had so longed to soothe in those long-ago other days when in her youthful ambition, and needing a good post after her father's death, she had used his every connection at the university to get herself placed in the Premier's secretariat, the youngest. How she had always gloried in being the youngest, the first: the first on her childhood holidays to run into the sea, the first in her schoolgirl set to fall in love, the first—with a self-forgiving rue now—to have herself seduced so as to "really find out." The first in her graduating class, the youngest. The best-qualified to have her heart broken, too, by the eternal female learning process of finding that her lover had added on for himself still a newer conquest.

She would dedicate herself to humanity, then. But even so she had had to be at the very center, and had managed her way into the secretariat. There, at every call for extra duty, whether in the dinner hours or late at night, it was Marianne who gladly agreed to stay on.

In those months of crisis—a doubled crisis for Vered,

national and personal too, because of the death of his first wife after a lingering illness—Marianne had almost nightly occupied a little secretarial office with a couch, on the top floor of the Residence. The ancient servants' rooms, each with its round window eye on the courtyard, had been refurbished, and there, still so young a girl, she would lie, filed away, waiting. Always one who worked late at night, Vered had been taken by an unremitting insomnia; he would continue dictating until three, four in the morning, and his faithful personal secretary, the loyal middle-aged Stéphanie, had had to admit she could no longer cope with the task. Others of the staff after all had husbands, and it was thought, too, that a young energetic girl would cheer his soul.

Marianne had done something else; she had become his friend. Within the shortest time—not three sessions, as it seemed to her later—there remained no barriers. In the midst of a sentence, on a suspended word, on a decision that had to be taken—to send arms to Spain or not, to send arms clandestinely but massively, or openly to intervene—he would turn to her. "What shall I do? I should intervene but will they follow me?" They—who were "they," the "they" that he invoked with every doubt? "They won't follow. The government will fall. What is my duty?" And he would look at her as though she were "they," she were the entire people. Yet his look distinguished, too, between her as "they" and Marianne as herself, for he knew her own sentiment, so that she could not feel free as "they" to press him, Do it, do it! For there was his duty to his party, to the pledge to work for peace that had brought him to power, to his own anguished pacifism, the poor man—the complexity of it all! And sending arms would strengthen the Communists, his own party would be pushed aside as the scapegoat by Dortolot, or even worse, by the extreme rightists. In the countryside that strange figure, the superpatriot, the leader of the devout, Auguste Rieber, was forming his followers into squadrons. And there was the cabal of the aristocrats around Albert du Caux; everywhere on their estates it seemed they had secret stores of arms, and they had family connections in Spain, and if he dared give aid they would create a chaos worse than in Spain itself. Then the Communists would rise, there would be revolution—and his eyes would fill with tears. Within a few nights he was no longer ashamed before her of this tendency to weep. "I have been a weeper all my life," Paul confessed to her. "I weep at parades, my dear girl, I weep at heroism, pay no attention." And impulsively she extended her hand.

Marianne had learned politics, indeed. How the forces were set so that the Premier could not, literally could not, do what he desperately at heart thought right. Each time, somehow, Vered found a crack, a tiny alley. A way to slip through a bit more of his labor program, of his welfare program, but if he went a grain too far, then there was the Parliamentary storm; there came the beseeching visits from his own party people. Even the leader of the young progressives, Remy, would appear to urge him to go a bit more slowly.

It was Marianne he called for almost every night now. "It is easier with her, she has the thread." And long into the night Vered would seek his way, and come to the edge, and hesitate.

But also there were times when he would have completed the file of dossiers marked URGENT, so that the bedside desk was clear. "No, don't go yet, my dear girl. Stay a while if you don't mind—perhaps you'll have a glass of milk with me? Or tea?" And then with his exquisitely balanced discretion, that never pried but merely touched at permitted openings, "I am ashamed to deprive so vivacious a young woman"—how understanding of him that he didn't say girl—"of her evenings," though it was after three at night. How was it, his eyes asked, that there was no impatient young man to protest her devotion?

She had blurted out then her whole banal heartbreak, so stupid for a girl supposedly so brilliant. "Why me? Why did he have to have me?" she had cried the eternal cry.

So he in turn had soothed her, telling her what she had already comprehended yet needed to hear sympathetically from a man. One thing that women could not always understand in men, he told her, was the trophy of virginity; for some men this became the proof of their superior masculinity, so that they had constantly to hunt down their virgins, and her friend, her first lover, had doubtless been such a one.

This little talk had somehow soothed Marianne, given her distance from the hurt, made it less personal. There had come to her a sense of womanly growth in this constant freedom of exchange with a man, not a father or grandfather or lover, though perhaps in the common Freudian jargon a father figure for her. He was in mourning, yet doubtless a sexual tension had existed in her, for more than once the touch of his hand, or a forehead kiss on parting, had stirred her. And then had come one night when she had already climbed to her room in the other wing of the Residence after completing their work. Vered had been somewhat ill, with what was nothing less than exhaustion over a prolonged, tormenting conflict connected on one hand with the pressure of augmented arms production, and on the other with his labor program for a shorter workweek.

In her sleep, Marianne had heard the telephone ring; the radium numerals of her clock showed four. An hour had passed since she had left Vered, but surely he had remained awake the whole time.

—Could she forgive him? His voice had a not-quite-controlled tremor, and Marianne had felt there was a confession in it of a loneliness so desperate that after a struggle he had called. He had been reading some newly published American statistics—and still on the telephone he had recited figures that proved how in heavy industry the shorter work hours had decidedly increased total production. Now, when Senator Joras tomorrow would again begin shouting guns or butter . . .

Marianne had not even drawn on her robe but had walked the corridor in her long nightdress, a quaint flannel gown she had loved for the feeling it gave her of olden times of innocence and peace. But her apparition in this gown had surely been a vision to him, perhaps bringing back an early boyhood angel image of womanhood, for Marianne had seen the rare smile of well-being that grew in his eyes as she entered the room. It was when he had completed his dictation and was lying back on his pillow that she had felt an overpowering wish to lie down beside him, not a sexual wish but a sense of something that would be finally and utterly fitting, so peaceful, only to lie together in surcease. He had known it, for his lips faltered. "My sweet girl," Paul had said, with a pleading regret, and she had only bent along the bed and touched his mouth swiftly with her lips, and felt her heart dumbfoundedly protesting as she took herself away.

Doubtless there was gossip, malicious, wise, even tolerant, depending on the politics of the gossiper. And in the secretariat the women began to defer to her, to let her settle any little questions as to the Premier's wishes or habits, as women defer to the known intimate. Marianne would never have done anything so foolishly hopeless as to deny a liaison; it was even a private jest between the Premier and herself, their "affair."

And with the competitiveness that was so sharp in Remy, it was doubtless this misconception that had first attracted him to her; like some warrior of old who in taking a throne had to make a consort of the queen.

But dear Remy had not realized the throne was being handed to him. Those were the anguished days when Michaelis in his papers had screamed that the nationalization of the arms industry was communism! The arms program would bankrupt the nation, Dortolot had predicted, while citing Marshal Philippe, who declared that the border fortifications were already impregnable and that the new type of armored division would be a total waste. An arrangement was possible with Hitler against communism, the diplomat Richard Delorme had proposed. All that was needed was the accommodating spirit.

And at the same time the Jew-cries had begun, surely from among the followers of Auguste Rieber. Walls were smeared with insults, and when Vered appeared at public meetings, shouts came from the rear, Hang the Jew!

At first his party had avoided any reference to such hooliganism. When Vered himself had brought it up in the party council, his colleagues had cried indignantly, On the contrary! His presence just now at the head of the government was the perfect symbol of liberalism as against fascism.

But night after night in torment he had debated with himself, and with Marianne as the listening and answering part of himself, whether he must step aside. Whether it was not a moral luxury to stand as a symbol at this time. Whether indeed a younger man, like Remy, would not be better fitted to deal with this growing crisis. Whether—

"But I never think of you as a Jew at all!" she had cried. Paul had stared at her as though she had said something completely incomprehensible. "I mean, it's just something that is part of you, like being a poet. It's nothing political." Then, "What sort of a Jew would you be? You're not religious, you're a freethinker, you've lived in a literary and political world, not with Jews——" And there Marianne had halted herself, feeling her cheeks fiery with embarrassment.

But Paul had taken that remark with particular interest. No, he had said, he had never felt especially Jewish. In all his adult years he had not been to a synagogue. On the other hand, not he, nor anyone in his family for all he knew, had ever felt separated, severed, from the fact and feeling of being a Jew.

"I don't mean that you would deny it. It simply never would occur to me—to anyone who knows you—that it could influence you. That it is important."

"Ah, but it is important. Not only that the Nazis have made it important; it has always been important. It is a component——" He had tried to formulate what this component represented in him and whether it could affect his daily life, his way of thinking, his decisions. "When I read the Bible," Paul had said, "it is my family chronicle for me. Though I am decidedly unopposed to intermarriage, I must admit that it was agreeable to me that the woman I fell in love with was Jewish like myself. When the Zionists come to me for support against the British who close the shores of Palestine to immigration, I find it terribly difficult"—and his voice had come to that quavering edge —"terribly difficult, to consider their requests solely as premier, and to rule out my consciousness as a Jew."

"But you have done it. Some say even too strictly."

"Ah, there you see, it's just as bad the other way."

Vered had never before as she remembered compared himself to Disraeli, yet now he remarked that Disraeli, though he had adopted the Christian religion, was in the end remembered as a Jew—so Jewishness was not really a religious matter, was it? Of all the questions that he had brought out and faced before her, this was the most impenetrable. He was sorry that he had not given himself at some time in his life to a study of the lore of his people. But in the end, this being a Jew was a part of one's personal life; why had it become a political issue?

She could only say: madness. Surely the world would not yield to it!

In the next crisis Vered had resigned, and to forestall the Communists, Remy had been made Premier. Then a nasty joke had spread, that Marianne, the secretary, went with the job.

Their liaison had begun long before Remy's premiership. It had begun, Marianne knew, one day at a full meeting of the Cabinet. Remy too had always been the youngest in everything, and so he had become Minister of Labor in his thirties, then Minister of War, and it was during the lengthy Cabinet report by the Foreign Minister, Richard Delorme, that dreary humbug, that their eyes had met over a particularly slimy repetition of his slogan about "accommodations with our neighbors." With the quickest sardonic wink, Remy had established a complicity with her. On emerging from the meeting he had made some request, an excuse to have her bring a document to his office, and Marianne had known that while she could send it with a page she would carry it to him herself. Remy had exchanged not more than ten words with her before he had come around his desk, embracing her as though they were already lovers, and that same evening Remy had come to her own place, the little apartment maintained aside from the room in the Residence. Again with scarcely a dozen words they had fallen upon each other in a fever of lovemaking.

Only then had she begun to realize why the term "making love" had always seemed inept to her. It was as if to say that love didn't exist as a pre-condition and as a continuation for the physical act. She did not want to use the same name for what was happening with Remy as for the most casual intercourse; to "go to bed" was an evasion, to "sleep together" just as inadequate, although at least it expressed what the body meant by the prolonged and needed closeness. Once, after Vered had made his remark about the Bible, she had been reading Thomas Mann's *Joseph in Egypt,* and had become immersed in the story of the suffering of Potiphar's wife. The yearning phrase used by the poor deviled woman, "Let us put our hands and our feet together," had seemed to speak of Marianne's own deepest need. So with Remy the sense of needed union had been instant and complete, from top to toe, their entire bodies confirming that sense of recognition conveyed in one little exchange of glances at the Cabinet meeting, an exchange that might after all have been only a moment of flirtation.

Compact, with dark strong brows, Remy exuded energy, willfulness; the phrase had already been coined around him, in contrast to the phrase about Vered and his generation, "It is not men of good will that we need so much just now, as good men of will." A politician to the bone, he had risen by energetic intelligence, showing himself outstandingly as a deputy, and moving quickly into the Cabinet. Remy's party, a small one, was a shade to the left of Vered's though not in the Communist camp. Indeed the entire political world, Remy liked to observe, consisted of socialist parties—each party clamored for socialism in its own terms just as each nation belligerently clamored for peace.

Was it true, as Marianne told herself, that in her first animalistic response to him it would not have mattered had he been a Royalist, a Trotskyite, or a Turk? It was a joy to accompany her plunging physical response with the thought that, although an intellectual girl, she now knew what was meant when women and novels about women spoke of that helpless, intuitive response, headlong, like letting yourself go down a ski slope.

Remy was married—Marianne had added a rueful "of course" to herself—married young to the mayor's daughter of his town, and from their arrival in Paris his handsome Carmela had achieved a notoriety for her way of inviting, to distinguished little dinner parties, people who were a shade above their social and administrative level but who could not refuse a young man so clearly on the rise. Two children, boys, whom he adored with all the tenderness of a man who had been inwardly turning away from his wife. From the beginning of the affair Marianne had known that Remy could not, would not, divorce, nor did he deny that he continued to "make love" with his wife. Used in that way, the term seemed correct.

This honesty, Marianne told herself, was at least the mark of a true liaison. In her little apartment Remy changed; there alone he could drop the constant burden of calculation, of playing his role.

It was not true of these affairs, Marianne learned, that the wife is the last to know. Carmela's tactic had been to multiply everywhere the tales of the little harlot who slept in the Residence but not in her own room. So the amused glances had turned to Vered. Remy himself at first had received with tolerant, sophisticated doubt Marianne's candid-eyed disavowals. "But why on earth should I deny it to you, if it were so!" Until, in a curious ceremony, as though blessing their union, the Old Man had invited them, only the two of them, intimately to tea one afternoon, with the woman he was to marry, a cousin of his first wife, herself a widow.

After the change of government, when Remy and Carmela themselves had moved into the Residence, Marianne had thought of resigning to go with Vered as his secretary, but this would surely have been given the worst interpretation by all the malicious tongues. Besides, the job itself had become part of her being. And she had even welcomed the vindictive feeling that Remy's wife could not demean herself by demanding her removal. "Now I am a whole woman," Marianne had thought in those days, "a bitch."

In the steeply accelerated series of crises the government reeled, swung, fell. Over his enormous war budget, Remy had fallen to Dortolot. It was then that Carmela had demanded that he break off with Marianne, and sworn never to give him a divorce. With the start of the war Dortolot had fallen, Remy had been summoned back, the man of will; the disasters had come, and in the last days, for the sake of the children, Carmela had agreed to be evacuated. So that at the fall, Marianne had been left alone with Remy.

For a short time, Remy had been confined to the Residence, but as he would not lend himself to the slightest pretense of a separate peace, it became clear that he would be sent away. Dortolot and others, they knew, had been sent to detention in honorable enough circumstances, in a castle. But Paul Vered was believed to be somewhere else, perhaps in a concentration camp. His newly married wife had insisted upon, and been allowed to accompany him.

It was this perhaps that had given Marianne the final sense of what a true wife would do, and she could not deny to herself the proud feeling that she would thus prove herself his true mate. Until Remy had been assured that his destination would be the castle, he had refused her importuning. But at last he had made the request that he be permitted to take with him his secretary.

Could the word of the conquerors be trusted? Would the German car that carried them away from the Residence indeed deliver them to a decent place of confinement, or might they at any moment find themselves behind barbed wire and—worst of all—separated? Would she then find herself alone, facing her fate, and not even knowing what had become of Remy? The anguish of that trip, the dread of that moment when the car crossed what had been their own frontier, would stay with her forever, and remain too as the greatest bond between them, something so pure that, Marianne constantly told herself, it would truly have been worth her life if they had come at the end to betrayal and death.

In their worst moments here this bond had already held, and saved them. For in their best moments Remy had confessed to her that he had known in his soul he had no right to put her to such a test, and no right to have her with him when all other prisoners were bereft of their women. Yet there had been such a fear in him to face his fate alone that he had conceded, he said, to cowardice and selfishness.

She would not let a man call it only that, and rob her. Had he not conceded, also, to love?

In these years their liaison had indeed become a marriage. The confined and binding relationship in the presence of others, the joined life in a single room, the lapses of passion, the irritation with small habits, even the tedium before what was utterly predictable in the partner, became endearing, the tension in the matching of mood and desire, the high period too of suddenly renewed intoxication, and the delineation of each person's areas of aloneness— all this, having never before really lived with a man, Marianne feared as a test for herself, just as much as the entry into imprisonment in the enemy land.

And there had come for Remy a long, desperate period of depression; early in the war she had been confronted with a deadened, hopeless man to whom inaction was unendurable. He had become touchy, querulous; the presence of Dortolot and the multifaced Joras had become insupportable to the point where Marianne had begged the Baron to let her have provisions for breakfast and lunch by themselves in their room. Even then Remy had fallen more and more into silence, and only a chance idea springing from a discussion with Vincent Maasi had saved him. Faithful and understanding, Maasi would come of an evening to sit with them; Remy would scarcely take part in the conversation, which was carried on between Marianne and their friend. Poor Vincent himself, Marianne felt, in addition to bearing the imprisonment so badly, suffered from a moonish attraction to her. Yet he came, puffed his weed-stuffed pipe, and talked of the flaws of Marxism and of the true needs of the common man.

Once, Marianne had noticed, Remy had caught a spark: something about the natural economic forces that persisted even during wars, so that in the most circuitous ways enemies traded with each other. After Maasi had gone, Remy had kept making remarks about this, and Marianne had fanned the spark, asking questions. From this, his interest had revived, quickened; a long-dormant idea had flared up. It was not political union but economic union that would save Europe. This was something to work for! Books, reports, statistics had somehow been obtained. The Baron had proved helpful. Remy had begun to study, to devour, and Marianne had plunged with him into his growing plan. It must not be idealistic; it must be simply the projection and acceleration of the natural economic process. The efficient combination of raw materials, labor, mechanization, transport, across political lines.

This work had saved him. And as the war began to turn, there had come the conviction that he would yet emerge and implement his plan. Remy had intensified his studies, grown, in her eyes, to a true thinker.

Through the whole of this war experience Marianne felt she had come fully to recognize, truly to know, her Remy. He was not a man streaked with greatness, like Paul Vered, but he was a truly admirable man, a man of courage, even with his human core of despair and fear, a man of resourcefulness, and despite his disavowal, a man of good will. She hoped only that it might be given them to continue their lives together.

Vered's eyes had opened; the peace remained in his face, and again it was of her own life that he spoke. It was his way to put this first, the life of those we care for came ahead of the fate of nations.

What she feared most with Remy, she told him, was outside their life together. The greatest danger would be the effect on him if he could not recover the leadership. There would doubtless be new personalities, leaders springing from the war, from the resistance movements. . . . Her voice hovered.

"Still, I believe they will turn to the past, but he need not worry over me," Vered reassured her. "I am only a symbol. Remy is the continuity. They will turn to him because that is the way for the nation to resume life, to say that the fault was not ours but the enemy's. Yes, I believe we shall see that this is the first desire, rather than a total new leadership." For example, even in the concentration camp men had talked of the manner in which destroyed cities were to be rebuilt. "They want to reproduce their towns exactly as they were before the war. Doubtless there will be modern conveniences, bathrooms and central heating inside the houses, but the appearance that the people hunger for is what was always familiar to them."

The familiar face in the ravaged world.

And she looked on his. Oh, how foolish it was to speculate, and already to measure ambitions. What was gained, what was real, was the warmth of this reunion, now, in this room, the clasp of this hand so miraculously surviving in the flesh, so surprisingly firm upon her own hand, which he ceremoniously carried to his lips, murmuring as in the old days, "My dear Marianne, my dear girl."

FROM THE BARON'S LARDER there came now each night a proliferation of surprises, a profligacy, a culinary pyrotechnics, as a finale. All the delicacies stored in the great cellars, the *foie gras* and the caviar, now appeared, if not in the form of a parting bribe, then in mutual celebration of the coming end to a long ordeal. Each meal began with exclamations of appreciative surprise, and with underbreath whispers, "the rogues, the robbers, the vandals." "No, I really believe this wine is from his own stock, prewar. Give the devil his due." And even the abstaining Marshal Philippe would be induced to try a little glass. As victory neared, the marshal's hesitations vanished, for it was no longer to the enemy's cynical generosity that they owed the good provender; everything here was as though already their own.

On this night the most superb of feasts had been prepared, for it had been expected as a farewell. All day the housekeeper had darted back and forth to the room of Maurice Astuque with gourmet secrets. But in the tension that had grown since the arrival of Kraus the festive atmosphere was only with the greatest difficulty maintained. The Baron had not appeared at the table. Clearly he would be dining with Kraus, and the uneasiness grew. Could he, if he wanted, persuade Kraus to depart? Was there still some chain of command among the Nazis, some headquarters in the redoubt to which the Baron could appeal?

Every beginning of a conversation soon became brittle and broke off. Marianne's absence was noticed.

She was keeping Vered company, Remy said.

What had happened between Vered and the Baron? The two had been together for the better part of an hour. Hadn't Paul Vered reported anything to Marianne? Auguste Rieber stared at Remy from under his heavy brows, as though Remy were withholding vital knowledge.

Remy didn't answer. He had had just about enough of Rieber's suspiciousness. Even at home, Auguste Rieber had always been making accusations of secret treaties, dark influences; he was one of those who believed the world was manipulated by underground powers.

Venison was served. For a moment, gastronomic remarks brought an air of animation to the table. "The Baron is really doing himself proud for our last meal," du Caux said pleasantly.

"Our last meal! You may be right!" Michaelis remarked, and the laughter was hollow. What if the Baron had already betrayed their refusal to Kraus? The mass executioner might appear at any moment with his gunman and mow them down.

"No, no, his driver is across the bridge getting drunk, and Kraus is getting drunk right here." Maurice Astuque always spoke with lofty calm, as befitted a man of high finance with inner information sources. The chief house-keeper, a firm-fleshed matron from the village, took personal care of his room.

Rieber burst out again. What if everything Vered had told them about Kraus was wrong? They were risking their lives on the word of one old man who was half out of his senses.

This time his words lighted little fires. Richard Delorme raised his voice to remind them waspishly that Vered had always been an alarmist, believing every rumor, and that the Foreign Ministry had had to take his information with the greatest caution.

Du Caux remarked that with all due respect for Vered's veracity, how could a man locked up in a concentration camp have learned all these Nazi secrets? And did it make sense that a man of Kraus's modest rank should have the power to operate so vast a program? Du Caux turned deferentially to the marshal, who nodded ponderously in agreement.

"Hallucination!" Joras interjected. It would only be natural for Vered to have become mentally disturbed over the murder of the Jews.

"We'd all be free by now," Rieber flung out, "if they hadn't brought this Jew here today."

"For shame!" Frère Luc shouted.

Michaelis shifted the line of discussion. Granted that the entire story of the mass murders was true—after all, the BBC had always proved reliable—what would the punishment of a Kraus and a few other culprits mean in balance against the millions of dead? To execute a few war criminals would only relieve the entire German people of their guilt, the people that had twice in the lifetime of everyone at this table bathed Europe in blood. What was to be done now with this people?

With momentary relief they plunged into the more general argument.

—Their teeth must be drawn, the marshal declared. They must never again be allowed to produce armaments.

"But we tried that after the last war," Michaelis reminded him.

"The nation must be broken up and put back into small agricultural duchies like this one," Dortolot offered.

Impulsively, Remy decided to test his overriding idea. Wasn't this the psychological moment to seize the leadership with something concrete, constructive, hopeful?

As he began, he felt curiously as if he were at one of the Cabinet meetings in the old days when many of these same men would be gathering into their chairs, and in the lull before the Premier arrived he, the youngest, sometimes tested himself by putting forward an idea. "We must think not in terms of fragmentation but of greater unity," Remy declared. "Unities, larger and larger in scope. A unified Germany would be no danger to a unified Europe—"

"That old pipe dream!" Dortolot exploded.

Remy swept on. The idea was an old one but it kept recurring because it was a natural necessity, and it would keep on recurring until it became a reality. Unity had been attempted again and again through force; the latest example was this war. But there was a natural unity that had to precede political unification. This was economic unity. The coal and steel complex was a perfect example of a natural economic unit—

"With Germany!"

"You want to marry the murderers!"

Remy saw Dortolot exchanging shrewd glances with Joras, as if to say, "Let him rave. If he goes on with this idea, he's finished. We're rid of him."

Remy plunged on. What had they fought in this war if not a hate-rousing racism—

Frère Luc, with glowing eyes, broke in, offering help that Remy felt he might well have done without, at this moment. After the bloodbath of the war, Frère Luc cried, the sense of human brotherhood must return. All Europe, being Christian—

"Religion!" The aged banker, Schall, suddenly screeched out of his withdrawn, vegetable quiescence. "After what God has permitted, do you think anyone will still listen to you?"

"Not God! Man has done all this!" Luc burst out.

"You, a priest, deny the punishment of God?" Rieber glowered at Frère Luc. At last he had caught him in his apostasy!

It was Dortolot who led the discussion back to Remy, tauntingly, to finish him off. "How much sovereignty do you intend to give up, my dear Remy? The army, first of all?"

"It is not at all a question of giving up, but of creating new entities, first, a supra-national economic body, then——"

"It may surprise you; you are a little younger than the rest of us," Dortolot remarked drily, "but this idea pops up after every war. Last time"—he nodded toward Vered's room—"it was your distinguished predecessor. I believe he even published a book on the subject."

"Of course!" Remy retorted. "People have tried to learn to fly, since Icarus. Now we fly."

He had scored a point. Dortolot choked down a mouthful of food—Remy wished Marianne were there to see it. "False analogy!" Dortolot spluttered, unable to find anything better.

Vincent Maasi entered the argument. "The worker understands with his stomach—he crosses national borders to find a job."

With the word "worker" the old hostilities exploded into the open. "Your workers! Your five-day week! When the Germans were working sixty hours to build tanks! It was you who betrayed us, you and your Vered," Astuque declared coldly.

Michaelis, Joras, Rieber joined the chorus. Vered! With his pacifist ideas, his collective security!

"Where were our tanks? Where was our steel?" the marshal boomed.

"You had steel. You put it into your damned defense wall instead of into tanks!" Remy heard himself trying to outshout them.

"Steel production actually rose under the five-hour week!" Maasi roared.

The marshal stood up from his chair, his face apoplectic. "My wall held them—waiting for your tanks and planes that never came."

"Planes!" Remy turned on Dortolot. "We ordered planes. Then, you were in power—"

"Ordered! On paper! With no finances, no factories—"

Astuque sat calm in the uproar. At him, Remy flung his accusation. "No factories. True. Because you wouldn't invest capital to modernize."

"Why should they," Dortolot thundered, "when Vered was nationalizing the arms industry?"

They were there. Back at the crux. The marshal sat down, a man whose point is proven.

"Everything goes back to him, to that—" The unspoken word hung over the table, pacifist, internationalist, Marxist, Jew. The hatreds lay like bones on their plates, garbage to be dumped over a sick, tortured old man. Remy found himself on his feet, pouring out his words, permitting no interruption. "You blame him, the scapegoat. You disregard all the facts, all your own errors. But I was his War Minister, you can't hoodwink me. It was Vered who pulled us out of the crisis when our factories were occupied with sitdown strikers. Have you forgotten? Have you forgotten the millions of unemployed? Have you forgotten that the entire country was bankrupt, that our industrial plant was outmoded, that the farmers"—he glared at Rieber—"had their gold hidden under their mattresses,

148

that the banks were afraid to make normal business loans? And what happened? It was Paul Vered who floated a huge national loan and persuaded the first big bankers to subscribe. That was what lured the gold from under the mattresses, and got the wheels turning again! It was Vered's shorter workweek that absorbed the unemployed —have you forgotten? What Roosevelt did in America, Paul Vered did for us. Yes, he called for collective peace, but out of strength! It was Paul who started the rearmament plan and forced it through when you all held back, even though we knew the Germans were arming! Yes, while he armed for defense, he called for peace. Is it a sin now to hate war? A sin to learn from our mistakes?"

Suddenly Remy saw that a change had come over their faces. No, they were not really with him, but a change had come. Then he knew. Snatching up his glass, he proposed, "A toast, then, gentlemen, to our elder statesman, whom God has spared to return to us—to Paul Vered."

They politely raised their glasses.

"Good appetite, gentlemen." How long had the Baron been standing behind him, smiling, in the arched entrance? Though he usually wore civilian clothes in the evening, the Baron tonight appeared in his most elegant uniform, his small feet in hand-tailored dress boots. And his holster, always empty, tonight bulged.

"We have been discussing a plan for a united Europe," Remy remarked.

"Yes. An exciting subject," said the Baron. His little smiling eyes moved from one side of the table to the other as he came into the room. Stopping just behind Remy, he remarked, rather privately, Would Remy and his two friends care to continue the discussion over coffee, in his rooms?

As the three men left with the Baron, the others turned to their dessert. The fearful tension re-established itself around the table; all the divided passion of a moment before seemed meaningless against what might now be about to happen upstairs.

For the first time in their years of detention here the three men crossed to the other side of the stair landing, passing the guard, who only half stiffened to attention for the Baron. In the Baron's wing the corridor proved a counterpart of their own, with the same floral pattern on the carpet, the same baroque foliage in the ceiling, the same gilded candle brackets transformed to electric fixtures.

Even in this crisis it was repugnant for the Baron to think of placing weapons in the hands of the enemy. Yet to order the guards to arrest the new commander might provoke trouble. Enough that he had got rid of Schreiter, having him take the colonel's aide into the village.

In the corridor here was his gun room, with his hunting equipment, and as they passed, the Baron remarked that the marshal might care to examine his wild-game rifles.

So the marshal was armed with a bear gun.

Remy, too, picked up and admired a long-nosed rifle,

incised with the Baron's coat of arms; the feel of the weapon sent a current of gratification through his entire body. In an antique cabinet with many little drawers, indicated by the Baron, were boxes of cartridges.

Dortolot, not to be outdone, possessed himself of a heavy six-barreled pistol, and so the expedition was ready.

Though he had locked the hallway entrance, Kraus had not shut the connecting door to the Baron's premises, should the old boy care to watch the sport. So it was that he did not even turn his head when he sensed a presence in that doorway.

He was riding strong in his favorite position, the bitch on all fours on the carpet. She was naked now; he too had flung off his clothes, and he had reached the great high plateau, the stage of inexhaustibility, the liquor as always giving him prolonged potency without need to discharge. The full Polish buttocks made a perfect, glowing globe; with her head down there was nothing else present for him from the female but this pink globe glowing red, the flesh fiery from his slappings; he was no damned sadist, he never used the strap, only good solid smacks with the palm, they loved it, a French bitch had admitted it to him. And this one too, her hair swept the floor and her stupid laugh gurgled up to him—*Ludern, ludern, nicht schmeissen,* she laughed—which meant good, she wanted it all right but not quite so hard. Oh, it was known, the Polish peasants had special hooks in the floor to tie their wives for the regular weekly whipping. Ride her! A fucking red-lighted globe, with a hole for his stick of dynamite, shove it in and blow the whole shitty world, let it blast to the end of perdition! So he rode her, oblivious, let the old fart watch, while she thrust back to his thrust. There was no fine delicate inside gripping and throbbing like his Hungarian baroness could provide, but solid peasant thrusting, and she grunted with it, thrashed and babbled and laughed, clawing the floor and circling under him, the blasted fucking world, tomorrow the final explosion— then all at once the flesh beneath him collapsed. A different gurgle came from the female as her face was raised from the floor, and he followed her head movement. The idiotic Baron stood there with his favorite prisoners. That was too much! Bringing them in here to join the party! Even if they *had* signed the document.

But the idiots were pointing cannons at him!

With a leap Kraus was upright, even as he heard the Baron stupidly declare, "I regret that I must put you under arrest." Kraus lunged for his holster, flung across his clothes on a chair, but the civilian, Remy, had already seized his gun while the marshal was poking a long, heavy hunting rifle almost into his belly.

"Traitor!" he shouted at the Baron, and in his first access of rage, every filthy curse he had ever flung at the Jew-shit came bursting out of his mouth; he did not even realize he stood naked as he spat the raw clots of malediction at them. Kraus heard his own voice screaming as though he were the Fuehrer himself, as though by sheer rage he would annihilate them. The female had scuttled out of the room, and suddenly he realized he was bare-skinned in front of their guns. His rage foundered, half rose again— the unfairness of taking him like this! They must have put the cunt up to it, he'd catch her yet and shove a gun barrel up her hole for real, he was not finished! And his man Gunter, and Schreiter—this cunning old bastard of a Baron had purposely sent them off into the village. What a dumb, stupid, easy idiot of a victim he had been!

He heard the Baron babbling on, the international convention on prisoners of war, the honor of the Reich, a threat against the safety of his prisoners and therefore . . .

The whole of it was: the Baron had sold him out in exchange for his own safety. The old crumbling turd. Then Kraus's fury turned on himself. Why, just this one time, had he broken his rule and let Gunter go to the tavern! Why, in his last move in the war, had he fallen into this most common, the most stupid, of traps, the cunthole! Or was it really his last move? Surely there was still something to be done. Surely there were still troops coming into the redoubt. If only he could get word . . .

"I will put on my uniform," he said as he made to complete his movement toward the chair. The three prisoners with their ridiculous, huge hunting guns swung with his turning. That ancient marshal looked as though he hadn't held a rifle in his hands in sixty years; if he pressed the trigger by accident—it must be an elephant gun! Kraus could feel his whole body exploded into flying chunks of flesh. Why had he even attempted this stupid maneuver? He should have stayed with the troops and fought. No, his own sense of duty had trapped him, carrying out his final orders, transporting prisoners into the redoubt when everyone else was throwing away their uniforms and taking to the roads. Home, home, going home, they all called as they walked inland, and in this instant Kraus longingly saw himself arriving, weary, hungry, a nondescript civilian figure; his wife with her good loyal face stood waiting in the doorway, and the boys rushed toward their papa the hero, and the girls came into his arms.

The bastard traitor didn't even let him take his uniform from the chair! That clown of an ex-Premier who had grabbed his pistol—Remy—whispered something to the Baron, and over the face of the sly old shit came a gleam, like when some pimply school kid whispers a frigging joke. "You had better stay as you are," the Baron said to Kraus. "I'll see that you don't catch cold."

They marched him, naked, down a back stairway, a winding stone staircase inside the castle walls; not a soul could hear you if you shouted your head off. The mouth of the elephant gun remained planted in his asshole. *No!* His entire record, his entire service career, screamed out at this indignity, this unjust, treacherous ending—to be locked up naked like some bare-assed monkey in a cage!

There he was, in the castle dungeon. Unbelievable. The middle ages. Would Gunter at least get wind and go for help? No, the bastards would have made sure of Gunter, probably shot the poor lout through the back of the head. Or perhaps they would still haul the fellow down and throw him in here? At least, not alone, then.

"Prisoner of war!" he shouted in scorn at his captors. "Very well, then I demand your precious prisoner-of-war status, according to my rank. My uniform——" And for the first time, his overwhelming slip of the mind came upon Kraus. "My box! My box!"

"Your box?" the Baron repeated.

"In the room. My personal belongings."

"Ah. The military strongbox." That dirty toad had caught on. "I must first make certain whether it is not the property of the Reich."

Their steps were already receding up the stairway. "You will receive your uniform and belongings back in due time," the Baron called. Then he was gone.

They had him. Kraus knocked his fist against his head. All the rest would be routine—some drumhead military court for "war criminals." War criminals! How could there be such a thing! Savage revenge! Gangsters, not soldiers. How soon would it come? A month? A year? He would stand in court with the best, the greatest of the Reich—but the thought brought little relief. Cursed and cursed and cursed be his stupidity. "Be careful, you are not always as clever as you believe," his wife had warned him. "My handsome Kraus." She had mocked him from the first. A handsome fellow needs a sensible girl. And a safe, sensible branch of the service, she had advised. Without too much competition. Specialize. Become an expert.

The Jews. Ideal. Close to the Fuehrer's greatest desire. He would advance, he would earn the gratitude of the Fuehrer himself. (Dead, dead, he's out of it.) And in a sudden access of resentment, Kraus wished he could have spat out of his life the entire organization, the whole rigmarole with the Jews. If she had let him alone, let him be a plain soldier—you take your chance, you live or die according to your luck, and with the shitty war finished you at least go home your own man.

He flung himself on the bench. There was a blanket. Mistakes, wrong turns. . . . If on arrival here he had only taken the Baron aside, offered him a share from the casket—the rich are always the greediest. . . .

With the key from the uniform's trousers, the Baron opened the strongbox. A surface of blue-white diamonds, rocks as large as sugar cubes. His fingers lifted out some samples from the top layer. What Jews gave their Jewesses. Pure jewels, here, freed from their settings, except for a few that still were attached to earrings or engagement rings.

This was indeed a fortune, into the millions. And digging further, the Baron's fingers touched on a substance of a different texture: warmer, more rounded things were there. He made a little hole among the precious stones and came to the second stratum, of gold. Scooping out some samples, he held them on his palm—gold wedding rings, men's and women's.

Still deeper in the box was something else, uneven, pebbly to his fingers. For a moment as he held a palmful, the Baron couldn't think what they were, these small nubs of gold that formed a solid mass at the bottom of the box. He rolled a few against his thumb. And then it came to him. These were dental fillings, removed from human teeth.

I T SEEMED OUT OF PLACE to laugh, and yet as Remy described what had happened—the poor Polish slavey scurrying off on all fours, the naked Nazi drawing himself up with military aplomb and demanding his rights under the Geneva convention—Marianne's laughter pealed forth as it hadn't in four entire years. Let this be the harbinger of their liberty! Still shaking with laughter, she turned half guiltily to Vered, for there was a melancholy in the incident too—that the immeasurable affliction his eyes had seen had come, when all was known, from such farcical nothings as this naked Kraus. "There is a time to weep and a time to laugh," Vered assured her, but as one who cannot yet join in the mirth. And Remy went on with the description, the march down the narrow stone stairway, and the imprisonment in the dungeon.

The marshal and Dortolot had recounted the victory upstairs, and now Vincent Maasi and Frère Luc came hurrying to Vered's little room. Presently, by some curious emotion of unity in their triumph, the others also arrived, the whole group crowding the bedroom as when Vered had first appeared. Marshal Philippe, still carrying his bear gun, stood beaming in the doorway, and behind him there was even Auguste Rieber, hanging about the fringes.

Marianne burst out laughing again. "Oh, I wish I could have seen him, naked, marching down that stairway—"

"I assure you he has an excellent physique," Remy declared.

She made a face at him. Joras had captured a flagon in the dining room, and a toast was proposed. In the rising excitement Michaelis suggested, Wasn't it the moment now to seize the entire castle, so as to hand it over intact and fully subdued to the advancing Allies?

Indeed, the marshal agreed, the possession of the castle could be of importance, for who could be sure that the enemy's plan for a last stand in the redoubt had really crumbled?

They must disarm Schreiter, Joras proposed, and his entire platoon!

Now Marianne felt alarmed. The escapade had gone to their heads. Could anyone imagine this group of old and middle-aged statesmen attacking Schreiter and his troops?

But no, Remy pointed out, the take-over could readily be effected through the Baron. He was now *de facto* their accomplice. They must convince him that the guarding troops had best be dismissed. Surely the men would prefer to go their ways than to be herded, when the Allies arrived, into prison camps. Or even worse, risk themselves in futile resistance here. For who could tell that another Kraus would not appear to command them to stand and fight?

All agreed now, for another approach to the Baron. Let there only be such unity when they reached home!

Promptly at nine, Gunter returned from the village, with the clear-eyed air of a soldier who has partaken of his justly earned relaxation and reports back to his post. The chief, he expected, would still be at it. The order of rank had never quite been abandoned between them in such matters. Though Kraus was a good fellow, and though Gunter might walk in on any scene whatsoever without embarrassing the chief, in such things it was not for him to take part—he could get his elsewhere. Indeed, as to some of the things he had seen, Gunter would not especially have wanted to take part; he was hardly straight-laced, he was not averse to having a girl here and there for the release of his sexual energies, but Gunter was in love, only a year married, with a baby on the way from his last leave, and he was somewhat ashamed of debauchery. Tonight he had a feeling there would be a complete letting down of all barriers for the very end, there would be a drunken sport going on in there, and the boss would even wave for him to take part, as though their army rank was already gone and they were back to being two plain fellows from the same sort of small town, simply one a bit older than the other. But just for a last few days of fun, Gunter didn't want to go back to his wife dirty. He even had a feeling of fate and reward about it—all sorts of things could yet happen, even a battle. For a bad sin he could still have bad luck at the end. Therefore right now he was going to have to be careful how he handled himself.

Gunter rapped, briefly, there was no answer; listening for a moment, he heard nothing. He tried the door—still locked. Then he went and knocked on the Baron's door. Excusing himself, Gunter said he was reporting back for duty. Could the Baron tell him—was his chief perhaps asleep in there?

The Baron led him into his suite; the connecting door to Kraus's room was open and Gunter saw at once that the room was empty. But Kraus's uniform, he noticed with astonishment, lay on a chair, neatly folded. He looked at once to the table. The treasure box was not there.

"Your officer has left," the Baron said, with his pleasant manner, as one might remark that a visitor had gone home early. "I provided him with civilian clothing." He entered the empty room, Gunter following. "I must dispose of this," the Baron said, laying his hand on the uniform, as though not quite sure what he ought to do with it. Gunter, too, stared at the garment on the chair. The side arm had not been left behind with the rest. Naturally. A man must hold onto his weapon.

"He gave no order for me?" The words had come out of themselves. Not that he couldn't think of what to do. But long ago in this war he had decided that the best way was to be ordered. It took all the cloudiness and moodiness out of life, even all the anger, and also the bit of guilt he had felt when first assigned to his special duty. An outstanding athlete in high school, a prize marksman in the Hitler Jugend, he had joined the SS, naturally, to be with the bravest, the toughest, the elite, and he had been surprised (not knowing that his sweetheart's father had used certain influence) when instead of being sent to the front he had been assigned to special duty as a bodyguard, driver, and aide to an important officer in a special secret section. True, it had to do with the worst and most cunning enemy of the Reich, the Jews, so it was important. Except for a couple of *Yupen* in the lower grades, whom he had helped beat up in the schoolyard, Gunter had not known any Jews. There had been a Jewish pharmacist in his town, and he remembered as a child watching the drugstore windows at night, for it was said that in the back of the store the Jew concocted poison to put into the medicines. In any case the druggist with his little *Yupen* who had been beat up in the schoolyard was soon gone, and the town saved from poisoning. When Gunter had understood the task of his special service he had felt a bit uncomfortable, but after all modern war was total war, as Kraus often said, and it could not be denied that the Jews were a terrible security danger in occupied areas. They blew up troops trains, the women were saboteurs, even children carried messages in the underground. It was necessary to round them up and transport them to concentration camps. There, the able-bodied were put to work, and the useless, who were merely mouths to feed, were, he learned, eliminated. This had jarred him at the start but the logic of it had to be admitted. A few times, driving Kraus into the elimination areas, Gunter had been offered a look through the peepholes but—as with the offered debauches—he had preferred to remain clean. Watching the smoke from the chimneys and smelling the smell was enough. As Kraus said, in war there were some hellish tasks, and the true heroes were not always those at the front but those behind the lines who did not shrink from whatever was necessary.

Kraus had always given him exact orders, even when he went out on leave. Like tonight. "Take three hours. Go into town with the boys from the post here, have a few drinks and get yourself laid." He had done exactly that.

What would Kraus have wanted him to do now? In a way it was clear from what the commander himself had done. And it was correct that Kraus had not waited for them to go off together; that would have lowered Kraus in the last moment.

The Baron now voiced his own interpretation. "I think the colonel meant that you were free to do the same," the Baron said. "In fact, he left something for you."

From his pocket the Baron produced one of the diamonds which he had removed from the strongbox with just this situation in mind. Gunter accepted the stone in his palm, gazing with only an instant of doubt at the Baron. Might it be that Kraus had left more than one stone for him? No, why should this wealthy nobleman cheat him? And besides, his boss had known that he was already pretty well fixed, for Kraus had made jokes about the full opportunities that had come Gunter's way from those swine-fed Hungarian Jews—they weren't even religious Jews, they cheated their own God and ate pork. When Gunter waited in Kraus's car outside the headquarters hotel, they would sneak up to him and offer anything, gold, jewels, property, if only he would use his influence with his commander to get a name stricken from the list. Gunter had sent home his gifts as they came along—this was his insurance—and now he could go home and live for quite a few years in comfort, buy himself a good business—oh yes, that part was taken care of. The extra diamond was doubtless Kraus's parting gift for good behavior, a present for his wife.

Yet now that the moment had come—and how he had dreamed of the day when he would head for his own little town, sleep with his own wife regularly in their own bed, waiting for their baby to be born—now that the day had come, everything seemed askew. Too sudden.

"I could find some clothes for you, too."

All the fellows were doing it, Gunter knew. At the inn, the fellows from regular duty here had talked of nothing else. Half the garrison had already slipped away in the last week. Nobody heard of men being stopped for their discharge papers any more. In fact it was just as easy to go in full uniform; all you had to say was that your outfit had been overrun, the officers had surrendered and you had escaped—if there was anyone to bother to ask.

Yet something felt unfinished. They had come here for

the last fight. He was going to be in a real fight for once, instead of just driving a car and guarding corridors. A battle such as he had grown up for. And to end like this seemed unworthy of all his school-day dreams.

The Baron must have understood. "We must suffer our defeat," he said like a wise father. "The Communists and the American gangsters, they were more than three to one against us. When you try to bring something great into this world you must be prepared that everything will be done to shatter it." He spoke reverently, without mentioning the Fuehrer, and Gunter was embarrassed that he had been allowing his own little personal problems to let him forget the tremendous grief that was upon the nation.

His eyes wandered, in shame. The colonel had left behind his fine boots, he noticed, and even his socks. "Sir," he said to the Baron, who was after all the ranking officer here once more, "if you could send me home on leave, and supply me with travel orders, I would go in uniform. That way everything would be correct."

The Baron smiled. Soldierly and proper. He would write out the orders at once.

Something pressed him, not only to get this fellow out of the way but to have the place clear of them all. At one time quite long ago, it might even have been in his childhood, a disagreeable smell had infested the castle, making itself known in whiffs in odd corners, at the turn of the stairs, in the hallway, in a bedroom, sometimes hanging on for a week, sometimes gone in an hour. The place had been scrubbed to the bare stone, every cupboard and every storeroom had been emptied, the plumbing had been taken apart in a hunt for dead mice, yet so far as he could recall the source had never been discovered. Eventually the smell had vanished; it had vacated the premises.

His oppressive sense of grief was returning, of needing to be alone with his grief. It was from the moment that he had put his fingers into the strongbox that he had felt this hopeless sense of ugliness, of shame, of the movement brought to shame, of the high emotions of the past brought to dishonor.

There—he had written out the order, and the young soldier, taking it, flushed, and finally got out another request. "Sir," he said, "since he left his boots, could I—"

"Of course, of course, take the boots!" The Baron went and handed them to the boy. A pity to have some American grab hold of them. With childish joy, like his own children so long ago over some coveted toy received for Christmas, the lad at once pulled on the fine boots.

He would, the Baron decided, get the entire detachment to leave, too. Right now. It was a good moment as Schreiter was off for the night. Tell the men on duty that he had received word the Americans might arrive by dawn. The men all knew that the enemy had special orders as to the SS, so that if captured they would be held longer than ordinary prisoners. Let the lot of them go, let this young Gunter take them off in the command car. The entire trappings of the war—cleared out!

Hurrying down with the soldier to the yard, the Baron called the few night guards from their posts. Odd—several of the men had their gear all packed. There was a flinging of stuff into the car. The men even bid him a hearty farewell, some with touching words about his good treatment. They would pass the word, they promised, to Schreiter on the other side. And presently the Baron let down the bridge and the command car felt its way, in blackout, out of his domain.

Unrealistic as he knew it to be, the Baron half imagined the Americans now pulling up, embarking their load of notables, and departing, at last leaving him here altogether alone, exquisitely alone, to roam through his rooms and set everything back in order as after a long roisterous absurd house party.

At least he had not taken off his wristwatch, and its numerals were luminous. They showed ten o'clock when Kraus heard, or felt, some sort of vibration overhead. The muffled effect of a vehicle came to him. Only one. He must be under the courtyard, and that was his own car, leaving. Gunter? Was Gunter deserting him too, leaving him naked to die like a starved rat in this dungeon? Then Kraus mastered himself. Gunter had discovered what had happened to him, and was going for help.

Before morning he would be back with Panzers, blasting his way into this toy castle. Then, Kraus saw himself marching up those stairs. Personally, he would drag out that old Baron, naked in his bones, and that old marshal, and those two cocky premiers, strip the lot of them and the blonde too. Personally, he would mow them down, throwing the old Jew on the heap for good measure.

The outrage still churned in Kraus, stirring his fury at his own mistake for dragging that Jew here. Always the Jew. Without the Jew he'd have been all right. Got away from here with a clean bill of health and his coffer.

Then—Kraus had an image of himself in the role of a mysterious wealthy wanderer. He was not deceiving himself; though with that statement from the prisoners he could have gotten a good head start, they had him on their list, and as long as the Jewish vermin were not completely stamped out they would be crawling after him, with their bug eyes and their feelers, hunting him all over the earth. He had known this all along. That was why his war task had been more perilous than any assignment at the front. For others the danger would be over when the shooting stopped, but his own danger would continue, even if there was victory, as long as there was a Jew alive. The dirty assassins.

Perhaps he would even have had his face altered by plastic surgery, although he had been careful about photographs, always stepping aside when the boys made their souvenir snapshots in the captured cities. True, once or twice some cunt had cajoled him into letting her take a remembrance photo of her handsome Kraus, but the chances were they would have destroyed the pictures anyway before their husbands got back from the war. So he saw himself, with his fortune safely banked in Switzerland, living in Buenos Aires for a time, and moving back to Europe, to Madrid perhaps, and in each city a luscious mistress like his Hungarian baroness—might he send her a message to join him? No, a new one, always a fresh one, younger. Or moving on to Egypt, or Damascus, a pasha, with harem girls, the Mufti would take care of him, and he could even finish his job on the Jews. And at home his children would grow. He saw himself like in an old Emil Jannings film, slipping back at Christmas and peering through the window at the family celebration, always careful not to be seen—for how many years would the Jews keep watch for him? No! Stupidities! Here he was, already caught! Locked in a dungeon. His rage turned back completely on the Baron; right now if he could get that stringy old neck in his fingers. . .

For one shuddery instant a forbidden thought skittered through Kraus, through his very veins, like some pestilential inner flea one cannot see or seize. A single, forbidden question: Could there after all be such a thing as retribution?

Left in here like this to die.

But with a thousand knives he slashed at the thought. Not one body had he ever personally done this to.

Besides, the Americans would come soon; they'd free him from this hole, even if only to make him a war prisoner. Wait! Could they even know who he was? Naked. No, there would be that damned Baron and that damned Jew and all the others to name him.

A trial then. A vast, lofty chamber, with judges sitting on high, and he would stand before the world. "What do you want of me? It was God's work I carried out!

"All right, I confess I have not been a good Christian; since I grew up, I haven't gone to church, prayed—but I have never forgotten that the Jews killed the Savior. They schemed and seized him and even when Pontius Pilate wanted to let him go the Jews screamed 'Crucify him!' They are forever accursed. God used the Romans to destroy the Jews, to wipe them from the face of the Holy Land. It is God's will, as everyone knows, that this people should cease to exist, for having murdered his only Son. Yet like bugs they are difficult to clean out. The devils crawled away to the far corners, all over the earth, and dug in and bred. Again and again God used the Church to wipe the earth clean of them, in the Crusades, and in the Spanish Inquisition. And finally the work fell on us!"

But a clever defendant must also test himself with the arguments of the prosecution: If the destruction of the Jews was God's will, why had the destroyer been destroyed? Why was Germany going down in defeat?

The entire image of the court had vanished; the question came from within himself, from Kraus.

A Christian might answer it was not God but the power of evil, the devilish power of the remaining Jews in the world, that had engineered the defeat.

His wife took the children to church, but did he still believe at all in any kind of God? Each man, Kraus solemnly told himself, must sometime face the deepest questions, and here naked in the dungeon was his time.

What God? All this shambles, the wiping out of entire cities, smashed from the air, women and children buried alive, and everyone suffering stupidity and injustice, and now defeat.

Did he believe in an afterlife? The tons of fine white ashes in the camp—that was the final answer. Man was on his own. That was himself, Kraus. The Jews would still try to destroy him, hunt him down, and by his own cunning and strength he must save himself. His answer to the court would be that he had been assigned to the Jew-question and his chief Heydrich had ordered him to draw up some population statistics and that was all he had done, out of the standard statistical books. He had read out the figures at the conference. The Final Solution had been adopted by the leaders and he had been ordered to work at the administration of the solution in the field. As in every military service he would have been put to a summary court-martial and shot if he had failed to perform his duty. He had performed his duty in the most humanitarian way possible. He had never acted on his own responsibility but could prove that each transport had been authorized from Berlin; indeed he had been nothing more than a timetable engineer and a sanitation expert. There was not one single case where he had personally raised his hand against a Jew, much less taken part in any killing. Once the bodies were assembled and placed on the trains, they still had their chance of life as laborers in the camps, so that it could not by any means be construed that he sent people to their death.

He was a soldier under orders.

On this he must stand. And it was true, wasn't it?

Then a peculiar thought came to Kraus. Why had he never been able to tell his wife quite what he did? She knew. She knew the damned Jews made his life miserable. Yet in a way she didn't exactly know. The children didn't exactly know. Always when a message came while he was on leave at home, a telephone call about a transport, some filthy bothersome detail, he had spoken of labor transports. When all that atrocity propaganda got around, his wife had had sense enough not to ask him the final questions.

And his sons—why did he still want to be able to tell them he had fought at the front? Why was there almost a wish not to go back to them now but to go into exile, into wandering, not to have to live face to face every day with a wife and children who would know what he had done?

Suddenly Kraus felt as though he were hanging from a great hook, a butcher's meat hook, by the collar of his coat. The lawyers were at him, tormenting him. They had found out everything, every last detail. What of that death march from Budapest? "After you had been instructed from Berlin itself to call back the march, did you not send it out once more on your own authority?"

"Fortifications," he tried to reply, but the way he was hanging from the hook, the words were strangled in his throat. By a great effort he heaved his body and the words burst out, "Earthworks. Advancing armies."

They sneered. "And the train from Budapest that was actually countermanded by Berlin. You sent it to Auschwitz. Were not the thousands of Jews on that train people whom you, even against orders from your superiors, sent to their death?"

"No, not on my order!" He twisted and heaved and his lungs opened to a great shout. "The Fuehrer's personal order!" And then there was a pause, an interlude in the courtroom during which they all quietly listened while he explained in a calm, lucid tone, so that for once they would understand. The order, from the beginning, came from the very top. Anything that might afterward intervene and seem to contradict the order was invalid. A man had to finish his job. When you pull weeds from a garden, if you leave one, the damned filth will start to grow all over again, and spread. There is a kind of weed, his father had shown him, standing over him when he was a boy, a weed with roots that spread underground. You have to dig them out to the very tip, it is amazing how far the roots spread. If you break off and leave only the least bit, the whole thing will grow again.

Therefore he had had to persevere. Everything that intervened, to make him stop, to make him leave a bit, was the work of the Jews, with their influence all over the world, with their gold sent from America, to buy off and to bribe even the high members of the party! Not him! To the end, he had carried out his job!

Despite the great impression his words made, the lawyer with his clever tricks was at him again. "You still pretend to believe, then, in the myth of a world conspiracy of Jews, over which your demented Fuehrer created the greatest mass slaughter in human history?"

"A myth? It is there in the books, in black and white! In their own secret books, admitted in their own words! In the secret meetings of the Elders of Zion, every hundred years. I have made a special study of this in my research duties. In the cemetery of Prague, with their cabalistic rabbis. And the next time with the Rothschilds in their palace in France. And the next time in Switzerland, the Zionists came from every corner of the world—"

"I put it to you that you know this is absolute poppy-cock."

Even as he hung there he managed a sardonic chortle. Poppycock. What about the Jew Paul Vered, upstairs, who had plotted with America and Britain to force Germany into war and destroy her? What about the Jew Trotsky who had seized Russia for communism and had then gone out to plot Jewish communist revolutions all over the world? What about Rosenfeld, the secret Jew who ruled the United States—

"Come now, you don't pretend to be as insane as Hitler! You don't believe President Roosevelt—"

"He was surrounded by Jews! I'll prove it!" And with a final superhuman effort, lifting himself clear off the hook, Kraus leaped down and unmasked his tormentor. "I prove it by yourself!" He pointed at the big crooked nose. "All you foreign lawyers are Jews!"

And a laughter, a sputtering laughter, welled up in Kraus at his own cleverness, and a weeping for his own valor. To your dying breath you must stick to your task, complete what you started; you must believe it or you cannot do it; if you let up on one Jew, then it was all a lie and each Jew you seized was a murder. No, there is no murder in war, there is soldiering, a man's job, perfection, completion, victory. Die spitting in their faces!

And then, in the night, the Baron came to him.

The sudden relief of a human presence was so great that Kraus momentarily lost his impulse to attack, to kill the old bastard.

The traitor knew he deserved to be killed, for while still unlocking the door he called, "Don't worry, I am going to let you go."

Kraus held himself wary. There the bastard stood with a strong torch, his claws on his Mauser, keeping his distance. No—too dangerous to leap at him; he was an experienced hunter, quick on the trigger. Kraus began his tirade. There was still a Germany, there would be a reckoning—

But the Baron cut him short. This was another voice he had, dry, decided. "I am going to let you go, but you will get out of my place. Your man is already gone on his way home, and so are the others. I want my place clean."

On his free arm he carried Kraus's uniform, and also a civilian jacket and trousers.

For a long hour the Baron had sat with the strongbox before him. And a nausea had established itself within him, like the polluted grief a man feels when still young, when he first knows for certain that his wife, like all other women, sleeps with other men. What was in this box gave him the sort of ultimate disgust that he had thought himself to have outlived.

Had the Fuehrer known of this? Something told him it was known and dismissed with one of those impatient side gestures, some sneer about trifles. Though at other times the most minute detail, even the design stamped into a button on a uniform, would be seized upon while war plans waited.

Then, pushing the strongbox away, the Baron had decided he had to let the creature go. Let the Americans find Kraus somewhere else. If they must find out about all this, let them find it out somewhere else. Not here, in the dreamed-of realm of a *Herrenvolk,* all noble, high engineers and cavaliers.

As Kraus put on his uniform, scorning the civilian clothing, the Baron sat on the stone bench. He brought himself to speak to this specimen. "Tell me, Kraus. The items of gold—I don't mean the rings—was this the Fuehrer's order?"

"To salvage all wealth and possessions. That was the order." Kraus demanded his boots. The Baron explained that Gunter had taken them, and instead he had brought shoes from Kraus's luggage. Frowning, Kraus put them on.

"And the detail of the teeth?" the Baron persisted.

What was this, already an inquisition in a war crimes trial? A jailer with a gun at your head demanding

answers? Kraus laced his shoes and stood erect, glaring
down at the shrunken old Baron. Already a thousand revenge plans—just let him get out of this place—crowded
his mind. "The Jews themselves traded their teeth in the
camps. Even there, they made a black market," he
snapped. "The Fuehrer's order was to waste nothing."

"Did he know of this detail?"

"How should I know! You were his personal friend!"
The burning, final retort was on the tip of Kraus's tongue:
Ask him! Angrily, for the first time with a kind of hatred,
he saw the Fuehrer in some bunker under the earth like
this one, blowing his brains out. To blow his brains out
and leave the whole mess! Leave the country in ruins!
Leave honest soldiers to be hunted as war criminals! "I
brought that stuff with me to turn over," he snapped at the
Baron. "It is my duty still to turn it over. I demand you
restore it to me."

The Baron nodded as though he had half heard, and
stood up, motioning Kraus from the cell.

What he would do with the casket the Baron still did
not know. To hand it over to the enemy—against that he
revolted. If not for the shameful part, a perverse flicker
within him told him the treasure might after all, as well as
anywhere else . . . no, he had never even entertained
the thought.

He marched Kraus in front of him up the stairs.

The hall was deserted, Kraus saw, not a guard on post.
The empty courtyard was unwatched, and even at the gate

there was no sentry. Once again he demanded his box, once again the Baron coldly replied that it was state property—did he want a receipt? In the last moment, as the Baron pressed the control and the gate swung open, Kraus suddenly took the civilian clothing after all, sticking the bundle under his arm.

The drawbridge had come down. He stepped across into the silent blacked-out town. On the other side he stood with a momentary feeling of disorientation. Now he was on his own. Behind him, he heard the subdued mechanical grinding of the drawbridge being raised.

Now he was free of that whole degenerate crew, the foul old Baron, infected by the enemy. He'd see the lot of them go up in smoke, soon enough!

The stroke of his steps on the cobblestones was the only sound in the village, and automatically Kraus touched down his feet so that the steps became scarcely audible. Not from fright but from the same impulse that makes one talk in hushed tones in a great empty hall.

The blackout reached even across the sky, starless, moonless. At least the town was not welcoming the Allies with a blaze of illumination and flowers in the street, as he had heard Germans had done outside Frankfurt-am-Main, to their eternal shame. Oh, he would like to give the bastards a blazing welcome! Fireworks and flame! Cannon and flamethrowers!

How alone a man felt in a silent town at night. Instead of crossing the open square, Kraus found himself walking around the sides, close to the shuttered shops. He came to the street opening and simply stood still; a moment ago it had seemed to him that he had a purpose, a plan. About the coffer. First, that traitor, the old ape, had no right to steal the coffer from him. Everyone in the outfit had taken stuff, even Gunter, and he himself had never touched a penny. This had been a way of proving to himself that he was in this particular service for a cause, not for easy loot. Nor would he have wanted to explain such treasures to his wife, who would have had to hide them away. At the end however, he had taken along this chest; he had a right to some resources in the future should he become a hunted man. He'd be damned if he would leave that box here for that mummified old traitor while he beat his way home empty-handed!

Suddenly the thought of the Russians swept over Kraus. The Russians had by now engulfed his area, his town. He pictured his wife huddled with the two girls, and his boys, the manly fellows, standing guard. He was needed there. But the Russians, too, must have him on their list.

Though the Jews were nothing to them, the Russians had their own account of the camps. The executed Russian prisoners were none of his affair, but would they even stop to know the facts? The black shudder that had passed through him at times, and gone, now took hold and remained. The damned Russians must be sitting there already in his house, waiting for him.

The mark on him was still in his flesh. Almost, Kraus was impelled to raise his arm and touch the spot of the SS brand, in the armpit. Indeed he had been witless. In Buda-pest, or a hundred other times in other cities, he could have had it taken out. In the last months when it had become clear that the end was coming, he could easily have chosen the greatest specialist, any of those damned Jews he had sent to Theresienstadt, and he could have had a little skin graft. None of the old SS boys talked about it, but in a drunken joke sometimes it came out—even as a dare: "Let's see yours, if it's still here! Let me see it!" A little skin operation; it could be done without a trace. If they could graft away a Jew's circumcision, this was nothing!

Well, it was still there, his mark, and, damn them, he would keep it! He would still show it to his sons; Kraus recalled the little fellows' fingers exploring there in his armpit, the mark of the bravest, the toughest, the elite. "Can I have it too, Papa, when I am big?" "Ah, but re-member, if you're an SS, you have to be ready for any-thing. . . ."

Shut out all this.

Standing, still unsure of his next move, Kraus was filled with a bitter foreboding. He would not escape them. From one side or the other they would come; he would be caught in their great pincers. Two days, three days were perhaps left before the claws closed on him, the Russians and the Americans clambering up on either side of the redoubt would link their grip and crush him between them. It was all false, all nonsense, that they would turn their guns on each other when they met. Nonsense, like the tales of the mountains here, filled with troops and secret arms.

What the Fuehrer had done was the noblest; in the end the Fuehrer had known the supreme act of courage, a revolver in the mouth. Rather than fall into their hands, rather than scuttle through the coming years a hiding rat, he should do it.

In his bones Kraus knew he could not.

But let death strike him from outside, a shell, a hail of steel that would annihilate him in one shredding instant so that he felt nothing. He was now ready for it. That was the best. That was what had appeared in his mind a moment ago, that had been his thought, his true plan. Death in battle! The fight to the last—for which he had come here! What was wrong with him, to have let the thought pass by! Why, he had his men, the guards on the last train! By now they must have arrived, not ten miles from here at the railway station. There was even armor on that train! He had only to get down there to take command, and he would return with force, smash the castle, execute that drawling beetle, the Baron, line up that whole lot of enemy Jew-lovers and mow them down with Vered together, and that blond cunt too; she had slept with all of them including the old Jew. He would cut them all to pieces, and when the Americans arrived he would smash their advance, give them a fight. He would battle on until pulverized, a hero for his sons forever.

Or perhaps he would even manage to get away when

the battle was over, and tell the boys the story himself!

Energized again, alert, Kraus started down the street. Yes, there still was something he could do, instead of crawling homeward without a penny, into a scummy life of hiding. And at once there came a token of the rightness of his decision. Looming before him, a blurred blacker lump in the blackness, stood his command car.

From within the shuttered tavern came voices.

NOW THAT ALL THE GUARDS had gone, a different form of quiet pervaded the castle. On other nights there had been silence, but one knew men were there. One listened for an exchanged word in German as one guard took the place of another. One listened even for the laughter of a girl slipping out of their barracks in the courtyard.

Now one did not listen. One knew they would not be heard. They were gone.

On this night there grew such a fullness of joy, release, and love in Marianne as she had never known before. Her feeling began with the sense that Vered was there, safe, alive and breathing within these same walls. It was as though she had been freed of an anxiety that had occupied her even when she had not been conscious of it, and had kept her from a total awareness of her life with Remy, an awareness of the last corner of his being that might until now have been untouched by her. She loved even the awakened remnant of doubt in Remy; it could not be called jealousy, but it contained that touch of the piquant that gave a woman an inner smile at her male.

She had changed into the one luxurious, feminine garment she had brought with her into exile, a long house gown of heavy silk, a flush of apricot in color. Marianne had usually worn the gown during her long reading hours with Remy. It was modest enough, not really a negligee, so as hardly to be disturbing if poor dear Vincent stopped in for a late talk or a cup of tea, that she would prepare on the electric plate provided by the Baron for this one domestic chamber.

Tonight she had brushed down her hair, and even applied a last touch of scent, and a little makeup. Though had she known that Frère Luc too would come to their room, Marianne jested with herself, she might not have given way quite so much to her bubbling voluptuous impulse. Perhaps she should even now scurry behind the screen and take off her lipstick? For despite his extreme liberalism, his robust attitude toward the world, she was certain that in a corner of his soul Luc felt distressed that during all this time, so close to him, this couple had been living in open adultery and sin. He must suffer, too, in the presence of her affection, though he should long ago have made his adjustment to his vow—if indeed a vigorous man could ever adjust himself to this constantly renewed urge. It had not seemed particularly provocative to allow herself an occasional hand pat for the good, adulating Vincent Maasi who after all had always been able to look forward to the day of release—so soon now—when he could assuage his urge, rolling together with his roly-poly wife. It was amusing and heartening to think of—Vincent was well into his fifties, and his wife only a few years younger, yet they had always let it be seen how they relished each other. But with Luc her nearness here didn't seem fair. Marianne had never been placed so constantly close to a priest, and like every woman, she told herself, she could not quite overcome the simple female curiosity about the way of a man who practiced chastity. Perhaps her feminine feeling—that in Luc as well as in Vincent her presence created a special tension—came only from vanity. Whatever Frère Luc suffered, it must be in the confines of his room, in solitude, for he showed himself always at ease in her presence. Yet had she known he would come in tonight, she would not have let her hair down.

Still, before Remy and Vered, she wanted to evoke all the softness, all the glow, of womanhood. With the chairs taken by her visitors, and having served tea, Marianne crouched on a pillow, leaning her head against Paul Vered's knees, and happily felt the returned warmth in his emaciated hand as he let it rest cupped over her head, occasionally stroking her hair with a slight movement of his fingers. It seemed to her that he was blessing her, blessing her union with **Remy,** and blessing her for having found the courage to come into this unknown with Remy and to stay with him.

With the blackout curtains drawn and the table light casting its glow, there was even a coziness in the chamber as the four men revived the past when their common view in the nation's crisis had brought them so closely together. Frère Luc it was who, when the industrialists had called on the Church to get the strikers out of the factories, had instead entered a steel mill to remain with the men, telling them "Christ himself was a worker and would surely be here as one of you." Vincent Maasi recalled, now, a remarkable Mass Frère Luc had conducted with a lathe as his altar. And it was Luc, after the strikes, who had been the first priest to obtain permission to take a job in the mill and live as a simple workman.

Without fail, Remy was off on his subject, the union of Europe, the task that lay before them. It was really for his old chief and mentor that he now spoke, for Vered. And familiar as she was with his every thought, Marianne had never heard Remy so brilliant, so well organized in the steps of his plan. Vered nodded, agreed, agreed at every point, expressed admiration at the way Remy had managed to obtain all his material even here in confinement, at the realism with which he was approaching his task.

Would Paul help toward it then? Remy asked at last.

Vered's fingers did not stop their gentle stroking of Marianne's hair. "I shall not beg off to you by saying I am too old and tired," he replied with his characteristic smile of candor. "With whatever strength I have left, I intend to work."

"Your strength will return. I feel it already," Remy declared.

But he feared, Vered said, that he would not be able to enter into so practical a campaign, for his mind, in these years, had turned to other problems.

What were those problems? Remy asked.

They were—he smiled—only the typical speculations that absorbed a man as he grew old enough to realize he could no longer affect the behavior of mankind. It was then that he sought to understand it. Without surcease he must seek to comprehend what had happened in the death camps, for this depersonalization of murder, he feared, might yet engulf the world. Man refused his responsibility. "In the camp, there was a sub-commander who considered himself a man of conscience. He would come and talk to me. After my wife was taken away, this man came, and he said, if all this was not God's will, would God not interfere?" Vered look to Frère Luc, and spoke as in the closeness of a family where all failings must be brought out. "Luc, I know that this same commander continued to go with his family to church, and that he believed himself a good Christian."

There was no accusation, only pain in his voice. Still, the room seemed to have become constricted. Marianne held her breath. If anywhere a group of friends could probe this wound, surely it was among these men.

"I know," Frère Luc said. "I have feared"—the words

came out in a choked rush—"I fear that your camp commander even believed he was performing his Christian duty in exterminating Jews. And many like him."

There it lay, the final, inescapable question. Remy tried to soften the priest's torment. Even here in their imprisonment, tales had come of many priests who had taken Jews into hiding to save them. Hundreds of good Christians had lost their lives for protecting Jews. But all of them in the room knew the myth that resounded to them from childhood, the myth of the accursed Jews. All of them had read the Gospels. The Jews, the Jews, the Jews demanding the death of Christ.

Frère Luc drew in his breath, sharply. He turned to Maasi. "Vincent, you are a Christian. How do you understand the question of the Jews and the crucifixion?"

"Sometimes it seems to me I understand what happened there, in Jerusalem, by what has happened to us at home in our own times," Maasi said. "The Jews were occupied by the Romans. They had collaborators, and they also had a secret resistance movement. The Romans must have feared that Christ, with his great following among the people, could be a resistance leader. What happened is that some collaborators among the high priests of the Jewish Temple betrayed Christ to the Romans."

The monk smiled at the way in which each man makes his own Christ. But his pain remained. Why had the Christ of the Church, why had the Christ of universal love, remained silent in all this holocaust, until there were Christians that could believe it was His will?

"Luc," Vered said, "I did not want to raise the question as a question of Christian and Jew—"

"It must be raised. As long as this hatred can grow from our Gospel, it must be raised. I myself mean to raise it." Frère Luc suddenly as by illumination saw his road ahead, a road of questioning and dissent, more dangerous for him than any of his arousals in the past, leading even, perhaps, to excommunication.

"It would be brave of you," Vered said, "but the question goes much further. These men carried out assassinations not only of Jews but of gypsies, of Russian war prisoners, of Poles, French, Belgians, of every conquered people. It is the will of God, some said, and others said it is the will of the Fuehrer. What is most frightening to me is that each man was ready to dispense with the existence of his own personal will."

It was at the use of the word God that Marianne's thoughts had stopped. For it came to her in despair that God did not, could not, exist, that the loving, universal God, above all creeds and religions, in whom she still needed to believe, could not be in existence in the face of so much innocent life extinguished in anguish. The thought left her with a sense of desolation so bleak that she could scarcely listen to what else they were saying. She rose and went to Remy, leaning against him. He held her hand tightly.

And yet she heard Vered speaking, answering precisely this dread in her. Virtually all religions spoke of a God who intervened, a God who punished wrong and evil, he said, but man had also developed beyond this conception of a bargaining God. He could still believe in a conception of God-in-becoming, of a process urging itself toward salvation, a vast force of love that must eventually override the inchoate and the destructive. A force which was not a completed and a judging entity, looking down from infinity, but which existed within all, and strove through all creation, through all good and evil, for perfectibility. Thus, human responsibility, the individual human will, which so many had forsworn and which people seemed increasingly ready to forswear, was precisely the entity that was God in us.

Marianne wanted to weep; there was in her heart the tragic pain one feels sometimes in the presence of a love that is utterly true and beautiful but that one knows to be, for some merely circumstantial cause, doomed.

Some slept. Senator Joras slept with Trudi, the Baron's cook, not young any more but a comfortable body. They had made their farewells, he had promised to return one day on a vacation visit, she had told him her husband had not been taken prisoner by the Russians after all, and would soon be coming home. So things had worked out quite handily for them and they amicably satisfied each other and afterward turned their backs, and Trudi slumbered. The senator felt his mind rumbling on, weighing the chances of the Remy faction and of Dortolot; perhaps the return of Vered, who would back Remy, made it best to ride along on their wagon, at the start.

Dortolot slept well. He had filled in his secret diary, which of course would one day be published, and he had given a sharp account of the argument at the table as to the responsibility of the left-wing leaders for the lack of preparedness in the war. This issue would be the one to raise, on coming home.

The marshal slept, content that he had behaved well, carried out an action, however small. He was well beyond retirement age, of course; on returning home, after getting his hands on the archives, if they had not been destroyed, he would write a study of strategy and tactics proving that his conduct of the early phases of the war had been irreproachable. He had been betrayed by politicians. Tomorrow, when the Americans came, he must be alert, energetic, himself.

Michaelis, Schall, Astuque, du Caux, each lay in his bed, fitfully or deeply asleep, or wakefully remembering, planning. Michaelis planned a news magazine. Schall wondered whether he might not simply stay on, or return to live in the mountains here. And Frère Luc kept vigil. The discussion had stirred the most profound doubts in him; he had even returned and read certain passages in the Gospels, with a new eye.

It was in St. John that the seeds of hatred burst open. He had always felt this and yet passed it over in his mind as a passionate form of expression, a burning anger against Christ's enemies. The other Gospels too of course repeated the story of the crucial moment in which Pilate declared, "I find no fault in this man" and the Jews demanded "Crucify Him!"

But in St. John the description was far more emphatic and provocative. The Jews were first pictured as hunting for Jesus to kill him. He fled from "the Jews" and hid. But was he not a Jew? Was he not hiding among Jews? "The Jews" schemed how to kill him. When they finally brought him before Pilate, it was, over and over, "the Jews" who were bloodthirsty.

Just as a deformation in someone we live with becomes unnoticed through lifelong familiarity, so it now came to Frère Luc that he had not noticed how the familiar description was deformed. Could Christ, could his disciples, have thought of his persecutors as "the Jews"? Were they not all themselves believing Jews, Christ, his disciples, and his followers? It was the high priest who feared the troublesome reformer from Galilee; it was, as Vincent Maasi had so simply put it, a collaborator who had brought Jesus to Pontius Pilate. The other Gospels indeed spoke more clearly of these specific powerful men who were enemies of Christ—and then suddenly it was the Jews, the Jews, the Jews. In today's light, could not one see this emphasis on "the Jews" as deliberate hate propaganda?

There was the explanation he remembered well enough from his studies. Since the Gospels had been written down when the Church was struggling for its life in Rome, since the authors of the Gospels had not wanted to provoke the Roman authorities by accusing them of the death of Christ, they had taken pains to exonerate Pilate, and they had thrown the blame on the Jews. By the time the Gospel

(MEYER LEVIN)

			March			
S	M	T	W	T	F	S
			1	2	3	4
5	6	7	8	9	10	11
12	13	14	15	16	17	18
19	20	21	22	23	24	25
26	27	28	29	30	31	

			May			
S	M	T	W	T	F	S
	1	2	3	4	5	6
7	8	9	10	11	12	13
14	15	16	17	18	19	20
21	22	23	24	25	26	27
28	29	30	31			

The Fanatic   813 L662f

The Harvest   813 L662h

The Stronghold 813

940.5315

G452

Monday

10

			April			
S	M	T	W	T	F	S
						1
2	3	4	5	6	7	8
9	10	11	12	13	14	15
16	17	18	19	20	21	22
23	24	25	26	27	28	29
30						

11

Tuesday
April 2006

Week 15

7:00

7:30

8:00

8:30

9:00

9:30

10:00

10:30

11:00

11:30

12:00

12:30

1:00

1:30

2:00

2:30

3:00

3:30

4:00

4:30

5:00

of St. John had been written, the quarrel between the Church and the Synagogue had grown bitter, and he had had no compunction about accusing the whole Jewish people of deicide.

Even in himself as a boy, Luc recalled now, the word Jew had aroused bitterness and anger for the killing of Christ, and the name Judas, so close to the word Jew, had seemed to stand for the entire wretched people.

How many Christians truly outgrew this first impression? In his own case, as he had grown and developed a passion for social justice, and come to feel his vocation was to spread it through the Church, he had overcome his early, primitive hate reaction to the word Jew.

Yet, was this not still being inculcated? Here in the Gospel of St. John it stood out brutally clear. And St. John was read beyond all others; some thought of this as *the* Gospel."

How could this hatred be undone, and could it ever be undone? Jesus Himself, so deeply a Jew among Jews— must He not grieve and shudder, must His soul not be in anguish over the slaughter done to His people, so often in His name, or in hatred grown from His name?

The weight of the coming struggle to have this hatred removed, eradicated through Christian teaching, already made itself felt in Frère Luc on this night. Could what had grown deformed ever be made straight? Could enough people ever understand why the Gospels had been written in the way they had been written, and could they, like Maasi, sense through their own lives what had really hap-

pened there in Jerusalem? Could there ever be enough
enlightened teaching about the true Christ, the preacher
among the people, the opponent of the rich, the powerful,
the ruler-priests who were losing the very meaning of the
Jewish religion?

Surely this was now his personal task, since it had been
opened to him, even more than the social task he had seen
awaiting him uncompleted from before the war.

Suddenly, in temptation, it seemed to Frère Luc as
though he were making this promise to a woman, a
woman with the soft, loving face, tonight, of Marianne.

If his struggle led to departure from the Church, Luc
promised himself, he must nevertheless continue in his
vow of chastity, as a proof to himself that underneath it all
he had not been motivated to provoke, by an extreme
campaign, his release, so as to secure for himself a release
from celibacy.

How unworthy to descend to this other struggle. He
thrust from himself the image of the woman in her soft
apricot gown, and remained on his knees, forbidding himself to lie on the bed. Sometimes, in the utmost fervor of
his prayers, Frère Luc believed the curtains opened, and
that he was admitted to Christ, into universal love, and in
such hours of elated exhaustion untroubled sleep would
come.

Maasi lay half awake; a bed had been arranged in his
room for Paul Vered, and he sensed that his old friend and
leader lay unsleeping too. He sensed that he must speak,

that he must in some way give Paul an assurance. But the words had not yet come to him. It was as though he were waiting for a thought transmission.

And in Vered there was his old recurring regret, the dreadful regret over the one decision about which he could not forgive himself, his decision to withhold aid from Republican Spain. Had he not known, as everyone knew, that it was the beginning, that the war to come might be quenched by firm intervention in Spain? Had this not been the moment when he himself had failed to exercise the crucial, the Godly interior force, the will of man?

There still rose to him the shouting, the raging, despairing outcries at a vast labor meeting he had attended to defend nonintervention. No use to repeat to himself all the factors, the tremendously weighty factors, the pressure from the great Allies to withhold arms, the plain fact that it was a contest between Communists and Fascists, the more potent fact that intervention, according to his own security police, would have brought right-wing revolution at home and that even a Rieber could have thrust for power. For beneath all the reasons there lurked the one that he dared not fully admit to himself even now. Maasi had come and heartbrokenly declared that the war in Spain was a war by Communist atheists against the Church. Even from America, Vered had been told that tens of millions of Catholics stood against intervention. And he had been turned from his inner conviction that he must intervene.

Was it because as a Jew he had not had the courage to

make a decision in what seemed a Christian issue? This, he
now accused himself, was for him the moral net, the resi-
due under the entire problem. In that one instance he had
perhaps been influenced by being a Jew, and he had not
admitted it to himself at the time. Yet the issue had not
been only a Church issue, nor had it been only a
Communist-and-Fascist issue, it had been the great human
issue of his time.

For this he accused himself. This would remain forever
his pain, his flaw.

From the other bed, in the quiet dark, Maasi's voice
came as though continuing some old discussion. "Paul, I
should never have pressed you against intervention in
Spain. That was my great mistake."

The slight tension between the two men was dissolved.
Both sighed, and slept.

Just as she sensed her lover's remotely awakened doubts
about the Return, and Paul Vered, so there was in Marianne too the awakened, remote doubt about Remy's wife.
Not the wife so much as the children. She hungered with
his own heart for the moment when he would encounter
them again, and she felt as in her own hands the hunger in
his hands to feel the shoulders of each boy under his fingers. Though she must not be present; she must send
Remy alone to that joy and that test. For perhaps there
was a need in a man's life as in a woman's—though yet
childless, she knew this—a need so profound that any dep-

rivation would be accepted for the gratification of having one's own young close by. That deprivation might be herself.

Marianne understood this tonight, as the test for the first time loomed imminent. And because of this her tenderness augmented, grew almost heartbreaking within her, and transformed itself into joy. Not for a long time had they been toward each other as young lovers who are aroused by every accidental touch of the fingers, even by brushing against each other.

Lying at last together with him, the love-hunger phrase from the story of Joseph and Potiphar's wife came back to her: Let us put our heads and our feet together. Then Marianne was astonished at Remy's movement, at the sign of transmission that is so profound a proof and comfort of long intimacy and harmony, for he twined his feet around hers as their mouths joined; they were entirely one flesh.

For this room of theirs too this night could be a final sacrament; how they might long for it in later days of freedom, long for these binding walls within which they had worked through all the difficult phases of the relationship between a man and a woman, the times of blank incomprehension when it seemed that one being could never truly communicate with another, no matter with how much sympathy and love one began, the times when she feared sexual staleness and even knew that Remy would like to taste the variety of ripe Polish girls enjoyed by the other men, the times of impatience with some simple physical habit that threatened to become abhorrent, the ghastly times when some streak of meanness, of smallness of character, would be revealed.

All, all was included within her tonight.

His fear that in the Return the people would now choose Vered. And his confidence that since he was young he would still have his time. And the greater, invigorating confidence that he returned with a plan to work for, an enlargement of the horizon for the whole nation. In their love pause, Marianne whispered a word of all this so as to be with him in his thoughts as they were together in their bodies.

And then in a new surge of love came a sudden springing of laughter; they had thought at the same instant of the naked Kraus, the enemy discomfited, ridiculed, conquered! A splendid carnality came over them, and Marianne knew that in this moment she was Julka for Remy, and she was every conquered German girl who was now being used by an Allied soldier.

But still further they were returned to each other, each only with the other, gratefully returned to the truest of all positions in physical union, his face above hers, her body wholly entered, and then with the movement stayed to a pulse of breathing within her, Marianne felt in a tremendous dawning surprise an understanding she had never reached before—why, something every woman must have understood from the beginning of time and love. In this moment of utterly balanced union between them, Marianne realized that his body within hers was like the one womanly knowledge she had not yet experienced: the male organ pulsing within her body was like the throb of a child in the womb.

How beautiful it was, how divine in its design, that the act of love should contain this paradigm, this evocation of the stirring of life. She was in bliss.

And this she would keep, as a woman must always keep some tender, intimate caress, or word, to offer to her mate in times yet to unfold between them.

Even the tardiness of her comprehension was a part of love, she told herself, for during the whole of life between a man and a woman there must continue to be new insights, discoveries, sudden understandings of mysteries.

Even within her bliss, a reality fluttered through to Marianne; this was not in her body a night for impregnation; but the bliss remained untarnished; she was complete now, forever complete; all was known to her.

Remy saw the smile that touched eternity that was on her face, and breathed to himself, "My girl," and knew this was a culminating moment in his own life too, knew he could never be more complete, more filled with the sense that life was good.

GUNTER HAD HALTED the command car before the tavern. He felt a trifle puzzled about the chief's slipping off like that without a parting word, after all they had been through together. Perhaps Kraus would be waiting here.

Besides, several of the men in the car with him had farewells to say, in town. One even had had a child with a Polish servant girl; half abashedly the fellow slipped away in the darkness, saying he wanted to leave her a bit of money. Nobody joked or laughed—that was a good girl he had found for himself, the men remarked, she had never let another man come near her; not all the Polish girls were cunts. Another of the men, of the elderly, fatherly type commonly sent to guard-duty posts, hesitated before the tavern door, sighed, and then shambled off under a hail of lewd admonitions, variations of "If you need help, send for the fire department." He had got himself entangled with an insatiable mother of five whose husband was a war prisoner and probably, as the boys said, wished he could remain one forever.

As Gunter opened the tavern's inner door, the volume of voices and the sudden light engulfed him; the whole town was crowded into this place tonight. Four years of entanglements couldn't be untangled in one stroke. And among the departing men, plans had to be made, decisions taken.

At the tables back against the wall, couples sat, in that curious silence when everything has to be said and yet nothing can be found to say. They smoked their last cigarettes, slowly. At the bar itself, knots of men disputed, one or two with their arms around a wench; there was beer-hoisting, even singing from the far end. The wenches, some of the girls and younger wives of the town, had their waists encircled now by one man, now by another, in the restless movement of the place. Now and again a behind was slapped, bringing a half-angry but pleased outburst. In all the uproar and confusion, the good wife who had kept the tavern in her husband's absence, and her thirteen-year-old daughter, managed somehow, their bare arms flashing through the entanglement of mugs and outstretched hands along the bar, to keep track of every penny owed them, calling out the sums from time to time.

At the nearer tables the men sat in threes and fours, some in uniform, some in army shirts and civilian trousers, some already looking like longtime civilians. Their discussions were earnest. A woman friend might pause by a table for a moment, listen and drift on, or pulling an empty chair from the next table might sit for a while with her thigh against that of a soldier who had been her lover for a few months, the second from the last, the last one having already gone off several days ago.

Things came out, in the earnest conversations.

Thoughts long put away, sentiments that couldn't be uttered yesterday, were cautiously brought out, unwrapped. Between the Communists and the imperialists, declared a shaggy-browed ex-schoolteacher, whose left cheek was shriveled from a wound caught in North Africa, after which he had been sent on guard duty here, he wasn't sure but what Germany's future belonged with the Reds. His eyes peeped into those of his companions, and he began to speak more freely. With German brains and Russia's raw power, the world could be held.

"*Ach*, what do you want with the Russians! They are ignorant, primitive—"

"All the better, that would leave us in control."

It was good to feel they were not finished. There would be a few dark years, but as long as there was a plan . . .

Heads bent, voices were lowered, voices were raised. Here and there a woman, arriving, found her man, touched him on the shoulder from behind. The man rose, there was a quiet word with his comrades—in three hours, an early start, well, better make it a few hours more, dawn. All right, here at dawn, then? And the couple departed. In the restlessness of this night, girls and women had appeared who had always held themselves aloof; word had spread that the men were leaving, and in the excited atmosphere it was as though any man was owed whatever he wished tonight from the nation's womanhood, for this was like a mark of reassurance to their men in their defeat.

And something else stirred among the more earthy of the women, in response to the tartness of the knowing jokes that floated and hung in the pleasantly stinging smoke. In how many of them, with that quick perverse glitter in their eyes, was there already the speculation, the anticipation even, that tomorrow they would not refuse themselves to the conquerors? Even a need to be possessed tonight by their own defeated men, so as most acutely, tomorrow, to sense the changeover.

And there were those of the men who knew this too; thus it had always been in war, thus they themselves had experienced it in conquered lands, and at the bar a drunken voice suddenly pierced the hubbub: "Ah, save it for tomorrow, you whore, you'll get an American bar of chocolate."

The scorned woman, Gunter saw, was the fatty he had been upstairs with an hour ago. She only laughed at the insult and moved on, putting her arm around some other fellow at the bar. She was no whore, Schreiter had told him, and indeed she hadn't accepted any money. Just a woman whose husband had been killed in the war, and she was making it up to herself, she had informed him; she liked especially, she had declared with a lewd burst of laughter as she looked down at his sex, new faces.

Gunter turned away now, lest she catch sight of him, for he didn't feel like going upstairs again; he was headed home now and would be clean. At the stairway in back, there was a movement of couples up and down, with a kind of signal between them, as there were only a few rooms and those who comprised the inner little group of the tavern were passing the beds to each other.

No one had seen Kraus, nor did anyone seem interested. But in taking his question from one man to another,
Gunter fell upon a fellow from his own town who had
been stationed here, and presently they were deep in plans
for the home-going, and even for opening a garage together. The fellow had a large shed, he said, and machine
tools which he had written his wife to bury, wrapped in
oilskin. He only hoped the damn Russians hadn't dug
them up.

Which roads to take? Where would the Americans be,
where the Russians? They fell into a trance of indecision.
Gunter feared the road he had taken this morning would
already be closed; the gap between the two armies had
practically vanished. And up north? From a corporal who
had just returned home to the village they got a few bits of
information. A map was called for, and finally the daughter of the place brought her schoolbook map. It showed
the Greater Reich, all Europe nearly, all one color, but
with a pencil Gunter traced back the old borders in the
north.

A Berliner joined them; he couldn't believe the Americans would let the Russians keep the capital. "They'll
come to blows over it yet. Maybe it will take a month or
two but you'll see, they'll start shooting at each other." He
winked.

The fatty had found him; she bent and stuck her tongue
in Gunter's ear.

Had she seen his commander? he asked.

What? Schreiter? Schreiter was still upstairs with his

sweetheart—there was a man who took his time! "I mean *Obersturmbannfuehrer* Kraus," he snapped.

"Kraus?" Her eyes glittered. That was one she had never met. An *Obersturmbannfuehrer,* too! Would he introduce her? And laughing, and reaching down and giving his prick a squeeze like a real whore, she circled away, her face suddenly sad.

Gunter kept glancing at the door each time it opened. When Kraus entered, he automatically rose and gave the *heil.* His commander returned it, and several of the men joined in the salute, some perfunctorily, even a few in civilian clothes getting up, with a kind of ashamed conformity. Only as Kraus reached his table did Gunter realize something was odd. Here was Kraus in his full uniform. "Excuse me, sir, but I saw it on the chair—so I—"

"Saw what, you dunderhead?"

"Your uniform. The Baron told me you had gone in civilians."

"Oh. He did."

"So that's why I took your boots."

A burst of curses came, in the fullest, foulest tradition, but not at Gunter—at the stinking degenerate traitor of a Baron. Around them the men raised their heads—already this had a good sound of old times. Sitting down finally, Kraus pulled off his shoes and accepted back his favorite boots. "You can have them if I get knocked off!" he half jested to Gunter, adding that there was going to be some shooting here yet; he was going to slaughter that renegade

Baron and knock over that castle if it was the last thing he did! The dirty old cocksucker had gone and armed the prisoners! "They arrested me! They stripped me naked and threw me in a hole in the cellar!"

All around now, men were crowding close to listen to the tale. How had he managed to escape? And even to get back his uniform?

"I'll blow his head off!" Kraus vowed. The whole crew of them, he announced, were going to go back with him and storm the castle, blow it to pieces, with the Baron and his Jew and his Jew-lovers together!

As though by warrior's instinct, Schreiter had now appeared, his heavy face as usual expressionless. But in Schreiter there grew a response to Kraus, first, over the dirty treachery of the Baron. Defeated or not, how could any decent German put guns into the hands of the enemy! And to have made an officer of the Reich—worse, of the SS—into an object of ridicule! No! Such things were not left unanswered! Besides, Schreiter had a few scores to settle with the Baron, that soft-handed old goat who thought that he was still ruling here in the Middle Ages and could stick his nose into every man's bed. Gossipy as a woman, every time he let a man have a night's pass he had to sniff out with whom he was spending it. It so happened that Schreiter's little woman belonged to one of the big families of the town, there were complications, things had had to be done in secret, and the Baron had put the family on the alert. Schreiter had heard enough from her, too, about the way the old bastard took his squeeze out of every shop, out of every business, out of every concession in the area. Finally, the idea of a good, smashing attack, a last blowoff, virtually with no risk, if properly handled, appealed to the soldier in him; he hadn't let off a shot since he had come out of the hospital after his troop carrier had hit a mine in the first great breakthrough into France.

As was his way, Schreiter began with objections to what he really wanted to do. The castle was not easy to attack, he reminded Kraus. The drawbridge was up, and the guns were still mounted in their emplacements.

"Who's going to man them? The marshal?" At this, one of Schreiter's old-timers reared up ramrod-stiff, in imitation of the military chieftain, and they all roared.

"Still," Schreiter declared, "we need a heavy gun, to break in."

Kraus leaped up. He had a plan, he told them, and by morning he would be back with all that was needed to tear the castle apart. There was no point in any of them taking too much risk over that treacherous fart of a Baron, and his "guests." "Keep an eye. Just don't let them get out."

Schreiter grunted. From his room upstairs he had an excellent vantage point covering the access to the drawbridge. "Let them try to come out!" As long as it was from a good safe position, he would be happy to pop off a few more rounds in this war. The Baron had given him a crawful, feeding goose liver and wine to the prisoners of the Reich, while at the front the men were on short rations.

Kraus was all decisions now, a combat officer. "You're coming with me," he ordered Gunter. With a handshake to his future garage partner, Gunter rose, in his stocking feet, carrying Kraus's shoes in his hand, and followed his chief out to the car, where he had his gear. A good thing he hadn't thrown away his own old boots.

With even the peep lights out, the car crawled down the steep winding road. Kraus sat rigid, holding his anger like some wound, denying to himself that if he had the damned strongbox on his lap, perhaps he would not bother to return. He was not in the habit of discussing his problems with Gunter, but the words burst from him: "The swine stole the box."

Gunter exclaimed at the Baron's swinishness, and heard his boss vow they'd get everything back. "Damn right!" he agreed. And then in a burst of honesty, and because if Kraus really succeeded in invading the castle and got hold of the Baron he would find out anyway, and that would be bad, Gunter pulled out the Baron's parting gift and showed it and offered to share the value.

No, no, it was his, he must keep it, Kraus declared. There would be plenty. But his face was dark.

Luckily the local detail map had been left in the car; using a pinpoint flashlight under the dash, for just tonight the enemy might be out to bomb the area, Kraus located the railway siding that was the destination of his train. Without a single false turn—Gunter was a master on strange roads—they came to the siding. Along the bit of extra track there was a short platform. Two empty flatcars stood there, at least evidence that something had recently been delivered at this place. There was no sign of Kraus's train.

Gunter banged on the door of the caretaker hut, and presently the attendant emerged, a one-armed pensioner of the First War, in a woolen undershirt, pulling on his pants with his hook-arm. He was exasperating thick-headed; all that could be got from him was what was clear to the eye—no train had arrived. No signal, nothing. Except two weeks ago, some crates had been unloaded and removed on trucks—he gestured—up there. Secret things, in crates.

Could he signal back along the line, still?

To the preceding station, this morning that had still been possible, but beyond . . . He chuckled like a fool at a graveside. Ah yes, another officer had come earlier today and demanded—

Another officer? What service? What rank?

With his good hand he scratched in his dense curly hair. A captain, he thought, but what service he couldn't tell and it was not his business to ask, but the captain had demanded contact with Innsbruck. He chuckled again, an idiot over spilled wine.

"You are cut off from Innsbruck? The Americans are already there?"

"I cannot even get the two stations before Innsbruck."

No, Kraus decided not even to signal the nearest station —who could tell but what the enemy was already that far? Why give them an alert? Perhaps his train had been captured and this was the end of his war.

It was Gunter who noticed the handcart on the rails. That would be the best way; they could carefully scout down the tracks until they reached the train, if it was halted somewhere within reach. Perhaps at the foot of the climb, for want of a second engine.

So they mounted, sitting opposite each other and operating the seesaw handle. A strange end for his war, Kraus kept telling himself, if he were to be caught like this coasting down into the arms of the enemy. And yet he felt a certain pride in his persistence; in the flat stretches, in the balance and swing of his movements, he told himself he was carrying on as a man should. Using whatever means was at hand, he was showing that he was no desk soldier; in the very end he was coming into his own.

And then indeed the mass of the engine loomed, appearing suddenly as they rounded a curve, so that they hardly had time to brake the cart.

With the squeak of the car's halting, Kraus leaped off; already a form was hurrying toward him—it could only be Werner, the only one of his crew who could be sure not to have deserted. And the dumb fat-ass appeared now, puffing. "At last you came—" and reciting a whole desperate rigmarole about the locomotive engineer who had refused to pull any farther unless half the cars were dropped off.

"Where is he! Put a gun at his head!"

The fellow had vanished. The train had been standing here since five o'clock.

From along the train, now, a sound emerged. It came

from behind the first few flatcars, that carried armor, and as Kraus hurried to have a good look at that armor the sound approached him as though sound could crawl, a low-pitched mélange, not of words, nor of groans, nor of whispers, but something throttled, and Kraus knew where he had heard it before. Long ago in the beginning of his special campaign he had inspected the work of an *Einsatzgruppe* that had cleaned the city of Lwów of its Jews, using the army method of marching them to the edge of the town and then shooting each Jew at the rim of a mass grave so that the body fell inward. This same sound had emerged from underneath the heap.

Indeed it was there and then that Kraus had determined on the more humane system of the gas chambers.

"They wanted to drop off our cars and bring only the armor," Werner was repeating, and just then the Panzer commander joined them. He was from a crack armored unit, the Avengers, and you felt this instantly even now. "Good you got here, or I'd have had to take strong measures." His red eyes were turned on poor Werner as though to annihilate the fat slug. "We must abandon the debris" —he gestured to the boxcars—"in order to reach our objective." He stood there, Luger in hand, staring angrily down the length of the train that melted into the blackness.

"It's *our* transport. We only gave you a hitch!" Werner protested, with querulous bravado.

"I have priority! Who needs your stinking load of corpses? It's insane!" the Avenger shouted.

"One moment. Exactly what have you got with you that can shoot?" Kraus asked the tank officer.

"We were caught in a lousy murderous defile by enemy aircraft. A whole bunch of staff cars got into my column and clogged it up, with their crummy high officers and their baggage. The Yankee bandits came down right on top of us and destroyed all but what I have on these flat-cars." The man seemed on the point of sobbing. "I was in the lead and managed to get out of the pass."

"I know, I know." Kraus had heard the story ten times when he had hitched them onto his train, outside Munich. The fellow was cracked with combat fatigue. Nevertheless he was his man. This man would never know when the end had come. "What is operative?"

"Only my own Panzer, sir, and I have an antiaircraft gun, but nothing to pull it."

"The tank can pull it," Kraus decreed; the dimheads, he should have been a combat leader the whole time. What resourcefulness he would have shown them. "Can any one of you drive a locomotive?"

Werner looked lost, as always when the slightest thing went out of routine. "Go down the line of cars," Kraus ordered. "Ask if there is a locomotive engineer." No, it was too absurd a chance. What Jew would ever have handled such a job? Werner obediently shuffled away into the night. Gunter clambered up onto the locomotive cab; it could not be so complicated, he was sure he could figure it out. Kraus himself climbed onto the first flatcar. The tank, its gun at a high angle, bulked vast on its great

210

cleats, an invincible monster. Oh, with this he had them now! He let his hand rest on the rounding form of the frontal steel wall, and it was as though his own body had been augmented with this power.

At the nearest boxcar, Werner tapped on the bolted door and shouted his question. "Is there anyone who can operate a locomotive?"

An intensified hubbub arose, as of a swarm of insects enclosed in a glass jar when a light suddenly shines on them. Squeaks, pleadings—*Wasser, Wasser*—beating on the walls, and the stench coming through stronger than ever. "I— I— I am engineer!" "Engineer, engineer!" The word shrieked through the boards. He knew their tricks. All would volunteer; they would claim they could fly to the moon, to get out of there. "Any bluffer will be shot on the spot!" But what did it matter to these wild beasts?

"Open, open, please, sir, a qualified locomotive engineer—" A particular voice managed to squeeze itself through the door crack. Already, from the cars behind, down the whole line, the sense that something was happening had provoked a growing clamor; even the subject of inquiry had somehow passed through all the car walls. "Engineer, engineer!" they shouted.

That voice from behind the first door, with a vestige of civilized intonation, kept repeating, in German with no Yiddish inflection, "Please, sir, I am a graduate transportation engineer. I hold a degree from the Breslau Polytechnic—"

Cautiously, Werner began working at the catch. As the sounds of the iron bar being moved were heard, the hysterical babbling and buzzing increased. He paused. "One. One only," he commanded. "The Polytechnic engineer. All others I will shoot. Let him out."

The bar slid farther back, a bit. Before he could move the door it was torn open, and instantly the entire gaping space was filled with tentacles, skeletal forms leaped into his hooded torch beam, arms no thicker than fingers grappled on him with ferocious strength. The door screeched, rolling farther back. The entire door space was agape and the contents of the car tumbled on him, the stench heavier than the bodies, the wild haggard faces somehow visible, teeth and eyes, hallucinatory. They fell over him, leaped over him, dead bodies tumbled on him; he was being suffocated in offal. *"Schiess!"* His mouth was smothered. His arms tried to throw off clots of forms like clots of shit, and his half-free hand kept firing and firing.

With a wrench the pistol was gone from his grip, and Werner heard the next shot fired, with hardly a break in sequence, as though he himself had pressed the trigger. "No, no, not me!" he screamed, a mistake, not he, not now, of all the absurdities not now. Nevertheless the bullet was in his neck, not as skillfully as when he had done it himself, the shot in the nape, and he was brought down amid all that offal, the blood pouring out of his mouth, a fatal shot.

The others, Kraus and the red-eyed tank captain, had come running, firing into the indistinct mass, and as

Gunter tried to find fat Werner, Kraus with presence of mind rushed on to the next car, for several of the freed shadows already grappled with the lock there. A few shots disposed of them. The remainder scuttled off, some collapsing of themselves even before they reached the trees.

At least the length of the train was now clear of them. If the rest of the cars had been opened, Kraus told himself, everyone would have been inundated; he would be lying underneath here like stupid Werner.

The Panzer crew had appeared; they had been stretched out in the woods, at rest. Kraus had their captain post them along the length of the train; there was scarcely a man to a car, but for the moment this would do. Where were his own men, the machine gunners on the train roof? Buggered off, all eleven of them.

They would have let his last train of prisoners go free. There passed through Kraus, at this thought, something like a volcanic tremor. He knew this feeling in himself. Whenever he was denied his purpose, it came. He could feel every muscle in his body crisped for an instant as by the passing of an electric shock. At meetings, when he was being lied to by highly placed Jew protectors, this anger had used to come within him, and he knew that after such a tremor he was always indomitable. His mind had a doubled clarity. In Hungary, when the scummy Minister of the Interior had countermanded him and called back that last train of Jews, this had happened. And he had fixed that dirty Jew-loving sneak; he had got those Jews on their way a week later, holding the stupid Minister in an endless conference until he was sure the train had passed the border and was well on its way to Auschwitz.

So now, Kraus surveyed the situation. The maddening squeaking along the length of the train, from inside the cars, was subsiding. Below the gaping door of the first car lay the little dark heap, like a pile of rags; Werner had been pulled out from under it. Kraus glanced into the car itself; offal; a clutter of dead in a corner where the others had shoved them during the trip, the usual thing. Only two or three days on the road and look at it; they were really the dregs, not worth transporting. And scattered on the floor of the car, a few more corpses, those trampled in the breakout a moment ago. At the far end, the pencil-beam of his torch caught a squatting figure, naked. There he sat like a small ape, huddled in fear, his eyes a fixed stare, the mouth drooling spittle.

Subhuman. With a growl of disgust, Kraus spat. The foul stench of them had coagulated into a vile taste in his mouth. He strode away toward the locomotive.

Gunter, in the cab, was touching the knobs and valves. After all, he declared in his unhurried way, calm in any breakdown, there is always a solution. "We can figure it out. It can't be so complicated." He fingered a handle that looked smooth from use. "This must be the throttle." In a moment he had made sure of the brake control. Now it was only a question of turning on the power. The Panzer officer joined them. Yes, Gunter and the officer were sure they had it.

"Good boys!" Kraus cried.

The red-eyed one swung down. He was going to un-couple the boxcars. At least it was lucky, he said, that the flats carrying his armor came first, as there was no siding here for switching the boxcars off. Indeed, it occurred to Kraus that from the very first, when the train had been made up, this fellow had had this in mind. Clever man, no wonder he had got out of that trap in the ravine, the only one with his Panzer intact.

The rusty old coupling needed all their strength—every last bit of machinery in the Reich was in rotten shape, *kaput*. Finally the catch fell open. The captain yelled ahead to Gunter, who tested the throttle, cautiously. The train jerked.

Standing on the forward half of the severed coupling, Kraus felt himself pulled slowly, definitely away from that black solid mass of boxcars. Yes. He was being detached forever from this part of his service. He had done his ut-most in it, to the last.

The locomotive moved with the flatcars, less than a hundred yards, and then he was almost thrown off his perch, in a stumbling series of brake jerks. No, no, every-thing was in order. Gunter was operating the train per-fectly; he had only stopped for the captain to gather the men who had been placed to guard the boxcars. As the Panzer commander yelled to them to come along, the nearest one yelled back, "Shall I open the doors, then?"

"Idiot! Do you want to get killed too!"

Leaving the cars locked, the men came hurrying along the cinders, and leaped onto the flat. Their captain—

Donnerwald was his name—checked them. All there—twenty-seven, the remnant of the most vaunted Panzer unit, the Avengers. Kraus gazed down on them, flopped on the flooring. His army.

"Forward!" he shouted to Gunter, as he climbed into the cab.

Only then, as the engine began to labor up the steep incline, did the thought come to Kraus that from among the prisoners who had freed themselves, some would crawl back. They would open the doors for the remainder, after all. The living garbage would flood out into the countryside, typhus carriers, infected with every conceivable bug, spoiling the land with their filth. It couldn't be helped. The dozen in the castle counted ten thousand times more than this trainload left behind.

There was a crashing, a screech, a jolt of the braked engine that knocked his head against the steel wall of the cab, while from behind came the cursing of the weary spilled-over tankmen. It was the damned handcar they had left on the rails. Grumbling, a dozen men climbed down, took hold, and in rhythm swung it off the tracks. Donnerwald glared at Kraus with contempt. Yet in Kraus, even perversely, a kind of joy was rising. How easily the men handled the damned obstruction. Ah, the German soldier —how could an army of such men have been stopped! And now as the train really got under way, up, up, into the clean mountain air, a wakefulness and cheerfulness came over the men. Jokes, snatches of song, broke out. The sky had cleared and was full of stars that seemed really, as in childhood, within reach of the outstretched hand.

Kraus looked at his watch; only two hours had passed since he had been sitting doomed in a dungeon, and here he was, with tanks, guns, a whole army, returning to the attack! A flask was passing among the men; it was offered him and he took his swig. Grim and hard, yet singing— that was the lot with whom he should have shared the war!

Now he turned his mind to tactics. A direct attack? Drive the Panzer smack into the town—no one would oppose them, that was certain. Unless the Marshal of the Armies—Kraus had to laugh every time he thought of his distinguished adversary—unless the marshal had moved out and taken possession of the village. But how? With whom? His doddering old ministers and his priest in skirts? If they even knew that Kraus had got out and was on the loose, those old farts were doubtless sitting quaking behind the barricaded walls. They probably couldn't even man the machine guns in the towers. Or perhaps they didn't believe he would come back and attack?

Should he drive straight to the plaza in front of the moat, and direct the Panzer point-blank at the main gate of the castle? Also, the antiaircraft gun. Could it be swung down to level fire? No, he had a better thought: He would plant the gun in the gully, below, on the back side of the castle. This would prevent escape, if they should take it into their heads to try to use ropes. He would have them pinned with fire from both sides. In terror, they would rush out and surrender.

Kraus saw them already, the crummy treacherous Baron at the head, letting down his old drawbridge and leading them out in single file with their hands in the air. Should he accept them as prisoners? Mow down the lot— the Baron, certainly! That baby-faced traitor—a man who had had the Fuehrer as his guest! Stand him against his damned heraldic post, stripped naked, the toad, before the whole town, and stitch him to it with a burst.

But then Kraus checked his fantasy. Suppose there was no surrender? Could he smash his way in and capture the lot? Make some kind of a bridge, an improvised war bridge over the moat? How long did he have, to break in and capture them and recover what was his? A day, still, before the Americans arrived? He was no fool, he had no intention of taking on the entire Allied army. But to knock off a few as they advanced—doubtless they would be careless now, overconfident—to give them a last bloody nose, and then vanish into the redoubt with his hostages—providing he chose to keep the beggars alive. Maybe only that blonde.

For his final escape, he must not forget, a good vehicle was necessary. He must pick up the command car at the station here. Higher up they would go, to the last fastness in the redoubt. There must be somewhere where the truly loyal had gathered.

The train had arrived at the siding with its little Tyrolean hut. The one-armed relic of the First War, now wearing his railway cap, stood signaling with a lantern, as though there were no blackout, the fool. As the locomotive halted, he ran up and down, worrying them for his blasted handcart, government property! "Back there alongside the track. You can recover it when we win the war, Papa," Captain Donnerwald advised him.

Impatiently, Kraus nudged at Donnerwald to get the armor down, the tank, the gun.

Suddenly the fellow snapped at him, "What do you expect, the Panzer to hop off by itself!" There was no ramp.

An improvisation, then. Hurrying around the little yard, Kraus searched for materials, made a dozen suggestions— tear up a few rails? Pry loose the platform?

No, the Panzer captain snapped, he had a better idea for Kraus, pile up some dead Jews and roll the Panzer off over the heap of bones.

Meanwhile he had pulled out an ax, and two men were already selecting trees to fell. It was slow work.

Midnight passed. For a while a surliness overtook the men, especially those who were not laboring; they flung themselves on the floor of the tiny station, failing to respond when Kraus prodded them to save time by unloading ammunition. But then, one by one, at some remark from their red-eyed captain, they moved and went to it. Kraus saw that he was going to have to be careful with these fellows. Well, he didn't blame them. War-weary. Let them keep to their own commander, just so long as the job got done.

Once the ramp was ready another mood came, an exhilaration over a nasty problem solved, and a second wind of night energy. As the tank treads safely clattered onto the ground a grunting cheer arose.

With Gunter, Kraus made a sortie in the command car to a neighboring farm; at gunpoint he commandeered a hay wagon, with two powerful horses, for the remaining stock of weapons, gear, provisions. Exalted by his success, he roused the owner of the next farm, too, and secured a second team of farm horses to pull the antiaircraft gun. Thus, at last, his command car in the lead, the massive tank like an elephant with its trunk raised towering directly behind, then the gun and the wagons, Kraus's army set forth for the final conflict.

All went as by charm. The unit rolled steadily onward, the tank's great gun snout, on the steeply pitched road, projecting like an arm raised in the *heil*. Donnerwald stood in the open turret of his Panzer, his field glasses ready in one hand, as though on parade. Now and again, from the farmhouses of the mountain folk, scattered back from the road, one could hear the opening of a window, a door. Over the barking of dogs, voices came. "The Allies?" Couldn't they at least say "the enemy" the lice? And then would come the sound of the same door or window being closed, even being slammed. Once there was the clatter of horses' hoofs, but not approaching—going away. Probably some deserter, escaping.

As they reached the turnoff to the road that mounted the last few kilometers to the castle town, Krauss called a halt. Here the pitch of the road drastically increased.

First, the gun must be dragged down into the gully.

Kraus tramped behind Gunter into the undergrowth. There were wagon ruts, but the slope was precipitous. The farmer who had come with his team complained that the animals would break their legs. Men must hold back the gun lest it tumble and drag the horses with it.

And so they began their labor. Pulling off his jacket, Kraus himself bent his back to the task—that was always the best way to keep men from exploding against a rotten dirty job. And he saw the effect at once; the weary, grimy soldiers stared at him for a moment, surprised at the way the *Obersturmbannfuehrer* shouldered into the brunt of it all. One of the gloomiest of the men, who had been faking it all along, lagging behind with a half-empty tin of gasoline when the heavy shells were being loaded, a deserter in the making, now shook himself as a comrade called, "Give a hand here, Felix." He plunged into the underbrush on his knees, sharing the weight of the gun with Kraus.

Bramble-torn, sweat-smeared, they got it there. As they steadied the gun into the dry riverbed—the stream had long ago been diverted into some kind of waterworks—the pre-dawn light could be sensed under the rim of the sky, and there, materializing in the mist, their target stood before them, outlined as though pasted on paper, the tooth-edged parapets on the sheer wall, the light coming through the bow slits. And the windows, dark rectangles through which the bursting shrapnel would soon scream its way, to imbed itself in the flesh of his enemies. Kraus could pick out the Baron's balcony, in outline, on the sheer wall. And there in the other wing, that blond cunt lay with her premier, snug after their last fuck.

Borrowing Donnerwald's field glasses, he stared at the solid mass of stone.

Just time, before daylight, to place and camouflage the gun. He was forgetting nothing. Here, under a rock ledge, almost as in a natural cave, was the perfect sheltered emplacement. Leafage all around. Excitedly, Kraus began to push and haul as though he would get the weapon there by his own muscle. The men, who had settled down, a few pulling cigarettes out of their pockets, slowly, grudgingly, came over to finish the job.

Then, it couldn't be helped, time had to be taken for breakfast.

Donnerwald told something of what he had heard along the way. The Fuehrer had got out in a plane and he was here in the redoubt. The Allied armies were being led into a trap, offered little resistance, but once they were drawn into these mountain passes they would be annihilated with the new, secret weapons.

Exactly! The new weapons! Donnerwald's news fit in with what Kraus himself knew.

From his jacket pocket, the Panzer commander pulled out a package of American chewing gum, remaining from the piles of supplies captured during the Christmas offensive. Yes, he had been there. This was going to be another show of the same kind, and with a better ending! Cigarettes, chewing gum, and fancy American ration packages, enough to last them for the rest of their lives! Unwrapping the gum and feeding the sticks into their mouths, the fellows made exaggerated chewing motions, like comical gangsters, and Kraus had a good laugh.

He sauntered over to his cannon. There was a great temptation in him to give them a salvo up there, to wake them up. But well he knew from all his labors in the war that the trick was first to get everything set and in place, your whole apparatus ready, before you started the fireworks. Otherwise the rats had a chance to run.

"To work!" And they clambered back up to the tank.

Only, not twenty yards up the side road, the monster began to slip. Donnerwald disappeared down into the interior. Taking the controls, he tried to maneuver his caterpillars into a sideward grip on the road, but an icy skin had formed overnight, and besides, there was a hairpin turn at a sharp incline. Gunter, ahead in the command car, had only barely managed it with a rush of speed.

The clumsy lump of steel skewed and slithered. Donnerwald cursed through tightly shut lips. Last Christmas he had dragged this battlewagon through a blizzard of snow and sleet up the worst slopes of the Ardennes, and he would conquer this blasted turn or let the shitty mess of scrap iron tumble into the gully. Kraus, squeezed in beside him, exerted the utmost force of his will, as if by sheer mental effort alone he would grip the cleats to the road. The churning iron tore chunks from the pavement, but could not conquer the turn. At last, Donnerwald backed the tank down to a flatter area and climbed out. Kraus followed. They stood staring at the torn road. "No use.

She hasn't got the power any more. I'll throw a track and then we're finished," Donnerwald said. Perhaps later in the day, if the ice cleared . . .

Impossible to wait.

An alternative. They had some heavy machine guns. Kraus would drive ahead in the command car and set them up, covering the drawbridge, preventing escape, and then they would reduce the castle entirely from the gully. Use the tank down there too. Even better than in town.

Donnerwald agreed. He had no liking for narrow streets; there was always a chance of some traitor lobbing a Molotov. The gully offered better cover, and they would have no deserters or civilians to contend with.

What faces, as the townsfolk saw the command car coming back, loaded with guns. Especially the women, opening their windows, poking themselves halfway out, still in their nightgowns with their tits hanging loose, expecting to see the Americans arriving, expecting to call the victors right up to their warm beds. The blank looks on their faces when Kraus and his men carried the weapons into their upstairs bedrooms and set up their positions, commanding the street, the plaza, the castle entrance, and looking straight down the road. Let the enemy just come riding along; he'd get some hot spit in his face!

The tavern was closed, at last, with that double-shuttered, dead-to-the-world look of taverns in the early morning, that seems to declare the owners have a special right to undisturbed sleep. Nevertheless Kraus relentlessly held his finger on the bell until the window opened, above. He demanded Schreiter.

The squad leader was there all right, and met him in the hallway, in his underwear. Agreed, leave the gun, he'd mount it. Don't worry, damn it—in half-asleep ill humor —he didn't have to be told where and how to mount a gun.

Kraus swallowed this one's lack of respect, too. The fellow was a damn good soldier and could rouse a dozen men in the place, behind him.

Down in the gully Kraus had a bad moment. Donnerwald's Panzer was so well emplaced and camouflaged that he couldn't even see it, and for an instant feared that the fellow had buggered off. But there, under the slope, the Panzer was in place opposite the antiaircraft gun, so that he had two angles of fire on the castle. There was hardly a corner of the damned fort that he couldn't smash. And not a peep yet from up on top there. Complete surprise.

Donnerwald had put on his helmet. In the day his face was less wild; it was sword-thin, a hard blade, and his red-rimmed eyes were small, with a sneer far back in the pupils. Still, he dug up an extra helmet from inside the tank and offered it to Kraus, who had climbed up level with the turret for a final discussion. As he strapped on the combat helmet, Kraus experienced an overwhelming desire to be inside the tank and fire the first salvo himself.

Donnerwald had seen this look many times before, the longing look of the desk warrior, and with that sneer even sharper in his eyes, he offered the colonel this pleasure. "You want to aim the first one?"

Kraus lowered himself inside. The captain came down and all at once, in a businesslike way, the metal roof clanged on them. Donnerwald kept watching him. No doubt—it gave you a feeling. To be caught and killed, locked in like this—it was not an easy way to die. You burned. But Kraus said nothing. He put his eye to the sight and, almost with natural knowing, manipulated the gun, raising the big snout until he had the Baron's balcony squarely in view, the cross hairs centered. The lazy fellow named Felix was inside; he had already loaded the gun, and now Donnerwald gave Kraus the nod. He pressed the release.

Though he was braced for the recoil, he banged his elbow, and lost the view at the instant of impact. Holding his breath from the stupid crazybone pain, he looked again. Part of the balcony's balustrade was crumpled, and the wall edging the window was now jagged. A nice bit of ruin. Perhaps the Baron was smashed up, inside there, too, amid chunks of his ancestral castle.

"Good shot," Donnerwald felicitated him. "Looks like they had you wasting your time in this war."

They were ready with the next one, and the crew's own gunner had brushed him aside. "Hold your fire," Kraus commanded. He had made up his mind: He did not want to smash them to pulp in there in the castle; he wanted to have them surrender to him. They must now be informed it was he. They must know he had come back.

I N EACH OF THEM, the first disordered reaction was of ghastly dismay. The Americans had arrived and attacked at once, without realizing who was in the castle! The Americans had taken it as a stronghold of the redoubt.

Stumbling into the corridor, each called out the same explanation, a horrible but natural mistake, as though the first care was to exonerate their allies. Remy in pajamas, Dortolot in his trousers, hopping into his shoes, the marshal pulling on his coat over his pajamas, Frère Luc in his cassock, rushing out holding a cross in case absolution was needed, the housekeeper in a bathrobe, starting out of Astuque's room, half pulling back, and then, as it was a crisis and as everyone knew anyway, saying, "Is anybody hurt?" and hurrying to the Baron's wing. Rapidly, the check was made. All, by wondrous fortune, were unscathed. Marianne was already with Vered and Maasi; the window in their room had been shattered, but the glass had not flown about; it lay in a heap against the wall, behind the blackout curtains. Vered was standing, in a pair of Maasi's voluminous pajamas. She must not be alarmed, he said; doubtless there was a strong basement —after all, Kraus had been taken down there to a dungeon. Wryly, he added, Kraus was the best-off!

"We must let the Americans know who is here," everyone kept repeating.

"Where did it strike?"

"On the Baron's side."

The Baron, like some apparition, came up the stairs. He had not been in his room, he had not slept. Still impeccably dressed, his cheeks smooth and shining, he caught sight of Dortolot, who was hurrying across the landing, carrying a sheet. "We must hang it out at once, it's the Allies!" And in the same instant the marshal, who had hurried back to his room, appeared with something even better than the sheet. His heavy cheeks boyishly aglow, he opened a full-sized flag before them.

Where had he got it? How had he hidden it? In the moment, as he stood with the flag, triumphant and admirable, his countrymen gulped. Some had tears in their eyes.

Except for a sudden intuition from the Baron, Marshal Philippe would have marched right out onto the battered balcony with his flag. "Wait, Marshal Philippe, don't show yourself!"

They all stood, puzzled. "Suppose it is not the Allies?" the Baron said.

Germans, arriving in the redoubt? Then why would they attack? How could they know what had happened here? Could Kraus's man somehow have found out, and gone to fetch troops?

"Nonsense!" the marshal declared. Stepping directly

onto the balcony, he draped the flag from the torn masonry.

Something was being hung out. A surrender, after this one shot? The exultation of that instant of release had not yet died away in Kraus.

"The swine! Their flag!" he heard Donnerwald curse, and in the same moment Kraus was elbowed aside, as by some professional who has finished with visitors and must now get down to his job.

Donnerwald's shell crashed into the balcony only an instant after Remy, by some instinct, had pulled the marshal inside. The flag vanished. Chunks of masonry flew into the gully.

Inside, the room was wrecked, with bric-a-brac, paintings, furniture smashed and torn by flying shrapnel. The group stumbled back farther into the hallway. "It's our turn for the cellar, I believe," Michaelis remarked, with bravado, and in that same instant Remy caught the Baron's eyes; the pupils were evasive. All at once, Remy understood. Seizing the old aristocrat by the arm, he demanded, "How did he get out?"

As he was seized, the Baron stiffened. His eyes became fixed. "It was not my place to judge him or to turn him over." He lifted his chin to the marshal. "This would not have been honorable."

Between the two men, it was clear, the code held.

"You let our prisoner go?" Dortolot intoned.

"I believed he would go home like the rest." Now the

Baron's voice changed, became almost plaintive; he no longer spoke as a man of the other side but as an inhabitant of the same house with them, under bombardment. "I had no thought he would do this; it was furthest from my imagination. If indeed it is he."

"This is exactly what he promised to do. Annihilate us."

The unspoken "Why? For what?" reverberated around them, loud as the shellbursts. What could possibly now be changed? Then, in the Baron's mind, an object appeared: the coffer. If the treasure were flung out to him, would the mad dog there in the ravine cease his assault and go away?

For the moment the Baron was too ashamed and too depressed even to make the suggestion; a fugitive desire was in him that the next shell might strike them all where they stood in a group, himself included, and explode them in one instantaneous annihilation, freeing him finally from his treacherous consciousness that was no longer, even in the most complex of its somersaults, amusing.

In the kitchen, with its stone walls warm-tinted with centuries of patina, Trudi, the cook, who had passed nearly her entire life in this room, circled in terror. Then the Americans were not going to be friendly after all? In spite of all the assurances of Senator Joras? The war was come here at last, in full storm. Someone must run down there and tell them their own allies were here. The Polish girl, Julka, was the one to do it; soldiers would not shoot at a girl. Never mind the pots and the breakfast, Julka must tell the Baron to let down the bridge for her so she could run out and save them all. But as the second shell struck the wall above them and all the stone vibrated, Julka doubled herself on the floor, scuttled under the table, and began to cry out prayers in her own language. The name of Maria, *Mutter* Maria, could be heard in every breath, and also the girl's saint's name, a Polish saint she had told Trudi about, in gossipy hours when she polished the silver.

The next shell came cleanly through the kitchen wall, as though a stone had been removed to give it free passage; it was like a bird that flashes by so quickly it is heard rather than seen. It was not the stroke of the shell as it came through the stone, but a shriek from Julka, that shattered the room. Streaking across her outstretched leg, the projectile left the flesh grooved as though an enormous bite had been taken out; already the shape of the hole was lost in blood.

The shrieking rose and rose, with unimaginable force, as the master, with several of the castle's inhabitants, the woman, and the monk, came thronging into the room.

Julka knew why it was she, out of all the house, who had been struck. The screaming—she let it continue from inside her, but her own screams did not fool her into believing that she was an innocent victim. She had been caught at last, like a thief at the moment of leaving a pilfered house, loot in hand. Because of her *ludern*. She had been letting herself imagine that after all of her lusty enjoyment, now with the war's end she would find her way back home and marry herself to one or another of the boys of her village, choose a good solid man and lie with him every night as though nothing had happened before in her womanly life; she would produce her children and be a good mother and wife, saving, in secret, the gifts of money that she had received from passing officers here, using it for an occasional indulgence in a new dress, a pair of earrings. All this she had intended, and see now how in the blink of an eye she was judged, found out, punished. No, it had been known all along. And she would not even die here of the fire in her leg; she would be returned home a hobbling horror, with a stump bound up under her skirt.

Marianne had come and was binding her; others too were kneeling around her, twisting down on her flesh, bringing water to her lips; a thousand times deeper than all the joys this flesh had ever given her was the pain it paid her with now, and momentarily her soul revolted, objecting—she was not worse than other girls, and she had never done bad things to people, she had done no hurt to anyone, it had only been *herum ludern*. The Baron—there was his face—he had wanted her to do it, hadn't he?

The Baron peered at the thrashing, screaming creature. It reached him that this was needless, a pity. These feelings always reached him as by a report. And then, the report was related to a personal reference in himself; the uneasiness, the shame in him, increased, for somehow this girl's suffering came from him, from the devil he had last night let loose.

The monk, kneeling on towels and newspapers, hastily spread by Trudi on the floor to protect his habit from the blood, was repeating prayers; Julka let her hand rest in his, clutching convulsively when new fires of pain flamed up; her body could scream no more. Her own prayers and contritions burst in little gasps from her, between the flares of pain. Though she did not understand his language, on the names of Christ and the Holy Virgin their supplications joined. His eyes were so intense, as though he bore the pain with her.

The poor child. Frère Luc exiled from his mind the eternal question of specific punishment for specific sin, nor would he listen to admonishments to seek shelter as other shells battered the walls; someone had said they did not strike twice in the same spot, or was it lightning? Oh, truly to be freed from distracting thought, and to hold to this soul that was in danger of eternal damnation. For however one pictured it, in Dantesque flames or in a concept of a weighed-down conscience eternally unable to free itself from its guilt and sin, here was the moment of possible repentance and absolution. This poor girl, had she not given these halls life and merriment in her passing, and had he himself not shared in her sin in the lurid imaginings that he had struggled against on some nights when her laughter had come from a bedroom window? Let her sin pass into him now and be taken from her; doubtless in her incomprehensible words she was now confessing her whoring within these walls, only last night with the evil one himself who had sent this shell. In his awkward German,

Frère Luc interjected a question: Sünde, sünde, *schlechtes?* She had learned a few words of German, and her eyes answered everything, in confession, and her hot hand clutched his, a child's hand.

There was no doctor remaining in the village, only a pharmacist; the doctor had long been with the army, leaving the town and the castle to be served by a physician from below, nearly an hour away on the Innsbruck road. The Baron was trying to telephone. Useless, useless, cut off; the Americans must already have come that far. But the physician had left an emergency supply of drugs and had taught Marianne how to administer a syringe of morphine; she hurried with it now.

With the wound partly cauterized by the shell itself, the bleeding had subsided; the girl would not die from loss of blood. But how white she was, the rosy-cheeked little peasant from Poland, and in her pallor, her lower lip hanging slack, she did not seem like anyone they had known here.

The morphine was already taking effect; almost everyone had retreated now, warned off to the more sheltered corridors, still hesitant about descending to the cellar, except for Schall, who was carrying down his miniatures, to enclose himself in safety.

Marianne and Frère Luc crouched by the girl. Vered was arched over them, with a haunted look that asked, "Is this because of me?"

The lower leg, without its blood supply—in a short while it would be finished. They watched as the girl faded into sleep, to awake a cripple, and with all their intellects and wills, leaders, messengers to God, they stood hopeless, knowing only that outside, in the ravine, one little man in hatred and fury could exercise his will while theirs were paralyzed.

"But she can't be left like this!" Marianne burst out. Up above in the mountains somewhere there must still be a headquarters, a surgeon. "If we can get her out through the village—after all, those men all know her—"

And to several in the hallway an additional thought appeared. Perhaps they could all of them escape into the village, take shelter there, hide, or flee.

As if in answer, a machine-gun burst came from across the moat, raking the upper floor of the castle. Schreiter, hearing the crashing sounds of the bombardment, had decided to have a last go for himself, too.

In his judgment, the marshal said, and his judgment would have to prevail as he was now responsible for their safety—as well as his own, he added with an effort at verve—very well, in his judgment the situation was serious but not at all desperate, and not necessarily perilous. Here in the hall they were fairly secure, as far as the evidence of enemy capability showed. Enemy fire had thus far disclosed two weapons placed at the base of the ravine. One could be identified by the unexploded shell which had unfortunately in its trajectory wounded the maid. It was a projectile from a heavy Panzer tank; judging by this shell, he noted, the enemy had not changed their model since the outbreak of the war.

At any moment, Remy felt, he would rush out. He would not interrupt the old drone but he would simply rush to the turret and spray the damned ravine. Finally to answer back. Even if the enemy was out of reach.

Armor-piercing shells, the marshal continued, had at a few isolated points broken through the more recent, thinner parts of the castle wall. But the tank gun's trajectory was limited; if he had a blackboard he could show them precisely the angle . . .

"The schoolteacher!" Remy muttered the old epithet for the marshal, who had for many years been head of the military academy. Nevertheless, to be just to him, in the First War he had distinguished himself in the trenches.

It was clear, the marshal went on, that the narrowness of the gulch made it impossible for the gun to pump shells into this corner of the castle; the tank would have to climb halfway up the ravine to do this and he judged the slope to be too steep. As to the antiaircraft weapon, it could not pierce the walls; its shells could enter only by windows or other apertures, and so long as they avoided such areas they were comparatively safe. Now, as to the weapons on the town side, again, the machine guns could endanger only those who exposed themselves in the apertures. Remained then the question as to whether the enemy could bring up further armor. In the marshal's opinion, an enemy stand here was not likely as there was no longer time for full-scale preparation. What was taking place was an isolated attack. And what was the enemy's objective? To recapture them as hostages? Possibly. To destroy them? It was not in the enemy's capacity unless he could force entry, and, most ancient device though it was, the moat . . .

What did he propose, then? Remy found the moment to break in. That they sit it out, here?

The phrase, with its echo of the strategy that had proved so disastrous on a grand scale in the war, came home to the marshal. The entire, indignant content of his mind in all these years of brooding swept to his lips. He would have delivered the total argument of all the closely written pages of the book he had prepared while here in prison, his thesis showing that assault was a state of mind that provoked action even when assault was foolish and wasteful of life. As against this stood the preservative mind. He was not afraid of the word conservative. Here this very castle—had it not endured into modern times as a witness of the effectiveness of a prepared, protected position? Unknowingly, the marshal had made a pulling-in movement of his head, like that of a turtle. "Yes," he declared. "We will man the defenses, so as to interdict any attempt at assault. We shall have to defend ourselves for only a few days, perhaps only a few hours until we are relieved."

Relieved. Rescued, he meant, as the entire nation had had to be rescued from without, because of such turtle-headedness.

The marshal, too, was at the same moment touched by the thought of the microcosm represented here, and pricked by the sense of failure that was never outside his consciousness. But he put against this the two other principles. The first, that a superficial similiarity is never proof that the outcome will be the same; the bad experience of a first occasion might indeed give one the wisdom to avoid crucial errors on a second occasion, and to prove that the principle itself had been correct, only the execution had been faulty. His defense wall had held, indeed it had never been breached. It had simply not been extended far enough to prevent the enemy from coming around the end, over the mountains. Therefore it was not a going-out to assault that had been required, but an extension of the prepared defense.

The wall must be rebuilt, the marshal conclusively proved in his manuscript, called *Legacy*. Strongly prepared impregnable positions were still the most important element in any defense system. Had the enemy himself not adopted the fortified perimeter defense in the Atlantic wall? It had been breached, that was true, but only with the most overwhelming accumulation of fire power in all military history. With better generalship on the part of the Germans it could indeed never have been breached. Conclusion—the border wall must be built stronger than ever extended, made absolute. That was the real lesson.

Now here, the condition was similar but not identical. Defense was all-around. The enemy could not surprise and penetrate them unless—perhaps Remy would even bring up this absurdity—unless by a pinpoint parachute drop! And for what purpose? Were they all that important? Was the nation's future really in their hands? Doubtless Remy thought so, but the marshal did not. He only wanted to clear himself of the past. And even if he were to die here under attack—his book would be found.

A second principle: For the true soldier—he censored the thought "truly great"—the smallest task was as valuable as the largest. It was as honorable for him to command this . . . this platoon of aging civilians, as honorable to map the defense of this single post, as it would be to marshal entire armies in their movements.

When he had rushed from his room the marshal had, without thinking, picked up last night's bear gun; now his fingers gripped on the barrel. And so he passed over to their own capabilities: a dozen men—and one woman; he bowed to Marianne, who had already demonstrated her effectiveness as an emergency medical aide. The men, including himself, were nearly all beyond the age of high agility, nor did they possess weapons capable of destroying the enemy armor even if—he gazed at Remy—such an adventure as a sortie were to be contemplated. The turret guns, he reminded them, had been placed as a caution against their escape, not as a protection against assault from without. They had no armor-piercing shells.

In Remy's eyes the marshal saw a retort. The fellow was about to suggest some homemade gasoline bombs. He had heard too many tales of the romantic resistance actions at home. The marshal did not want to devaluate such heroism, but in military measure the results unfortunately amounted to nothing but pinpricks. The capability here was purely defensive, but, he judged, adequate.

He passed on, then, to the disposition of his forces. In the first watch he placed Remy in command of the turret facing the enemy emplacement in the upper rooms of the tavern. Thus, the marshal felt, Remy could relieve his hostilities with an occasional burst of answering fire. With the young ex-Premier, for the sake of harmony, he placed Vincent Maasi. At the farther tower he stationed Dortolot, with Frère Luc. He himself, the marshal said, would take up his position on the parapet overlooking the ravine. This brought something of a murmur from Michaelis—was it advisable for the commander to take the most exposed position? Gripping the bear gun, the marshal shrugged and smiled. They would stand four-hour watches. The relief group had better now try to rest.

He took out his timepiece. As the others all waited to coordinate their watches, a shell was heard striking the wall. The sound came from the far end of the dining hall, the limit, as he had declared, of enemy capability. This time, scarcely a window shook. It seemed a good omen. The marshal announced the hour, the minute, the second, and the men stood to go to their positions.

Marianne spoke. What of poor Julka?

The casualty? Was she not resting well?

They had carried Julka to her bed, but a fever was developing. "She's breathing so heavily—I—we must do something."

"The wound should not prove fatal, I believe." He knew what they thought of him, this woman and Remy. They would imply he was callous. He was as sensitive to loss of life in combat as any man. Was this not at the root of his entire career: a search for a military defense that would minimize casualties? What right had she, with that expression on her face, to accuse him? The Polish slut would live. Doubtless this one was distressed for her, that with only one leg she would be limited in her sexual activities. Let them rather hope that this would be the worst of the casualties here!

Could not a way be found to get her out? Marianne persisted, her voice rising. "I can't take the responsibility for the girl's life!"

Get her out? Over the drawbridge, perhaps, so that the enemy could meanwhile rush in?

"They'll let us send out a wounded girl!" Remy declared. And the thought of the men on the other side hovered in the room: almost every one of them had made use of this girl.

The Baron, remaining nearby if he should be wanted, had not attempted to enter their conference. Nor, he was aware, could he offer to join the defense, though the castle was his, and of them all, he was the huntsman. That swine out there—to hunt him down would be the way.

Farther up in the mountain, the Baron now reminded them, there was the sanatorium. He was still attempting to telephone. Though no operator answered, there was a buzzing on the line; it was not dead.

Kraus knew exactly what he would do in their place. He would try a sortie along the top of the ravine. Protected by the brush up there, he would creep along and when just above the Panzer, he would hurl his explosives. Probably that young Premier who thought himself so clever would try it, fixing the Panzer's position from the fire flashes.

Never in the whole war had he been outmaneuvered. Even that train of Budapest Jews. In spite of all the double-crossing tricks of the Hungarian Ministry, he had got the train on its way. Now he had the same feeling; he would outwit them in every trick they thought to play against him. A real soldier, he would outgeneral the general of generals, outguess the enemy on every move. Let them creep along the top of the ravine—he'd fix a reception for them!

Among the boxes of supplies he had made note of a crate of nice flat pancakes that you could plant, and cover up with a handful of leaves and twigs. One step and the blast came up, right between the legs.

Along with Gunter, Kraus set out to plant the mines. Each carried a dozen in a sling, and they stepped with tender care, picking their way up the side of the gully. Just one misstep, a fall against a tree, and even though the mines were not yet armed, it seemed to him the whole lot might be set off. They must be careful, too, not to stir a twig, because the bastards up there had certainly manned the guns, and they had a direct line of fire along here. Kraus kept imagining what a chance hit on his sack would do to him.

But to plant the mines was good. You could just see the

path those swine up there would take, a footpath below the ridge of the ravine, meandering among the trees. Let them come, those clever premiers and ministers and marshals. Maybe the Baron, too—the great hunter would be showing them the way, that baboon, with his face of a baby just pulled out of the muck of the crotch.

The earth already felt warm to his hands, with springtime, Gunter said. What a beautiful romantic path here, so still and deserted, in the high morning, with not a mark of humanity on it, only wildness, each leaf living its life, and with small budding flowers among the stones, opening to the spring.

"I didn't know you were such a lover of nature," Kraus said.

Ah well, he had always been a mountain-lover, Gunter told him. This had never come out between them. Oh yes, he was even a bit of a climber, Gunter said, and they worked on.

A new idea came to Kraus. Once they had made themselves secure from assault, they could try their own assault. A charge of dyamite, under the retaining wall of the moat, on this side, and the castle's protecting ring of water would vanish into the gully, like from a flushed toilet. It was crazy how a few yards of water could keep you from assaulting your target. All right, with the moat empty and dry, a quick rush under plenty of covering fire, and he'd grab the lot of them in there. Good evening, Baron. Good evening, Marshal. Just to see their faces!

"Listen to the turds." Donnerwald, wearing his headset, sat intent, his eyes in a fixed glare. "I haven't heard their crap since Christmas in the Ardennes."

So it was the Americans. "Where are they?" Kraus demanded.

"They are at Z for Zebra," Donnerwald spat.

"Near?"

"I get them clear."

"They may not even come to this place. It's a side pocket."

The tank commander gave him a dirty glance. "It's a pocket," he said. A lousy hole in which, it was clear, he had no intention of getting stuck, to engage the American armor. But surely, Kraus told himself, there was still time for one last blow! A quick assault. For the casket. That was the way to convince the red-eyed bastard. And Kraus spoke of the strongbox, stolen from him by that traitor to the Reich up there, the Baron. Diamonds, not one of them smaller than four carats, each stone enough to set a man up in a nice postwar enterprise.

A look of curiosity had come onto Donnerwald's face. Kraus turned to Gunter. "Show him."

Gunter pulled out the matchbox and held it open in his palm. Donnerwald nodded, and turned his eyes on Kraus; they were a shade harder than before. "So that's what we've been after. A box you left behind. Why didn't you mention it before, Kraus?"

Naturally, he had always intended to share! And with the hard eyes still on him, Kraus plunged into his plan for the attack. Now at least Donnerwald's eyes did not ridicule him. And as Kraus heard his own plan it sounded practical enough. A short climb from the side nearest the road, where the trees were thick. The climber couldn't even be seen from the tower; certainly not at night. A dynamite charge under the shelf of concrete. Then a concerted attack across the emptied moat, from front and rear—

"And they can pick off every man."

"They'll surrender when we blow the moat. They have no idea how many we are. We don't have to expose ourselves. I told the Baron I had a division on the way."

It was up to the men in town, Donnerwald decided. Just as after the last war, things were going to be damned difficult, and it wouldn't be bad to go home with a little starter. If the fellows in town coordinated, if they also carried a charge and blew open the gate the moment the moat was emptied, there was a fair chance nobody had to get hurt.

A few volleys had been exchanged across the plaza, nothing but reminders from each side: We are here, alert. So they sat, Remy and Maasi, grumbling to each other over the ineptitude of their military leader in this tiny situation as in the great war; it was fascinating, Remy repeated, how a man is ruled by his character so that every action of his is consistent.

But the other side, Remy was certain, would not sit and wait. To bring up a tank only to blast away a bit at the castle didn't make sense. There would be a surprise. The only hope was to forestall Kraus with a sortie, risky as it might seem.

And then Maasi caught sight of the command car climbing to the town. For one brief moment as it took the turn, Remy fired furiously. But he had swiveled too late.

They knew surely now it was Kraus. Frantically, Remy yelled across the roof, even exposing himself, gesticulating for Dortolot to catch the vehicle as it entered the village.

It did not appear.

Cursing the nerve of that band of decrepit politicians with their stupid wild shooting at him, Kraus had ordered Gunter to halt just below the peak of the rise. On foot, keeping close to the walls under the shopping arcade, they made their way to the tavern.

The pounding of the castle from the ravine had raised a certain grim merriment in the *Gasthaus,* partly dispelling the depressing atmosphere of defeat that had lain over the empty chairs and tables with the stale-beer smell of morning. Good, let the old Baron have a few jolts. And if a few heads were blown off, in there, all the better! Whatever was said about Kraus, after all he was no quitter!

Schreiter hurried down to greet the hero: Well, what had he come back for? His jewels, no doubt! the sergeant jested, from some remarks that Gunter had made.

Why not? Kraus replied with the proper verve. There was loot for everyone. For himself, it was more than a question of loot. He had a job to finish. And he launched into his plan.

At each phrase, Schreiter nodded, but his nodding became slower. "They won't know which way to turn, front or back!" Kraus insisted. "They'll rush down to where we blast the moat, the whole gang of them, and right then you can make a safe attack on the gate. Why, they've got the shit scared out of them already with the bombardment. We'll capture the whole caboodle."

"Somebody could get hurt."

With good coordination from both sides, Kraus insisted, the whole thing could be done without a casualty. Even the Panzer commander had agreed. "We'll all go home with diamonds in our pockets."

Schreiter snorted. "Still, if they turn the floodlights on, we could lose some men."

"They'll be too scared to shoot, I tell you."

"Hell, if they're so scared, why don't you ask them to surrender right now, with all your bombardment?"

Just then as though by some fatal connivance, the young daughter of the place came from the back room, telling them in an awed half whisper that a call had come through from the castle.

Hovering over the Baron at the dead telephone, Marianne had almost given up hope for Julka when suddenly there came an operator's voice. A repair must have been made somewhere. And though the sanatorium could not be reached, and the pharmacy did not answer, at least the tavern responded.

The Baron began his explanation. The little Polish girl, Julka—Schreiter himself had been friendly with her . . .

When he had explained, there came a long wait. Then the conversation was resumed, and the Baron's face changed, puckering more than ever, like a baby's when it hovers uncertainly on the verge of tears. Covering the mouthpiece, he said, "It's Kraus himself. They demand that we surrender."

Already, word of the telephone contact had brought a circle around them. The marshal replied firmly, "No question." And he turned to the others. "If they believed they could seize us or destroy us, they would not call for surrender."

"It's only the removal of poor Julka!" Marianne cried into the telephone.

It was that bitch, that same little bitch that had tricked him, naked. And in his fury, what Kraus really wanted burst from him.

"Give me back what I came with, and we will go!"

"Came with?" the Baron repeated.

"My coffer, and the Jew. Give me the Jew and my coffer!" Kraus heard himself shouting. "Or else it is all finished with you! The hell with your wounded!"

Startled, the Baron held the receiver from his ear, letting the roar escape into the room. The others had moved in a step closer, and with them was Vered. Through the outheld receiver, the words came reverberating, "Give me the Jew!"

Kraus himself was as astonished as they, to hear the ultimatum that came from him. He had not prepared it. Yet in the same instant his whole being accepted this as his absolute. This was his truth. It was not for the loot that he was carrying on this final battle, no, that would have been unworthy. It was for the rightness of all he had done.

The cry had come up from a man's bottom need, from the deepest rage of all, the demand for self-justification. And now Kraus told himself his instinct just now had known best. His instinct had acted on what he had learned but not fully realized, in those few hours he had spent in the castle. If left alive, this Jew would be returned again to the highest office in his land. It was this one, this very Jew, that the enemy would appoint again as their premier. Not any of the others in the castle, not Remy, not Dortolot, but Vered. The final shame, the final annihilation of all that Germany had fought for, the final annulment of all his own work in these years. A gigantic, blasphemous jest at the very memory of the Leader. And deliberately, in spite, they would do it, like spitting in the face of the great dead Fuehrer, the great idealist—they would elevate a Jew to their highest post.

And even worse, the greatest shame of all—as ruler of the victors this Jew would decide the fate of the vanquished. The Jew would extend his arm over all the Germans.

The dark ember of his mission flamed up again in Kraus. His life must have a meaning after all. In him alone was left the purpose to fight against this final disgrace, this final shame of all his kind. And he would fight. If he were left all alone here in the end with nothing but a pistol in his hand, he would find a way to destroy the Jew.

They had hung up.

It was Marshal Philippe who had stepped forward, at the reverberating word, and taken the receiver from the Baron's hand, setting it back on the instrument.

Over the little group there settled a listlessness, as though they were confronted with some tragic, immutable condition of nature, as when one hears the results of a crucial medical test on someone one has known: cancer, inoperable, hopeless. Each takes the word into himself, deep into some inmost corner, for examination. Could it also in some way touch his own being?

No, in his own case it had never gone so far, the Baron told himself, and it was finished. Yet he looked away, so as not to see Vered.

The marshal stared directly at Vered, one might have said as one expecting approbation. But something was working in him. He had never been a quick student; instead he had come to pride himself in the attitude that once he grasped a thought, an equation, it was part of him solidly and forever. In all his disputes in the years gone by, with Vered, he had never thought of him particularly as a Jew. This man had been a socialist, a *littérateur,* a civilian, a politician. Of course the marshal had known that the epithet, Jew, had been applied to Paul Vered, and he had known that the Premier was a Jew by birth, though fortunately of an old distinguished family, but he had never listened to any insult in the appellation as it applied to Vered, for it was simply, to him, a bit of dirty politics, and in the marshal's own code of honor, anti-Semitism as such was no longer approved. Naturally he did not care for the Jews, as Jews. The grubby commercial kind, the over-clever kind, the pushing kind, the foreign kind. There were none such in the army. If there were some officers who were Jews by birth they were, like Vered, persons who simply were not "Jews" in the pejorative sense.

The whole enemy campaign about Jews had been segregated in his mind as something that was not military, and no concern of his. Indeed, when the radio stories about the death camps had been heard, he had felt a reluctance to enter into any discussion of the massacres, for profoundly within himself there was a flicker of response to the wish to get rid of the "Jew Jews." And yesterday, when Vered had appeared, alive, his first thought had been that at last even the Nazis had realized it was a mistake to consider such as Vered to be "Jews." At least, not "Jew Jews."

Yet when Vered had told of how his wife had been taken to the gas chamber, the marshal had felt the beginning of that stirring, the stirring that came when he was about to grasp a hitherto incomprehensible theorem. This distinguished, sympathetic woman he had known, this well-bred woman of a fine family, a perfect dinner hostess . . . and a shock and pang had come. He had many times been her guest.

Now, staring at Vered, the marshal was telling himself:

But this too is what is meant by a Jew. And inexorably the theorem was taking hold of him. There had been those failures of reaction at the start of things, when something within him had refused to revolt at the boycott of Jewish shopkeepers. But could all that outcry have been part and parcel of the cry he had just heard, "Give me the Jew!"? Could they already have meant Vered?

With the best of his restraint, Vered held back the words that rose in him, "I am ready to go."

No, no, it would be a gesture of false heroics, for the others would not, could not, let him yield to the barbaric demand of the defeated enemy for a last sacrifice, even if it truly meant saving their own lives. And for him to suggest that they had it in them to yield would be a betrayal on his own part, a nullification of all that had been fought for, far beyond the fate of the Jews.

Even though he could sense how in some corner of the soul of a Rieber, a du Caux, his words might touch off a momentary sense of relief, the impulse was absurd. Doubtless some of them would even tell themselves that if he yielded it might not mean death, but trade for a high Nazi. And that in any case he was quite old. But it was too late in the world to permit such self-deception.

Yet under all this another logic gripped Vered, and as it dragged him downward he could lean on no one here, not even Marianne. "You have no right, or even wish, to escape the fate of the Jews," the logic said. And the enormous weariness that had begun to lift from him yesterday, when he had felt the warmth of his devoted friends, of Maasi, of Remy, of Luc, the dear affection of Marianne, indeed when even Dortolot and the marshal had been glad of his survival, the warmth he had felt of being among people from his own life, of being home in a sense—smothering this warmth, his weariness now seeped back, engulfing him. He recognized—he had sat face to face all too long with it—the wish for death. Not death itself but the wish for death had a form, and the form was again present, though to some extent a man, a being, could hold it off by recognizing and naming it: "You are the death wish." And in a surprising echo, the child-heard Hebrew name occurred to him, the *Malach Hamavet,* heard in some grandfather's tale, from the time when there had been a believing Jew in the family, a real one. The *Malach Hamavet,* the Angel of Death. There could come a time when the name was no longer used to send away, to exorcize. The presence remained, sat with you, acknowledged by you, and self-acknowledging. And then it would become a comforting presence, and then it would embrace you, and at last as you yielded entirely to its comfort, the angel would carry you away.

Yes, he was ready by now—he had perhaps too long been ready—to agree that the evil in mankind was too much for him to understand; let others contend with it henceforth. Most of his life he had trembled—did the belief of a single person matter? Yes, it did matter, it must matter—on the border between agnosticism and atheism. The last shred of human dignity, the final intuition of the soul, demanded that there still could exist the possibility of God. God, impervious to evil and to this monstrous accumulation of suffering? The remnant of God that remained was a conception of a spirit that came upon matter, trying endlessly to blow into matter something of itself, with the fire catching hold, flaring up at times, at times dying out. And if he had at last perceived this, perhaps he had gone as far as he could, and had no more need of life. But he could not offer that life now. He must not.

STRANGELY, THE TELEPHONE RANG. The Baron hesitated to pick it up, wearing the expression of one who feels sure the call must be for someone else, and as one man looked uneasily to another, Marianne, with the ridiculous sense that she was still playing the role of a secretary, picked up the receiver. It was not that voice of which they were all so apprehensive. Instead, Schreiter stated that he was ready to receive the wounded girl; two men would come to the bridge, if their safety was guaranteed. "Of course! Of course!" Marianne cried. "At once!"

The others would have intervened with their doubts. Could it be a trap? "Agreed, agreed!" she repeated.

From above came the brief clatter of machine guns, and

Remy appeared for an instant on the stairs, shouting down to them, cursing himself. Kraus's command car had got past again, on the road, returning to the valley.

In the guards' quarters they found a regulation stretcher. Frère Luc and Dortolot, their watch relieved, lifted the girl, who seemed on the verge of awakening, muttering Polish words in her delirium, then a cry in German, *"Hund, du hund!"* And her head rolled, while her breathing came coarsely. There seemed no way to secure the torn leg, so that Marianne had to stand between the men and lift the limb like a separate object. Pathetically, even now the other thigh seemed indecent, and Marianne held down the edge of the girl's skirt until the body was placed on the stretcher. Already it seemed a corpse, smaller, more childlike, than in life.

With the marshal, rigidly watchful, standing at his side, the Baron let down the drawbridge. Across the plaza they saw Schreiter himself advancing, with a comrade in half-uniform. Above, it could be seen that the window in the upper floor of the tavern was manned.

A number of townsfolk had gathered in the doorways, venturing no farther, so that they could dart back inside if trouble began; a child, a boy not ten, started from his family group and was pursued by an elder sister and pulled back. "It's a truce, they're not allowed to shoot!" His voice carried over the entire area, in the still air under the high sun.

Crossing the bridge, Luc and Dortolot deposited their

burden between the two heraldic pillars, and as Schreiter came near to take over, Dortolot managed in a few quick words, an offer. "We'll pass you the valuables. Get rid of Kraus."

Schreiter turned his face to the politician, stonily. He could not, even in the end of this putrid war, let himself be bought by the enemy. "You picked the wrong man," he said. He'd get his loot in a soldier's way, tonight in the attack.

The girl's eyes had opened. On her face, as Schreiter leaned down to the handles behind her head, there came a mixed expression, something close to a childish leer, the leer of the still-innocent who wants to pretend that she knows all the secrets. And at the same time, in her look, there was a swift communication of her bitter knowledge of all that awaited her in the remainder of her life, a crippled woman.

Her eyes had recognized him, too. During several months, when she had first come here, Schreiter alone had been her partner in *herum ludern.*

The bombardment had resumed. It was Kraus's journey to the village, then, that accounted for the lull. And why had Kraus come up? For some concerted plan, that was clear. An attack, with darkness, Remy was certain. Their last chance.

Meanwhile the shelling increased. A direct hit carried away part of the parapet where the marshal had again taken his station. Everywhere there was flying stone and shrapnel; it seemed at times to beat like hail on the old castle walls. The bursting antiaircraft shells, futile against the stone, nevertheless sent murderous slivers through the partly barricaded windows. An increasing jumpiness and terror grew among the besieged, as no help came. They spoke less and less to one another, and in the silence, the unavoidable conjectures, the unavoidable thoughts, seemed to stand clear in the eyes of more than one. If only not for Vered.

Vered sat with Frère Luc. All through his hours of duty in the turret, the monk had struggled with himself, in the appalling understanding that had come to him. At one moment, he had attempted to pierce the mind of the good Christian who manned the gun with him. For Dortolot was a good, practicing Catholic, the routine sort, Luc knew; one must not ask profound and mystical belief of him, but soberly and responsibly he had always held to the Church. And Dortolot was a believer, Luc knew, for Dortolot had confessed to him; the man did not trouble himself with the complexity of dogma, but he had a true and untroubled belief in the Savior.

And so Frère Luc had spoken to this man now. "Tell me, Robert, of what Vered related to us—that there were Christians, men who believed themselves to be Christians, in the camps, slaughtering the Jews. And that some of them surely believed they were doing God's work. Can you believe this?"

"I can believe they believed it, unfortunately, yes," Dortolot replied. "Man can make himself believe almost any-thing."

Luc would not let him evade. "But as practicing Christians?"

"They were wrong, of course," Dortolot said. "Christ said that all were forgiven. But it is not too difficult to see where they found their rationalization."

"We were told the Jews were accursed, yes. We are told they were outcast, yes. We have taught that they can find salvation only in accepting Christ the Messiah, yes. But we have never been taught to kill them!"

Dortolot's face had closed. The subject was painful, complex, and what use was there to pursue it further? But in Luc the dialogue continued: "Have we ever been taught not to?" "We have been taught not to kill, and surely that included the Jews." "Even a Jewish teaching!" "And yet for centuries we killed Jews, in the name of Christ." "That was all in the Dark Ages." "And now?" "It was a Nazi decree to kill them, not a Christian decree. Some Chris-tions, taking part, were misled by myth and superstition into imagining Christianity expected the death of the Jews." "But did the authority of our Church raise its voice against this mortal error?"

Unremittingly, insistently, the conclusion that had touched him yesterday fastened itself upon Frère Luc. There was unmitigated error. There was mortal error in what was taught about the Jews. Doubtless, it was through faulty interpretation. Had the Savior not died for all man-kind?

Then how, then why, was this error allowed to persist?

Impatiently, Luc had waited out his hours behind the gun, to speak again to Vered. Face to face with the Jew, he found his turbulence, his sense of immeasurable error, somehow being contained. The tragic error was perhaps not hopeless. It was not universal. It was not irreversible. He was far from alone in his faith to see it. Indeed, those who were mature in Christianity had seen it in themselves and dispelled in themselves any hatred of the Jews. Vered himself pointed this out.

"All my life I have lived among Christians and I was not made to feel I am a hated Jew," Vered remarked, with the slight accent of irony which Frère Luc realized he would not, before the war, have characterized as Jewish irony.

"Yet we too had our waves of the most brutal anti-Semitism."

"Earlier. I believe that, in general, people are ashamed of its vestiges."

Then Frère Luc said, "I asked myself now, if Nazism is gone, if its teaching of Jew-hatred totally disappears, is this hatred really finished? And it came to me that there remains one place where the hatred of Jews is still systematically inculcated, where every child absorbs it." Almost sobbing, he added, "My own church. We repeat it every day."

Vered leaned to him and touched his knee in sympathy.

"I believe this must be my task," Luc said. "To labor to bring an end to such teaching. It is not the Jew as Judas, but Jesus the Jew that must be seen. Will you help me?"

From Paul Vered's eyes, the eternal Jew looked at him; not the former Premier, not the *littérateur*, not the patriot, the fighter for social reform, the ironist and the agnostic, only a world-weary and time-weary Jew who said, "In this, my good friend, how could I? How could a Jew possibly help you?"

There was another who brooded over the Jewish question, the cry from the telephone unceasingly in his mind: "Give me the Jew!" To Auguste Rieber, Vered had always been the Jew, and to Rieber, it was not for their campaign against the Jews that the Nazis were at fault. He too believed in a nation purified and cleansed of foreign elements, strong in itself. But with that, let each nation remain to itself. The Nazis had no mission to conquer other nations: it was only in this that they had been evil. And as to the Jews, had not the Lord used one evil to destroy another, as was often seen in nature? Could the destruction of the Jews be anything but the will of God? Could so vast a decision be human? What everyone looked on with horror, the vastness of it, the conception of an entire people being eliminated root and branch, was indeed the very proof that a divine and not a human plan was in progress. This was from God, as had always been known and predicted: the time had come. And the Nazis, having been used for this primordial task, were themselves now destroyed for their sins. Give them the Jew! Let them be destroyed together, and the good people saved!

To propose this to his countrymen was useless. Even the man of the cloth, whom he considered to defile the cloth, was in the toils of the old Jew's hypnotism. The only way was to act by himself. Open the gates. "Come and take your Jew!"

How and at what moment to do it was the question. No one could be trusted to help, not even du Caux, not even for this. To open the gate was not difficult: it was unguarded. He had only to press the button for the drawbridge to go down. He could slip into the courtyard when his tour of duty was ended, and do it. And then? The loudspeaker, carrying his voice into the plaza. "Come!"

But Remy, Dortolot, Luc, Maasi—all the Jew-lovers would be on duty then on the roof. What if they started shooting as Schreiter and his men came across the bridge?

Could he himself in some way seize Vered? A compunction rose in Rieber's flesh, as though some shriveling power would come from the Jew if he but touched him. Or could he arrange the affair when his own group was on duty on the roof? Could he get du Caux and Astuque to agree to hold their fire, and then run down and open the gate? Suppose the others caught him at the control? There was even a manual control to let down the bridge, slower; but there he could lock himself in. He was not yet certain how best to proceed. Only, he must be ready to seize any opportunity that might arise.

Through the storeroom, Remy prowled and searched. There were grenades, and he dragged a crate up into the hallway. Flares, too. If an attack came they might be needed; he carried some to the roof. But still he felt the essential was undone. To sit here and wait to be attacked, to be annihilated, was unendurable. He must break out.

Again in the storeroom, he stopped before the tins of gasoline. He saw himself hurling gasoline bombs. Where and how the opportunity would come he did not know, but he must find some empty bottles and make ready. At least he would feel he was doing something.

Night had come. The way Gunter did his climbing was admirable. Not a twig snapped as his form filtered upward among the roots and rocks beneath the moat. As he reached the concrete span, he was like some upside-down insect with glue on his paws.

Kraus waited below, rigid.

Schreiter too was in position, covered by the heraldic pillar, with a dozen men hidden on the other side of the plaza waiting for the instant to attack. They were all he had left, ready for a bit of adventure and a share of Kraus's treasure.

The bugger's plan was not bad. One minute after Kraus's explosion at the rear of the moat, Schreiter's man, in the power station, would cut the current to the castle, eliminating their floodlights. That one minute would still give the defenders time, in there, to rush down to the site of the explosion. The front would be unwatched. That would be Schreiter's turn. As the water rushed out from the moat, he would wade across, carrying the charge for the gate. Once the gate was blown, his men would follow him inside.

And now, perfectly on schedule, the moat erupted. Great chunks of concrete whirled up in a geyser that shot erect in the brief red flare. "Good boy!" Schreiter cried out involuntarily. He began to count the seconds.

From the turret, wild shooting into the valley began. On his side, Remy fired at the area of the explosion, but, unable to depress his gun to a low enough angle, ran onto the roof and flung two grenades. His entire body was trembling with a fury of confusion. The time for action had come and he was momentarily at a loss. A breach had been made somewhere down there, an attack would come. He must rush down to meet it. Already, he saw Luc vanishing down the stair hatch.

"Stand!" the marshal shouted. "Man your positions!" He himself was still firing into the ravine.

With a clamor that sounded like full-scale war, the tank and gun added their fire to the explosion. Remy found himself flat on the roof from the air impact of a shell passing hardly a yard over his head.

"Idiot! Take cover!" Yet Marshal Philippe himself rushed out onto the open roof. The ancient, solid lesson had come back to the marshal: every attack could be a diversion. Look elsewhere. "The floodlights!" he called.

Dortolot turned on the switch. The lights glared down onto the empty plaza.

Now, now, Rieber realized, was his moment. Running to the sentry box that controlled the gate, he released the drawbridge, and at the same moment shouted into the loudspeaker. The bridge began to separate itself from the wall, while startingly, in the plaza, directly over Schreiter's ear, Rieber's words came out.

"Come and take—"

At that instant the current was cut. The remaining words, "the Jew," emerged only in a strangled guttural, while the bridge remained frozen at a high angle. The briefly illuminated area went black. Groping, Rieber tried to make his way toward the hand controls.

Schreiter, clambering over the side of the moat, crouching, had only moments to wait as the dark waters, greenish-tinted in the night, were siphoned downward. The way the bridge had started to come down was surely a sign of surrender. There must be real panic in there. But some were still shooting. Should he put the current back on, and call for them to come out? But a change of plan would confuse Kraus. And somehow the idea of placing his charge and blasting the gate, a great big blast in their faces, drew him on.

Rieber's cry had echoed to the roof, and Maasi, peering down in the momentary searchlight glare, had noticed the bridge parting from the wall. Instantly, Marshal Philippe had stormed down the stairs, reaching the sentry box an instant after everything went dark. "You miserable traitor!" he shouted, flinging himself at Rieber, his old sinews filled with the power of his rage, bearing the half-crouching man to the ground, even trampling on him.

Meanwhile Remy had thought of his flares. Suddenly a glowing, phosphorescent ball of light hung in front of the castle, and there, in the bottom of it, a figure stood in momentarily arrested motion, a soldier holding his weapon aloft away from the water. Schreiter had waded into the moat.

Flung from his bed by the explosion under the moat, the Baron seized his rifle. The geyser had drenched one side of his room, and now a brilliant glow engulfed the opposite window. Looking down, he saw the attacking figure in the midst of the emptying moat, his gun held high, and a long pike, with a charge on the end. In some momentary atavistic way the figure appeared to the Baron as the eternal, primordial, rebellious and attacking servitor, the peasant, the *Lumpenproletariat* of the hungry years after the First War, the entire threat of mankind, and taking quick easy aim, he brought the figure down.

Schreiter tumbled into the water, his arms flailing, trying to get a grip somewhere, his whole being seeming still to be strong, protesting, "Why do this to me, I am not so bad," while the swirling blue-black current rolled the black lump of him over and over. He caught himself for an instant on all fours, but his arms buckled under the pain of his chest wound. A great sucking lunge of water carried him along through a jagged gap in the concrete, that left a long tear on his side as his body plunged unseen, enwrapped in the waters, into the abyss.

From across the plaza a wail had arisen, anguished, awesome, a howl of women echoing into the mountains the eternal cry of those who watch the sacrifice pitched into the maw. And within the cry arose the shriek of a single voice, from the woman who was the victim's own.

They had waited in the dark windows above the tavern, to watch the gate explode, but instead, as the flare light swelled over the area, touching even them, turning their faces into pale lemon hollows, this death had come.

Their howling and the single, endless wail pierced to the Baron. With the glimpse of Schreiter falling engulfed in the water, his momentary satisfaction over the shot released, over the good hit, had vanished and there came to him a dreadful sense of error, of dismay, of his having committed an unspeakable transgression in killing one of his own, his own serfs, and the shriek of the harpies confirmed his crime. He had done an irretrievable wrong among his own villagers.

As much to hide his shame as to remove himself—a target—the Baron drew back into the room. The dark castle was enlaced now with terrified callings, names to names—Are you there? Are you all right? Paul, Marianne, Philippe, Albert—and opening his door, the Baron saw scurryings with candlelights, matches that flickered out and on, while with an oil lamp from the kitchen, Trudi climbed up faithfully to make sure of her master.

The monk's form had come blundering down from the battlements, pausing only for an instant on the stair landing where the others were clustered. All on the roof were unhurt, he told them. But an attack would certainly come now, below. Frère Luc clattered on downward, leaving them standing there confused.

Marianne stood at the turret stairs calling to Remy. Paul Vered, in response to something wild and self-endangering that had been in the monk's eye, felt his way down the stairs after him, calling his name, Luc, Luc.

In the midst of his cluster of men, Kraus had lain high on the slope watching the blast. The great spurt into the air had given him something of the same sense of accomplishment as a filled train departing. Now he waited for the moat to clear. The group of fighters close around him, the low-sounding laugh over an occasional war joke, the great *aah* when their blast went up, and the crisping together as they readied for the attack—all this heightened in him the feeling that he was at long last in the peak of combat; the war had not passed without his truly taking part as a man. In the next instant, a real officer, he would leap up and wave his warriors forward.

The terrified old fools on the roof were firing wildly, throwing grenades in all directions after the blast; next to Kraus, a corporal half reclining on his back, was sure he had picked off one of those fuckers up there, silhouetted in the back glare of the floodlights. But then the lights had gone out.

Then the bastards used a flare. Suddenly, with the orange ball of glowing light hanging over the emptiness, Kraus knew what was missing. The explosion at the gate. Something had gone wrong. Or was that blasted Schreiter holding back because of the flare?

This was his own moment to lead his men. Whether or not the gate was blown, this was the time to attack from the rear. If by some freak bad luck something had gone wrong with Schreiter, the command lay doubly upon himself to rush in and help.

From every man around him Kraus felt the expectation. Just next to him, Gunter was already half up, in a crouching position, and at Gunter's movement, Kraus felt as though he too were pulled up. He poised himself on his knee and even raised his arm. Now he must go forward, the first. There was no alternative. Yet in sheer equilibrium, just as Kraus felt the forward expectation of his men, he also felt everything that pulled in them to give it all up, to mutter to hell with it and crawl off down the side of the ravine rather than strike out from their security into that ball of illumination. He was not certain the men would follow him.

So it must have been in every assault of the war, he told himself. This was the moment of an officer's worth. Mastering himself, he stood upright and moved. A few men were rising. Unevenly, but nevertheless with certainty, the group formed behind him. And the inward glow he had felt with the explosion now returned, augmented. He was an attacker! He stormed ahead and his men stormed after him!

Chunks of concrete from the blast lay piled under the hole, leaving a gap nearly twice a man's height up to the underbelly of the moat. On another man's shoulders, a fellow could scramble up into the empty trough. Kraus must be the first; this action lay inexorably upon him.

Tilting his head and looking up through the hole, he could see the edge of the cloud of phosphorescence. At least, at the outset, he would be in the shadow. Making sure his holster was open, Kraus raised both arms upward, and like a dance chorus encircling the star, the men boosted him. He stood on Gunter's shoulders. His head was through the aperture. He smelled the slime in the moat bottom, greenish under the pink-tinted night, and planted his elbows on the muck. This was combat. Now he gathered his strength to heave himself upward. Did he hear the men below joking about his clumsiness? Doubtless if Gunter were doing this he would already have sprung clear of the hole. As Kraus tried to lift his full weight, he felt his elbows quake.

Just then, Frère Luc saw him. The monk had reached the shattered kitchen window, directly opposite the hole in the moat. There, rising from the gaping black hole in the bed of slime, was the enemy. In the irreal, yellowish light, that eerily glowing, narrow pointed face was nothing other than the face of Lucifer.

From behind himself, Luc heard his name called; he heard the distressed voice of Paul Vered.

It was for the Jew they had come!

Frère Luc was aware he was allowing himself to be swept into allegory; he knew the form he saw was Kraus, and yet for all his realism, in this instant the mysterious and the transcendental became flesh; something within him triumphantly cried, "This is how the Lord works!" and in absolute response he leaped down into the emptied moat and flung himself at the emerging figure.

A machine pistol had been in Luc's hand, but in his scramble he had let it drop. Only a combat with all his being, now, could overcome this evil apparition.

At the monk's assault, Kraus was halfway out of the hole. His trunk was stretched on the slippery concrete, while his legs still hung downward, and he could not, on the instant, reach his pistol. Below him, his men could scarcely make out what had happened, nor could they fire without endangering Kraus. As Frère Luc hurled himself upon him, thrusting him back into the hole, Kraus locked his arms around the torso of his assailant, at the same moment feeling himself undermined by a furious sense of the ridiculous. To have at last come into hand-to-hand battle only to find his fingers gripping, not a uniform but the skirts of a priest!

At this instant a second flare was thrown from above, as though purposely to illuminate his shame in its full, awful glare.

From the roof edge, Maasi, Dortolot, and Remy looked

down on the writhing figures. With the white glacial peaks standing ghostlike behind them, the two wrestled as in some embodiment of the Inferno.

They must find their way down to Luc. They must guard here against a frontal attack. From the stairs the marshal shouted up to them to man the guns. "Luc!" they cried.

As he struggled, Frère Luc, doubling his body forward, managed to lock both hands firmly on the head of his adversary. With all his might, then, he pushed the head downward, and Kraus, under the weight and pressure, with no way to brace his dangling legs for resistance, felt his body inch by inch grating against the jagged concrete downward. Momentarily he let go of his hold on the priest's body, to steady himself and resist the fall. In that moment, their faces were so close that their eyes seemed physically to pierce each other. No hatred Kraus had ever felt was so great as the rage in him at this contact. Stupid blathering eunuch, interfering in the battles of man! Sin, sin, he had not sinned! And in that same instant, with all their force, the huge hands whose very bones he felt crushingly against his skull gave him a powerful shove. His hold on the concrete was broken, he was falling. With a convulsive effort Kraus seized the ankles of the monk, protruding from under the muddied cassock, and with his own entire downpulling weight Kraus yanked on them so that Frère Luc, his handhold broken, unfolded backward like a sprung jackknife, and came sliding down with Kraus into the hole.

Instinctively thrusting out his elbows, Frère Luc just managed to stop his descent. It seemed as though his arms would be torn off at the shoulders, yet there he hung, his elbows on the concrete, with the full weight of his adversary loaded onto his feet, stretching him as on some ancient torture rack, while the jagged ends of the broken concrete dug into his breast.

He must not give way. He must not give way to the weakness for martyrdom that lurked in every brother in Christ. And from the window from which he had leaped, he heard Vered's voice calling his name. He saw his old friend's face there. The voice called out, with all the authority that Vered had been able to evoke in the days of the great crisis in the factories, the authority that he seemed to call up within your own self, "Luc, don't let go of your life!"

Even in the increasing pain of the downpull in his legs, Luc's consciousness wondered how Vered, a Jew, had sensed this one temptation that threatened to weaken him, a Christian. Or was this the sum total of all Jewish wisdom, the secret of their presence? In a glowing haze of pain, Frère Luc heard the words as perhaps the final command addressed to mankind, "Don't let go of life!"

Summoning all his remaining energy, he managed to pull up his knees and deliver a sudden kick. The heavy shoes struck Kraus in the face. His hands let go the ankles, and he tumbled among his men, while Luc, freed of the downpulling weight, heaved himself out of the hole.

The fallen Kraus at last got his hand on his revolver;

one shot caught the monk before he could pull his legs clear. It shattered Luc's left ankle bone.

All who were not on duty on the roof had stumbled their way to the kitchen; Joras and Michaelis, clambering over the window to go to Luc's rescue, leaped back with the shot. But as Frère Luc, on all fours, dragged himself away from the hole, Joras, wearing a German battle helmet, bravely let himself down into the empty moat, scuttled across, and got the wounded monk half onto his back, helping him toward the outstretched arms that pulled Luc up into the kitchen. Marianne, by the light of her candlestick on the floor, carefully cut away his blood-filled shoe, and began to clean the wound.

I N THE FAR CORNER of the kitchen, which had proved to be out of range of the shells, they were gathered drinking tea while the marshal summarized the situation, which he still deemed to be grave but not desperate. Only du Caux and Astuque were on watch on the turrets, as the marshal felt that for the moment there was little danger of a renewed attack. Flares had been lighted on all sides, so that the entire castle seemed suspended in a great reddish ball of light, whose reflections seeped inside, giving the interior an eerie cavernous atmosphere.

The enemy had been repulsed on both fronts, Marshal Philippe reported with a constrained smile that asked their indulgence for his describing the skirmish in such lofty terms. But all had fought well. There had been two casualties, one civilian, evacuated as they knew, and one, if he might say so, military, though a man of the cloth. A traitor had been apprehended trying to open the gates to the enemy, and he was now imprisoned in the cellar.

So far as the enemy was concerned, one casualty was known, Schreiter. As he had been the commander in the village, the enemy's capacity to mount a frontal attack was presumably seriously affected. However, the castle was still under fire from front and rear.

"With the moat empty, we are open to assault on all sides now. We have fewer effectives than before. But we have no alternative. We must stand guard ready to repulse any assault, until we are relieved."

Again: sit and wait. For a whole year before the war, Remy had torn himself in an effort to drive this entrenched dunderhead into action. Out there, Kraus's bitter-enders—give the bastards credit—had tried an assault, and they would probably try another. One man, at most two, had set the charge and blown up the moat. One man alone could go out and blow up their damned Panzer, instead of sitting here under the pounding shells waiting for rescue that still might be days away.

"We can't just sit here—" he burst out.

"What do you propose, my dear Remy? That we attack the tank, bare-handed?" Marshal Philippe asked.

Marianne spoke. "Someone must go out and bring the rescue. I could do it."

As was her way, Marianne had first completed the thought in herself so as to be able to rebut all objections. Since the moat was dry, it was possible to slip away without lowering the bridge in front of the attackers. The Americans could not be very far off; if she took the way to Innsbruck, she would be bound to encounter them. No one else could go without weakening the already sparse defense, nor could they attempt a mass escape, because several were not strong enough for the venture. Her German was good. In any case a woman stood a better chance than a man of getting through unnoticed. Numbers of German refugees, fleeing the Russians, had already come into the area; if questioned, she could pass as a refugee.

They listened. She kept her face averted from Remy, knowing it was hurtful of her not to have spoken of her plan to him, first. But then he would have found some objection. Perhaps—and something in her wished this—he would even have forbidden her to go, so that whatever their fate, they would share it. Yet as she spoke, Marianne knew, more certainly than before, that her plan was now so necessary that it superseded everything that concerned only herself, or herself and Remy.

She turned her eyes instead to Vincent Maasi, to Vered, to Frère Luc, beseeching her friends not to offer objections.

The marshall spoke. "Though I am confident we can take care of ourselves, I would not deny that to establish contact with our allies would be desirable." But he could not spare a man, and he would not take it on himself to send a woman. The mission was certainly not without danger.

With that, and gazing somberly at Remy, he left the group.

It was odd, how little discussion came. Remy was silent, for whatever he said would seem to come from a personal motive. That her offer had raised all their hopes was clear. And from the tart ex-Foreign Minister, Delorme, there came a half-audible remark. Perhaps Marianne would be in less danger out there than here.

Marianne stood for a moment with Paul Vered. He pressed her hand in both of his; perhaps for once Delorme was right. Then Remy went upstairs with her while she dressed.

To Remy, she could not know, her venture gave him freedom for his own. It would be many hours before Marianne could possibly bring help, and that might be too late. He meant to act the moment she was on her way.

A heavy wool skirt, two sweaters, stout shoes and an old coat, her hair combed plainly under a peasant kerchief, doing everything quickly, hastily, so as not to lose courage, Marianne was soon ready. A little bundle with bread and cheese, a water flask. "Will I pass?" she asked Remy.

Examining her—how a woman could alter herself so immediately and with such small means he would never know—he would have said this was a woman from hereabouts, anybody. Indeed he would not have looked twice, he would not have felt any attractiveness. This thought Remy pushed away as a worthless intrusion; his own girl stood inside this garb, she peeped through to him now, and in their parting Remy was swept by a total feeling of their life here together. And there might be no other life for them; he might be unlucky in his sortie, or might be smashed in this house before Marianne could return with help. What a pity—Marianne deserved all the rewards that could come now. The reward of presiding in the end as his true lady, at diplomatic receptions in the Residence, should he come through tonight, and win again at home. But how could he imagine Marianne had even dreamed of rewards when her self, the very self of herself, was exposed to him now; more than any link of naked bodies, her utmost loving self stood before him in farewell. Was he cheating her in this moment, in not telling her of his own plans? Could he let her go under such a withholding, such a deception? Yet it would have to be a man's doing, alone, and he could not bring out a word of it.

Wrapped in the trench coat, Vered sat at the side of the kitchen window, on watch over the gap in the moat. He could cry out as well as any other, he had insisted, and there was strength enough in his fingers to fire a gun. As Marianne approached he stood, and they repeated each other's names, in blessing. "Marianne." "Papaul." He leaned and touched his dry lips to her forehead.

To help her over the farther wall of the moat, Remy slid down before her from the window; Vincent steadied her as she climbed over the sill. Vaguely illuminated, like actors in the penumbra of a spotlight, Marianne and Remy darted across.

He had even brought a stool; clambering up on the far side of the moat, Remy stretched flat and reached down to her. As her hand tightly grasped his own, there was a dark flash of misgiving in him; was he actually helping Marianne into disaster? But she had drawn herself up and was beside him. A few steps from the moat, and they were among trees in the Baron's parkland. Now they could not be seen, even from the castle, though the orange haze still enwrapped them. The last impulse, in both, was for him to go with her. To run out together and be free of the bombardment, the dark halls, the waiting.

Holding her, Remy said, "If I could—"

"I know you can't."

Yet, his final resolution she could not know. As he kept his own plan tight and remote within himself, Remy's tenderness, as he sent her off, had to contain his secret farewell to her in case he, and not she, should fail. No kiss could speak differently enough for such a parting; against her lips his own said the ritual words, "My only love." And then she resolutely broke, and turned, passing from him, and in a moment passing out of the lighted haze, and away.

He hurried back across the moat.

In almost a run, a scuttling, as much of terror as of haste, Marianne followed an earth path on the forested mountainside. One reason against her going on this mission she had withheld, telling herself that her terror of the woods in the dark was laughable, too feminine, even childish. Only, she could not quite control it now. The fear swelled up in her like a panic fear in drowning, a panic fear of heights; oh, she was not at all an outdoor girl, she was an indoor woman, she had always jested, though she had a deceptively athletic air about her, and wore sport clothes well . . . as long as they were not for sport, she used to laugh. The old persiflage was a good distraction for her now; she must think of other funny inconsequential items from the time of the world of peace.

Piercingly, an animal howl cut through her little defensive thoughts. Marianne nearly shrieked, and fled against a tree. The Baron hunted here, she remembered. The trophies on his walls bared their teeth to her—wolves, wild boar—she couldn't tell what she had heard. How would a city girl of today know the cry of a wolf? Nervously she tried to continue her jesting to herself: the wolves were giving her the wolf call, as in American movies.

Everything depended on her steadiness. Frère Luc with his shattered foot, Paul Vered after what he had lived through, her return to Remy. All depended on her not giving way to her growing impulse to run back. Her mind enumerated her aids: the torch, the pistol; if a wolf really appeared, didn't you shine the torch in his eyes? Another scrap of lore from somewhere. Or was it lions? At least there were no lions here. But deer. Of a deer she was of course not afraid. And mountain sheep and goats, the herders kept. Much not to be afraid of. But dogs. If sheep, then dogs. How quiet the nights had been in the castle; she had never noticed. These same noises must have been around her. Yes, of course, she had noticed them the first months, and been afraid, but being afraid inside the house was a feminine wile, a coziness, a way of having a man put his arms around you.

She had to halt again. She was going too fast, descending, and her knees felt wobbly. There was the water bottle in her shoulder bag, and the pistol, and as a last resort she had taken from Remy two grenades. It had been no weight at all, the bag, but already it made itself felt biting into her shoulder.

Now came a shape, a herder's hut. She would circle away. All at once there was the bellowing of a dog, each bark a thrust at her in the night. Marianne stood frozen, trembling. The dog must be leashed or he would already have been upon her. Distinctly, a door creaked. It was so near! Or, on the clean air, all sounds were near. And a man's voice shouted, "Who? Who is there?"

Surely he would unleash the dog now, and come searching and seize her. From not so far behind her, she heard the tank firing, and was swept with guilt, above her fear. For in the first few moments after she had climbed out of the moat, there while still in the park enclosure, Marianne knew she had felt a rush of pleasure. To be out! To be out of that house, that prison. However peaceful, however luxurious, the place was a prison. Year after year. And an exultation had come to her despite all the desperation of this night, despite the responsibility of her mission. She could have sung.

This was her guilt now, paid for in terror. But the thinking out of it had partly calmed her, the barking had slowed to a questioning growl, and the door had closed again. Man and hound would not hurt her.

Then in relief Marianne began to sob, her shoulders, her entire body, convulsing in hushed sobs, as she felt herself, so small against the tree roots, small as that mutilated Polish girl. Oh, I am only a woman, a girl. Why did I believe I could do this? A man should have gone. If I fail, all of them will die, surely Papaul.

With a gasp she realized this was not hysterical babbling but truth. The image of Kraus came, with his pistol at the back of Paul's head. Pulling herself upright, Marianne began to walk, calmly, carefully, better now.

And what of his children?

As she grappled with this thought, unaware, Marianne increased her pace. She thought of the thin, carefully kept folder of envelopes with the stamps of the International Red Cross, containing the letters of his sons. She remembered the special smile, that she had always felt certain was a trifle forced, with which he showed her their letters. Not that she saw all of them. At times he only read her passages, and she understood this too, the hugging to himself of the one entirely unquestioned love a man received.

If only the meeting, so soon now, would not be a disappointment for Remy. How many such meetings waited in the world! Men and their children. And men and women. Parted so many years, could they find each other again, on their meeting? A failure between two people who had held onto an image of love—that could be the greatest grief of all; and how lucky, how extraordinarily fortunate, she had been—she had not even measured this luck till now—in that she had spent these years when others had been separated, close together with her own.

And now, if between herself and Remy a new cycle began, and a child . . .

A fear came upon Marianne, a fear no longer of the woods alone, but of the malevolent world. Could things come out so well?

Of a sudden the forest ended, and she stood at the edge of a gently sloping meadow. The mere profile of the moon had appeared, a bluish ring among vapors, yet it made the field seem magical, and she stood in awe. But how peaceful, how poignantly beautiful was the earth and the world! It was as though she had come to the end of her mission, and here was security and peace. Not a dwelling was in sight; the sounds of the cannon were no longer heard—

how many hours had she been on her way? Something within her warned Marianne that she still must be wary of this sense of peace, that it was more dangerous to her than her terror; she must not stand here and lose time. But the clover smell! She allowed herself a full, profound breath, inhaling all that was here, and there coursed through her entire body a contentment, like that in the after-love of last night. So an assurance came to her now, that her new-born understanding from last night would carry itself into the rhythm of a long relationship, and the time would come for a child. In her belly, and down through her legs, there flowed a return of the sweetness of that night. Here she stood, a creature totally alone in a shimmering bluish field of clover, alone in the universe which in the end nothing, no effort of man, could destroy.

And not so solitary: Remy was with her. For after so many years, for them now to lie together with an ardor utterly new—was that not the rarest proof of a true mating between man and woman? Her lover's encourage-ment and strength were in her, and she would prevail.

She was not really tired, yet. She would eat something, walking, so as not to lose time.

Yet, which way must she go, out of this field?

There was no more valley. Nothing led downward.

In their hasty, anxious preparation in the castle, they had not found a compass. But Remy had shown her, again, the dipper pointing to the North Star. She must go with the star on her right; then she would be walking west.

Marianne found the star, and began to cross the field. It

was far broader than she had thought, and at the end there were trees again, and the earth sloped upward.

Surely it was only a ridge of some kind; she would climb a way and find the descent to the west. As she climbed, the ground gave way to rocks; there was no path at all. The wind penetrated beneath her coat, her sweaters, and her fingers felt chilled. When she reached what seemed the top of the ridge, another ridge loomed in the bluish moonlight, beyond. Should she go back down, then, and try a different direction? Southward?

Fatigue seemed to liquefy all her bones. One must not give way to cold, to fatigue; it was dangerous. She looked at her watch. She had walked for something over two hours.

Then, atop the next rise, the ground flattened, and to her astonishment, Marianne came against a fence.

At the top of the world. In this end of nothing. She stood against the piled row of stones, and allowed herself to laugh. She must laugh, it would help her.

Within the fenced area was a field cleared of rocks. The stones had been carried to the perimeter to make this wall, this enclosure. It was as though she had come upon some troglodyte marking, as though she had journeyed back close to the beginning of man.

A wall of stone. Why here? Against whom?

This was all border walls, all nationhoods, all war. And she didn't want any more to find the reason for anything.

At the far side a slight, blessed downward slope began. Clouds had now drifted across the sky and she had lost her sense of direction. The slope did not go the way she had been going, she felt. Not westward. Perhaps to the north? But it led downward, and below there could be some change, some break in the imprisoning peaks of rock and earth.

And then, once again, the shape of a hut.

No dog's bark assaulted her. Marianne stood still, waited. No sound whatever. Nothing. Hardly even a hut; a shed—for when some shepherd, or whoever it was who planted this field, came to stay for a short time.

Timorously, and even grasping her revolver, Marianne advanced to touching distance of the log wall. She breathed, and glided to the window aperture. Her fingers touched the black surface; the pane was whole.

Then she made her way to the door. Surely the place was empty. But what should she do here? Wait? Rest a little? The door hung slightly ajar on a broken hinge. The shriek of rust, as she pressed it farther open, made her hand drop. But she was safe.

She stood within.

A form was there. Something in her at once knew that it was not sleeping but was inanimate.

Marianne approached. The form was curled on itself, a small heap. Even if alive, what strength could it have had to harm her? Stooping, taking her light and pointing it downward so as to leave no reflection through the window, she saw what was there. The form wore a cotton garment of some kind, thin, with long stripes. The skull had only a stubble of hair on its top, and there was stubble on the taut skin of the cheeks. The mouth had fallen open, and remnants of yellow teeth were there, and the eyes in deep hollows were glazed.

Then she knew, as though Paul were beside her to tell her. The striped flimsy garment, the shaved skull, the skeletal form. A Jew, of the death camps.

But how—here—in this end of nowhere?

All terror shrank away under some ghastly understanding, and compassion for this last creature. Whatever he had been had somehow escaped, somehow crept this far. And as in the strange rock-surrounded field, there came to Marianne a sense of being within touching nearness of the heart of all the mystery of the way in which man had doomed himself in the universe, but never given up hope.

Was there in his mind, Remy tormented himself as he watched her form descending the steep slope like a form being lowered into a pit, yet brave and upright, holding herself strongly erect for his view—was there nevertheless in his mind some acquiescence to the possibility that he might never see Marianne again? That this was the final image for him to hold forever? This shadowy, unwanted, forbidden feeling—could it even be a secret half hope? No, he told himself, the thought was only the product of shame, a punishment of himself for having let her go. It came from that calculating area of his mind which he hated and disowned, which persisted in reminding him that if she did not return he would, though with a heart turned to stone for the remainder of his life, have no impediment to a household with his sons. Even a *modus vivendi* with his—his wife, though he should attach the word "former."

All the problems would come now, on the return: divorce, custody of the children. And if a loss of the children to him resulted, would he not every living day resent Marianne? (Something in him tormentingly whispered, Better to mourn your love than to resent your love. Oh, what a horror he was.) And would such a strain not spoil their relationship? So that these years of seclusion in the castle represented a perfection in their lives; could they ever be so well again together? They had, in their frankness with each other, even discussed this fear, and determined that they would know how to face a more complex life so long as they were aware of the danger. The greatest love, Remy told himself in order to shake off his shame, at times included the wish for separation, even the fantasy of the death of the partner.

And surely, far more powerful than this doubting, scheming side of his character was the dreadful heavyheartedness he felt, the profound fear for her safety. What a brave girl, what a spirit, as she went off alone into the darkness that she so dreaded. And there still could be German troops in the area and it needed only one brute, one bitter-ender with a gun, one shot—Remy shut his mind. Despite all the reasoning that he was so desperately needed here, a man did not send a woman off on such a mission. Only when he would have gone out on his own mission, more hazardous than hers, would he know that there could in the future remain no wound from tonight between them.

Bent over the kitchen table, the marshal made pencil marks on the chart he had drawn of their fortress. To Remy and Dortolot he explained that he must now alter his dispositions. The central turret facing the ravine had suffered a number of direct hits, chipping away the masonry. Better to place a man on the second floor.

"Excellent," Remy approved distractedly, for his mind was only on his own purpose. It was his turn off duty now; could he go without informing the marshal? It would be incorrect—wrong even—but suppose Philippe should refuse to let him go? And just then he caught, from the commander, an opening.

The worst problem remained, Philippe grumbled wearily: that he had no knowledge of the capacity of the enemy, even his numbers, out there.

"Isn't it the time to send a patrol?" Remy demanded.

The marshal looked up at him quickly, the look of a man who is at least glad to hear his own language spoken. Yet the glint faded; he was utterly without the means for proper war.

"Let me go," Remy proposed.

Their eyes met, in a different exchange than ever before. Behind the mention of the patrol, the look acknowledged something else. After an attack, a counterattack. The marshal's gaze clouded over, and his head began to shake. Wasn't it even a little cruel to remind him of his lack of means?

Above, there came a thunderous strike. Great chunks of masonry were falling away, spattering on the bottom of the moat with terrifying reverberations. The three men leaped to their feet. In the hall, Maasi, who had fallen exhaustedly asleep in a large chair, stood, startled, making vague protective gestures with his arm in front of his face. Then the voice of Joras, even now oratorical, came thundering from above them. "The central turret. A direct hit through the aperture!"

How right the marshal had been to have it abandoned, what a miracle! Anyone inside would have been pulverized. But within the very glow of this escape there spread the sense of increasing doom, and of their helplessness.

Remy caught the moment. "Let me go, Philippe," he asked again.

The aging marshal placed a hand on his shoulder, and suddenly Remy felt there was in this military man a human understanding to which he had never given full value. "You feel you must do it, Remy?" the commander asked.

"I must." Someone had finally to attempt to silence that gun.

"You are among the few I have here who . . ." All the arguments hung suspended between them, even the memory of the bitter disputes at the outset of the war when, as now, the civilian had insisted, Go out, attack, go out! Ah,

Remy would see now what it meant to go out, to attack with insufficient force.

"And how will you get back?"

He would be well above the enemy, Remy pointed out, and if they pursued him, they would first have to climb the ravine.

"Bullets climb quickly."

There were some risks a man had to take.

All the while, Dortolot had been silent, as a man who does not interfere in a private conversation, though he is present. Now he declared, "It would be best if I go, too."

The marshal reacted at once, pained. "No, no, you know I cannot risk two men, or even one."

In Dortolot just now, as in himself at the moment of Marianne's leaving, Remy knew there must have flared, unwanted, rejected, that shred of speculation: What if Remy should not come back? Then Dortolot would have no rival. To exorcise that selfish thought, he had made his offer. Remy smiled to him, and shook his head.

"Good luck, then, old man. And caution." Remy felt the marshal's strong old fingers tightly squeeze his shoulder. "If you see it is too risky, don't hesitate to turn back. Remy, we need you."

Dortolot pressed his hand. "Better to come back with nothing, but to come back, old man." They looked honestly at each other. All differences were after all unworthy.

Strapping on his equipment, loading every pocket, Remy also kept in mind how everything should be jettisoned should he need to run. Already, Marianne's absence was felt in this room, and his movements were urgent, as though to catch up with her. He thought to speak to Vered, to Luc, but no, no farewells. Dortolot and the marshal came along to hand him down into the moat, and Maasi, in the hallway, remembered to give him the comradely kick for good luck.

Clambering over the ledge, he knew instantly the loneliness that Marianne must have felt. But no exhilaration as yet came to him at being released from the imprisoning walls; the force of the release was in the explosives that he carried on his body, and this force pressed him to almost a delirium of purpose.

Moving off on the opposite side of the ravine from the path Marianne had taken, Remy walked swiftly. The ground was mossy, soft, and this area too was wooded. He paused at intervals to watch for some movement, to listen. There could be scouts. Behind him, the systematic bombardment continued, with the sound of crashing stones after each impact.

He had come far enough so that in looking back the structure was part of the landscape. Under the lighted haze —which, though it gave them immediate protection, boldly outlined the castle as a target—the broken sections of the wall already gave the impression of ruin.

All at once Remy had a sense of himself, this creature standing alert and alone in the nowhere, a creature with knobs and bumps of mechanical devices protruding, dangling, attached, giving him a form and shape of nothing in nature. And what was he, with his little popgun and his handfuls of explosives, on this earth, under this sky of pinpoint worlds, a little man of politics, with a ferment of schemes and ideas to put this and that together, to be a leader again, to sway all the men who had scarred and chipped this part of the earth, and spilled out the contents of their arteries? And what were they? One strong rain would wash away all the volumes of blood they had spilled, and in one season, foliage would overgrow the ruins they had made. Seen from above, the total destruction of the war, cities flattened, must still be like the havoc of a passing hurricane. How good the clean air smelled; perhaps he should simply wait here until the war was over, and retire with Marianne to a small country house, have children with her, and live his life.

He moved forward, his hands touching his tools of attack to make certain he was ready. What he did here was an integral part of his existence. To emerge from the war years and return without having struck one direct blow at the enemy would have left him without a sense of his right to speak, to lead. It was even great luck that on this last night the opportunity for action had come to him.

Remy edged over toward the rim of the ravine. He must judge his distance. The balance was between nearness, to throw accurately, and distance, for his lead in withdrawal. The force of his throwing, fortunately, was hardly a factor, since he was above them.

Another shell flew and he imagined he felt the recoil in the earth under the soles of his feet. In the instant of the fire flash, he saw the entire enemy encampment as in a picture slide that appears and is pulled away. They were not many. The nose of the gun pointed through a frieze of branches, and the forward part of the tank projected into the open; this part he must strike. The hatch was almost directly beneath him; a man stood with binoculars watching the shell's impact. In an instant now, if he did his work well, this man would vanish, disintegrated.

Around the tank a half-dozen men could be seen in various attitudes, a few in movement, two carrying shells from a wagon that seemed nearly empty, three men sitting on a tree trunk, relaxed, talking—they would vanish midsentence. And in that moment Remy felt not pity nor compassion, but a kind of regret for them, for the way they would die, torn, without really being aware of the event. Behind this group, he had only a blurred impression —perhaps some canvas, under which a half-dozen more might be taking their sleep.

Now Remy considered whether to make his throw in the next gun flash, or to light the area so as to give himself a surer target. But this would also give the enemy an instant of warning and—if he did not act quickly enough —the instant to reply. He could be cut down in a sweep of fire.

The first and highest necessity was to strike and silence the gun. With a few men killed, they would make no more attacks on the castle. Light would blind them, panic them, make them feel they were under a larger attack. He must prepare both in his hands, the flare, the bomb, throw them in rapid succession, then throw his grenades, dodge quickly behind his chosen tree, clamber away and run for it. To confuse them he would run forward, and not toward the castle.

Cool-minded, wholly himself now, Remy stood in position, a man released, able. His arm swung. In one breath, the whole bottom of the ravine stood glowing, the human figures transfixed, the foliage so clear he could have counted the leaves on the trees. The clarity surprised him, too, as though he were down below and this had happened to him. Then, angry at the half instant lost in his own surprise, the bottle already in his throwing arm, Remy hurled the bomb directly downward, moving his arm back for a full swing with such force that he awakened his arthritic pain, and the unexpected shock of the pain slightly impaired his throw.

Already, he could hear firing below; it seemed to have nothing to do with him, pop shots. The tank's machine gun swung his way but he expected to see the whole of the Panzer burst into flames. He would not have been able to hear the bottle strike. Automatically, within the paining of his arm, he carried out his planned intention and tossed a grenade, a second, a third, heard the first burst, saw bodies in suddenly altered attitudes, one crumpling in rising, knew his gasoline bomb had missed the tank—because of his arthritis, surely—and flung himself backward to his tree.

In this movement, Remy's heel struck metal under loose earth. The mine's explosion ripped his back; he felt the pain like a tremendous electric pulse, while his body arched off the ground and collapsed face upward. His only consciousness was a startled impulse to respond, as in parliamentary days when some clamorous interruption came from the back of the hall. An impulse to cry out, "Let me speak!"

BELOW, EVERYONE UNHURT was shooting with whatever came to hand. Even the great barrel of the Panzer was swinging toward the wall of the ravine, while the body of the driver, who had been watching with the binoculars, lay embracing his beloved monster from on top. A grenade fragment had cut his throat.

From inside the tank, Donnerwald pulled down the body of the man, his comrade of war. He closed the hatch now, and something closed within him. His war life was finished.

The men kept shooting; carbines, pistols, machine guns scoured the sides of the ravine. The flare hung against it, revealing a mocking immobility of rocks and earth; even the leaves failed to stir under their fusillade.

Was it already the Americans? An advance patrol?

Had they in the end waited a shade too long, because of that damned Kraus with his jewels and his Jews?

Kraus, that first moment when the emplacement had been illuminated, had been sitting on the ground with his back against the caterpillar tracks, the picture of the weary commander catching a moment of respite in the field of battle. He wasn't through with them up there. If not for Schreiter's failure he would have made it. He would still go back. There were still men who would follow him. Let Donnerwald keep cutting them to pieces up there, and he would simply walk in and take what was his. Then suddenly, startled as by a light switched on in a bedroom, he had leaped cursing to his feet, pulling his pistol and firing toward the castle. The gasoline bottle had fallen directly in front of him, shattering and splattering him. It had taken him a moment to realize what it was. Then, hearing someone cry "Molotovs," he had jumped back as from a snake, but in a moment had begun to scuff earth over the fluid, even bending to throw handfuls of dirt.

He had not at once noticed the effect of the grenades. Of the three men who had been sitting on the log not far from him, the last one lay faceless on the ground, attempting to shriek his agony; only a gurgle came. The man who had been next to him kept shouting at Kraus, at the world, "Did you see him get it! Right at my side!" For a second

Kraus didn't know whom the soldier was talking about. He had not seen. It had happened too quickly. He was still apprehending, picking up scraps of what had just happened. The third man, spitting curses, was crawling up the side of the ravine, stopping every moment to rake the ground above him with his Schmeisser. Only then did Kraus situate himself. He shouted, "Be careful, it's mined!" and the fellow flung back at him, "You shitty idiot, I mined it!" Why, it was Gunter. Simultaneously, the mine above exploded, and exulting, Gunter shouted, "We got one!"

The faceless one lived, and was being pulled back into their cavelike shelter. Now the cursing cries—Where? How many? Where?—began to slacken, and a conclusion began to spread: not a raid in force, only a few, and already gone. Kraus climbed up the side of the ravine, feeling men at his sides and above him. One of them stood up, in the top fringe of the aura of illumination. He kicked at something and growled contemptuously, "Only one." And, puzzled, "A shitty civilian."

Reaching the place, Kraus looked down and emitted a short, easy laugh. The fucker, the smart fucker, the one who had his woman with him, the one who called himself the Fighting Premier. Remy. One of the brave gang who had marched into the room last night and captured him and driven him naked to the dungeon.

Now a glow arose in Kraus at the justice of war, the absolute and appropriate retribution that could come and would come here. Gunter stood with him; with his boot,

297

the lad turned the body over. In the rent clothing, the clotted back flesh was mingled, all the way up along the spine. "We got this one all right," Gunter repeated, including Kraus now in the combat achievement, for had they not together laid the mine?

Proudly, Kraus told the rest of the men who this was. "One of their premiers. Thought he would make himself a hero."

"He got two of ours," the soldier replied, staring down at the body. Then he too rolled it over with his boot; now face up, the body seemed unharmed.

The blasting and firing had died down. Two more of Donnerwald's crew clambered toward them. "Careful—don't spread out!" Kraus warned. "We mined it." Disregarding him, they came and stood over the kill.

"They're bound to come looking for him," one remarked, as the beginning of an idea, but yet as something routine. He was a fellow they called Papa.

"Who? They'll be afraid to stick their noses out."

"Or when the Americans show up. If we leave him here. Just wait!" The man began to clamber down. For a moment Kraus failed to understand his intention, but these fellows around him were all real combat veterans, with war-hardened faces, and Kraus did not want to ask, to show himself ignorant. Instead he watched the remaining men as they rifled the body. Nothing much of interest. The usual wallet with photos—two boys. Not even that blonde from the castle. A few cigarettes. Gunter and the other men divided them, offering Kraus his share—he let it go—

and they squatted down for a smoke.

The fellow called Papa climbed up again, with a small cylinder in his hand. First his comrades gave him his share of the smokes. Then he and two others stooped to the task. Carefully they scooped a shallow hole under the arm of the corpse. The cylindrical mine was placed there, and the trigger cord attached to the bottom side of the sleeve. Then the arm was carefully arranged over the booby trap. When the body would be lifted . . .

"There's a last little surprise for them." With the air of a man who has evened the score, Papa stood up from his task, and blew a full breath of smoke.

They all climbed down. At last, Kraus felt, he had come to the real war. He had taken part.

The only true burial would have been with the Panzer itself: to place his comrade in the driver's seat and let the man and the machine together sink into the earth forever. Donnerwald had known his comrade would be killed in the war. For two years he had known it, and the Snout had known it; this had been the whole crew's joke in the last weeks with their daily rumors of the war's end: "Hah, look there, Snout is still around. The war can't end until he's killed." True, it had been an exorcism, a charm against this very death that had caught him now, in spite of it all. So the fate they had sensed had indeed awaited him, or had they brought it on? Their jest had come from his daring, his recklessness. "I'm going to die in this stinking war anyway." And so even tonight he had been sitting up there, a target. But no, all of them had exposed themselves, and Snout had been hit not by aim but by a random piece of shrapnel.

Put it away. Donnerwald put away the futile speculation, and with the same gesture he felt himself putting away the war. An enormous apathy engulfed him. This dirty-business Kraus, with his box of jewels, there, or his precious prisoners—all that was put away too. There remained the after-war task of seeking out Snout's family, in the exchange of promises they had made to each other: You must be the one to tell them how it happened. And from the clothing of this corpse, too, there came the wallet of snapshots, already familiar to Donnerwald, a sister surrounded by her little girls, a father with a mustache, a mother with a fixed motherly smile, a sweetheart also. Snout had kept her picture but the sweetheartship had long been finished, one of those things of the war: "I am not worthy of you . . ." And already Donnerwald felt himself in a period of reminiscences, sitting with a comrade over a beer (Snout, that was to have been): "Remember the day we crashed through the Ardennes into that village—what was the name of the bloody place?" —and your old comrade supplies the name—"And remember how Snout, sniffing the air to get his sense of direction, would head straight for some door where he smelled pussy? And it never failed." That one! He had a special approach. He had fixed a feather-lined eggbox inside the Panzer. His brag: in ten thousand kilometers he had never cracked a single shell! And, entering a town,

Snout would take a few eggs in his hand, smell out the proper house, and, smiling boyishly, ask the woman, "Will you cook my eggs for me?" It never failed. Then he'd call in his Captain Donnerwald, and if there wasn't an extra woman around, why, like brothers they'd have their eggs cooked in the same pot! The big joke was—and Snout would roar with laughter when he'd show the woman the next morning—he didn't like his eggs cooked at all, but drank them raw! Ah, what a fellow! What a driver, too! The debacle then, the trap in the pass. The enemy planes a thundercloud overhead, and your eyes bugging to follow the air battle up there, but who could cut them down when their fighters filled the sky and their bombers came in droves, flung into the air by a power that had numbers without end? It was to tear your heart out to see the few of your own dart and weave against such a swarm. Still— "Look, good! Look, the sonofabitch trying to parachute!" And a clatter of a thousand machine guns, pistols, yours and Snout's among them, executing the murderous gangster, come overseas to spoil the already-earned victory, to ruin the war. Still their boxcar bombers came on and on, diving on top of you, dropping their loads, and the road became a line of explosions like a string of Chinese firecrackers, one after the other. The battlewagons leaped and fell over like struck lions, and self-propels and troop carriers lay on their heads, and nothing could move, the road choked with dying armor. And in that hell, Snout had thrust and twisted this old Avenger as though she were turned into rubber; through a narrow hole between a general's Mercedes and a flaming troop carrier on its side, and then, teetering and balancing, straight over a pile-up of trailers, and then, while the murderous bastards returned overhead for a cleanup mission, to burn everything alive with napalm, Snout had maneuvered at an acute angle up the slope of the pass, and when he came to a gully, plunged across like a jumper—he had made it out, past the entire destroyed column. And that, Donnerwald realized, had really been the end of their fighting war. They had had to carry on until now only because Snout, old Snout, had to be killed. Finished.

Donnerwald tore across the snapshot of the sweetheart who had defected, and let the pieces drop from his fingers. The family photos he placed back in the wallet.

That criminal idiot, Kraus, had clambered onto the Panzer again. His face was in the hatch. "Avenge your comrade!" He really believed the boys would walk into fire for him now, for a box of baubles, or whatever he had left up there. "Fuck yourself," Donnerwald muttered.

Kraus climbed down. A few of the men glanced his way. It was the moment for him to call, "Follow me!" To stride forward. But this last time, would they follow him?

"He's done it! Remy's done it!" They watched the pinpricks of fire down in the ravine, then the hanging balloon of light, and they were sure they heard explosions amid the distance-dimmed rattle of firing. Yet where was the great red blot of the burning Panzer?

It was all over so quickly, with an after crackle, another pop or two—what did it mean? The binoculars passed as always from the marshal to Dortolot, and he would have handed them on to Remy; he handed them to Vincent Maasi.

The shelling had halted, that was true. Then Remy had done it, he had silenced them. Yet his absence deepened. They waited, alert and ready with covering fire, for the sound of his approach.

And in all this the Baron had taken no part. He sat in his office, under the hunting trophies, comparatively safe. A lantern stood on the desk.

How had it been? Through the mouth? That absolute deed—he could never quite get his arm to do it. Not even with an unloaded pistol as a test. And why should he do this, now that the shelling had quieted? If there was no further assault tonight, and if Marianne succeeded in her mission—a capable young woman, she would succeed— why then, his position toward the victors was enhanced in that he had saved his prisoners and even allowed them to defend themselves.

And he would have a task before him: to restore the castle. It was the wounding of the structure that depressed him now, he was certain. The gaps torn, the bruises in the masonry, the entire center tower destroyed. That was something to live for—was it not?—to repair, restore, so that the place he loved would be exactly as it had always been. If he took his life, who would perform this task? The place would remain a shambles, who knew for how long? Until some American millionaire acquired it as a summer estate. Or would the Communists come and turn it into a rest house for workers, stuff up the holes with tar paper?

There was no longer even a malicious satisfaction in watching what stupidities mankind could perpetrate.

The fellow's box, with the lid up, was there on the desk before him. This, he knew, was the source of his dreadful sense of abhorrence, of contact with filth.

And Schreiter. A good German, a good soldier, already accepted as one of the village, dead by his hand. And from the village, from his villagers, the black sense of repudiation. He was no longer theirs; they were no longer his; he had destroyed the immemorial compact, the faith. An ideal had existed. The *Herrenvolk*. Like himself, and in himself. Masters of domain. An entire people, bred constantly to greater strength, health, beauty. Young men, each an ideal: stalwart legs, straight back, the clear and fearless eye—beautiful. Such as his sons might have been had his wife brought him sons. A nation, a folk, all knights, all rulers! The vision of ordered beauty as in ancient Greece, of ordered mastery as in ancient Rome, heightened and extended, projected into the realm of machine power with only the *Herrenvolk* as masters of the machines. The loved one's vision rose again within him and filled him. How close, how very close, it had come to realization! And these—these Kraus louts, these inadequate helpers, had been the flaw. With venal stupidities like this casket. This was what had dirtied and desecrated the great vision, the way obscene scrawlings desecrate a beautiful design.

Almost, almost, the great dreamer, the daring creator of the modern plan for world order, had imbued the ranks with this vision. But the human material he had had to work with was flawed; the folk had not yet reached the approximation of a *Herrenvolk*. The Kraus kind prevailed.

And so, below the street surface of Berlin, withdrawn into his most private chamber (the Fuehrer's female companion was excluded from the Baron's mind, or given the place merely of another attendant in the bunker) there, the final gesture had been completed.

To do the same would be the only way to hold to the vision as though it were unsullied. If a gun in the mouth was abhorrent, there were after all quieter ways.

And the task of rebuilding? Was this not simply an excuse? An evasion? Could knighthood, could love, ever be rebuilt?

THE RAILWAY TRACKS had come shining before her as a mirage. Lost, moving on mechanically in the blind hope of coming to an end of the forest, with the trembling muscles of her knees threatening to catapult her at every down-climb, Marianne all at once found herself in an open corridor amid the trees. She had nearly stumbled over the track before it came to her that here was the railway. The flooding sense of relief was so great that she spoke out loud, "Remy, Remy, it's all right!" And she began to leap along the ties, as in a childhood game.

If only nothing had happened up there during the night. Marianne was sure they had held out, sure she would be in time.

To heighten her sense of release, the predawn light now came, suffusing the sky bowl; behind her the horizon turned mother-of-pearl. She was going in the right direction.

And there before her, solid on the tracks, was the shape of a train. A whole chain of boxcars, standing, without an engine. Marianne slowed. There seemed to be no one anywhere near the train. A freight train, left standing by the Germans as they dragged their supplies into the redoubt?

The doors gaped open on a blackness within, emptiness. As she edged closer, the dawn light reached obliquely into the car that stood before her. A heap was there, of forms like the one in the mountain shelter. Supplies for the last redoubt.

And as she moved away, in the periphery of her vision, at the end of the line of cars, a figure moved. In soldier's uniform. Not German. Surely American. He had seen her, and as she ran toward him the soldier approached, with a puzzled uncertainty in his posture. "Help us!" she tried to call, but could barely control her face, keep back the gush of tears, stop a hysterical attack of lip twitching. Marianne halted, taking large breaths to regain her composure. The soldier, an officer, had so striking an expression that her emotional seizure passed. His eyes seemed still to be seeing into the train; he held some record sheets in his hand—had he been counting the corpses? From his entire being there came only the question: Why this too?

Suddenly it came over Marianne that he took her for a German woman, and this thought so shook her that she regained her clarity. "You are American?" she asked in English, and before he could reply, she burst into her story: Aid was needed at once, important prisoners, three former premiers, the war marshal, Cabinet ministers, under assault by an SS commando . . .

Hurrying her even as she talked, to a small open vehicle, he repeated the names, whistling. Remy, Dortolot, Vered, too, alive! The vehicle leaped over holes, rocks. He was not a combat officer but a chaplain, he said, actually a rabbi for the American Jewish soldiers, and just now he occupied himself with the fate of the Jews. To find Paul Vered—!

With an abrupt turn that nearly hurled her from her place, the jeep, as he called it, pulled up before a guarded villa, the headquarters, he said. Marianne followed into a hall where the young rabbi interrupted an officer—he seemed on his way to breakfast—a man with a boyish face but whose cropped hair was gray. The story poured out.

"Hold it, hold it, Harry. Now, who did you say they were?"

"Remy, Dortolot, Vered—" The names, she saw, meant nothing to the commander.

"Marshal Philippe!" Marianne interjected.

The officer eyed her. "You sure she's on the up and up? Could be a trap."

"The SS is attacking—" she begged.

"All right, all right, lady. Tell you what I'll do." His brigade was at rest in its final position here. He had no orders to go hunting big-shot war prisoners. But he would telephone back to his division chief. "Now, you come along and have some breakfast."

To stop to eat while up there . . .

At least the young rabbi understood. While the telephoning proceeded, they were in his jeep again—going toward the division headquarters, he said. Long minutes passed. Suddenly the rabbi halted his vehicle. A large military car was speeding toward them; it was a Major Cassidy, he said, already answering the call. Then there was good in the world after all!

She rode with the major. He was Intelligence, he said; he already had all those big names on his list and he would have come perhaps tomorrow. Big scientists had first priority, he apologized; the Russians were combing the redoubt grabbing off the top German scientists.

A professor in civilian life, with heavy glasses, he asked about everyone. Ah, Kraus! Yes, that fellow they wanted, very much.

At the villa the professor halted; he had to get troops.

"I'm through losing men for nothing in this war!" The

crop-haired commander wasn't going to throw his men at a bunch of fanatic SS without taking every precaution. A full striking force must be assembled.

Slowly, reluctantly, the men moved. A whole unbearable hour. But at last two light tanks turned onto the road. With Major Cassidy's car between them, they would race up to the castle and effect the rescue while a larger force would follow and strike at the SS in the gully.

Heavy tanks, self-propelled guns, antitank guns, troops with mortars and flamethrowers were ordered out. On the telephone, the brigade commander called for air support. Grumbling, leaden-eyed from their exploits with the *Fräuleins,* the soldiers took their places. In the lead tank, a Texas gunner explained to his comrades for the thousandth time a little trick he had that had worked all across Europe: You get into a town, you see a good-looking woman, you take a couple of eggs in your hand, walk into her house, "Lady, will you cook my eggs for me?" Works every time!

Marianne heard not a sound from the valley as Major Cassidy's car and the two light tanks swung at the hairpin turn, and climbed. Could the attackers have departed? Had the castle fallen?

The village too was silent, all shutters tightly closed. She had given warning of the machine-gun nest above the tavern; the first tank crawled forward, its guns pointed. Nothing.

And suddenly, from the castle, shouting, cheering—all were safe, then! The drawbridge was slowly coming down.

The marshal strode out first to greet his allies.

In the confusion, the elation, Marianne ran across the bridge calling Remy. He was not there in the hall where most of the others stood with their suitcases. And as Maasi advanced toward her she already understood.

There was no need to worry, really, he said. It was Remy who had gone out alone during the night and silenced them, below. He had not yet returned. But there was no need to worry.

Maasi's large round face, seeming to grow larger and larger, told otherwise. His huge arms rested heavily on her shoulder.

Three, four of the men at the same instant had caught the distant iron tread of the advance American vehicles, before Kraus had recognized any sounds. Indeed, after they had called out and begun to scurry, he still could not identify what they heard.

Donnerwald had rushed up the ravine. In his binoculars he could pick out the advancing specks. Should he swivel and take them on? But where there were two or three, more were certain to follow.

As though on an agreed signal, the men were vanishing. He did not even have the heart for the last gesture, blowing up the breech of his tank's gun. With a final curse, Donnerwald walked away into the woods.

Kraus had already started changing into civilian clothes. As he pulled on the old trousers, he knew that the moment of his defeat had been when he failed to throw away this damned bundle as the Baron handed it to him. Or, more finally, last night as he had pulled himself up through the hole and been unable to reach his gun to get rid of that priest. Then at least he would have ended his war in victory. His whole being was being proved the other way now. What he was, was proved all the way back to his maneuver to get into the special section where he would not have to go into combat.

"Scheiss!" Kraus cursed all fate, the fate within himself, and what lay before him. In their bloody Bible they had already known of him, they had already prepared their mark of Cain.

"Gunter!" he roared, but his last man was gone; that lousy little devil had vanished, and taken with him that last diamond he had said he would share. Alone, Kraus must hide in the world now, wander far from home, hide himself until their manhunt was over, and he did not even have his gold.

The last to leave, Kraus glanced up the side of the ravine to where he had left his final message for them. He had paid them back after all, a premier for Kraus. If not the Jew, then a damned Jew-lover, with his shitty democratic ideas, all people are equal and all the rot that went with it. Why, Kraus had seen for himself what they were, turned them around his fingers, the blockheaded Poles, the bootlicking Romanians, the sheep-smelling Greeks, all the crawling peasant vermin of Europe, Hungarians, Slovaks, every inferior breed. Why, all alone the Germans had conquered the lot of them, and the time would come again! And the American gangsters too. Maybe a few of the American boobs would spatter into the air for good measure, when they found this last message of his.

But he did not dare to wait to see it go off, and he scuttled—a drab, nondescript figure, the most ordinary-looking of men, in a worn forester's cap—through the underbrush, the way the others had gone.

THEY WOULD NOT LET her go alone to search for Remy. It would best be done from below, they said, and the Intelligence major helped her into his car. At the juncture with the main road, a swarm of armored vehicles had halted and spread; men were unrolling telephone wire, and others were setting forth, calling to each other through radio machines carried on their backs, and under no circumstances could she descend with them into the ravine; she must wait here.

The American rabbi went.

Harry Bercowitz walked along with a medic. At once these two Jews had fallen into familiar discussion, the young doctor surprised that a rabbi also had so many years of graduate work to get through before entering his profession. As for himself, the little doctor said while they picked their way into the ravine behind two soldiers who carried mine detectors, "One more year for psychiatry. That's the coming thing I want to get into." This war had made him wonder. It was the human mind, more than the human body, that needed to be studied.

The patrol leaders had espied the Panzer, its gun still pointed at the castle. Cautiously, holding their mine detectors before them like magic wands, and circling the instruments over the earth as in an incanted ritual, the soldiers made sure of the approach. The huge tank was deserted.

More relaxed now, the men sent their message back to the command post. "Signs of a scrap . . . not too much . . . maybe a couple of grenades. Yah, two fresh graves. There's some torn bushes up the other side of this ravine. They must have chased somebody up there."

Even more slowly, more carefully, the men with the mine detectors climbed the far side. And then the first one halted, holding his machine out rigidly. "Mines!" he yelled.

The bastard Krauts. Couldn't be satisfied the war was over.

Several more men came, cursing their task, lying flat, gingerly unearthing the foot mine. Bitterly, the men with the mine detectors groped onward, while behind them white tape was unrolled to show where the path had been cleared and was safe.

Then they found him. "Casualty!" Must be the one that blond dame was looking for. Civilian.

Even up to then, the organism still lived. In consciousness and out of consciousness, in tumultuous black waves of pain, in fleeting life images, and in sudden commands to himself, piercing yet somehow blurred, of something urgent that he had to do, some great plan that he must carry out, Remy lay there, his body paralyzed.

Hearing the men yell, the little Bronx doctor interrupted himself in the midst of trying to explain to this rabbi chaplain how, though he was definitely not religious, he still could not say he did not believe in God. In spite of the war, in spite of what had been done to the Jews, he still could not say no. "Wait," he said, for he still wanted sincerely to ask what a young modern rabbi like this one could believe, about a Jewish God, but first he moved up step by step along the taped line to do his job.

The body had life. There had been a great loss of blood —no color left at all, but life. Even as he bent to turn the body over, to seek the wound, a soldier called, "Watch out, Doc!" He had grasped the arm, and, always a shrimp with little strength, he exerted himself.

The explosion shattered through both bodies, with blood and flesh spattering on the watching soldier, who had fallen back against the tree. "Don't move! Don't move!" he screamed.

Presently, with infinite caution, stretcher-bearers climbed along the white taped line, and the last two dead were carried down.

In a single swoop, a plane passed over the gully and the castle, and after it was gone, leaflets floated down to the area. Some fell on the road where the battalion commander had set up his post, and Marianne picked one from the ground. It bore a horror photograph of a dead German soldier with his mouth fallen open. "WHY GET KILLED IN THE LAST DAYS OF THE WAR?" the caption read, and the text exhorted surrender.

After she had identified the remains, they took her back to the castle to gather his effects.

In the first moments, as the American soldiers had poked through the castle, putting souvenirs and trophies into their pockets, the villagers had come hesitantly, but soon there were a number of girls and women, the kitchen was filled, real coffee was coming out of American ration packages, laughter over language mistakes was heard.

In the confusion no one had thought of the Baron, but then an officer had opened the door to the little office, and found him. He slept dead in his chair, his face, with the smooth baby skin, utterly cherubic. His hand still lay on the table, holding an ornamented antique pillbox. On the table, also, was an outpouring from an open metal casket. Diamonds, a heap of gold rings, and a mound of small gold nuggets. At first no one quite knew what these nuggets were. The soldiers could not take their eyes from the treasure, as though by staring they would absorb some of the jewels for themselves. But the major had already placed a guard on the room.

In her dazed state, through the courtyard where Dortolot and Joras and the marshal and Astuque and some of the others were already loading their things onto American army vehicles, Marianne passed with Major Cassidy into the hall of the castle; several of her countrymen left their baggage and came to press her hand, but she scarcely knew who spoke to her, and then the major led her into the little office—the only quiet place, he said, since he had put guards at the door. He said something about the Baron's having already been removed.

Paul Vered sat there against the wall, waiting, and near him sat Frère Luc, his bandaged foot on a stool. Papaul rose; long ago she had believed that in his wisdom he could explain everything, but now in her anguish she could not even press herself to him and weep, and she half turned her face away. He stood there silently too, his eyes at first on her, then slowly lowered, in shame at eternity.

She sat down at the table. Distractedly, Marianne began to touch the rings that lay there in a heap. There were men's wedding rings as well as women's, and her fingers touched them, moving one kind against another. Her eyes followed her hands among the rings, and Marianne wondered, then, which from among all this heap of wedding bands might in life have been pairs.

Through waves of physical pain that came up from his shattered foot, Frère Luc clung to the knowledge that there remained, there had come to him, something that was for him to do, something difficult, vast; that might shatter his very hold on faith, yet in the end he would regain and know what was truth. The error he now knew. He had heard it from his own people; it was deeply rooted, embedded in the very stronghold of faith. He had listened to Auguste Rieber. A believer. A man of complete literal faith in the World. The will of God, he vowed, his eyes fixed. How could it have been otherwise than the will of God? It was written! How could the Nazis have killed millions of Jews unless it was ordained?

But did they not kill Frenchmen and English and Russians and people of all the world? Does not the Gospel tell us that there will be wars until the evil in man is conquered? Does not the Gospel tell us that Christ died for all and that salvation is for all?

Yet Rieber's eyes had glittered with knowingness: not for the Jews unless they accept Him! Are you a priest? Can you deny the Church? God put his curse on them!

And in those sneeringly triumphant eyes Luc saw the Jews as Jesus, as Man being perpetually crucified.

All he was, all he could give of himself, must enter into

this struggle to rectify a horror and to cleanse a hatred that had entered deeply into man. Not the cause of the Jews was in question but the horror that taught hate in the very name of eternal love. Luc felt he could not even look to Marianne, or to any human being, without revealing the depth of his doubting. The war in him was beginning only now.

What could he give of himself? Vered wondered, refusing to give in to despair. What could he consecrate in the last of his years? How could he find the lever on which to exert his remaining strength, in some way, in some infinitesimal way, to help the poorly evolved nature of man, so slowly, so painfully, detaching itself from chaos, in learning to control the dread energy of life itself?

Something urgent, something possible that he could do, seemed almost on the point of appearing to him. He hardly dared lift his eyes as the question echoed through him: What can I do? It was the same question he had cried out in the past years when perhaps he could have done something, when, if he had gone one step further, if he had exerted one more ounce of will against all who counseled "No," so much might have been averted. But that way, in such speculation, lay eternal guilt.

What can a man do? What can I do? What must I do? he wanted to beg, as he had begged in those other days when this poor girl, this woman in her anguish now, had been the presence of womanhood listening to the helplessness of man.

He must not wonder whether the thought could come to
Marianne that all this was because of him, of his failures,
of his presence.

Because of what, then? Of whom? Of Remy himself? Of
Kraus? Of a nation? A leader? Of existence itself? Of
God?

He turned his eyes to Frère Luc. All they could say to
each other was for now in abeyance. Yet some link remained that both separated and bound them: in each, some
vow, some urge, inextinguishable, unbroken.

For Meyer Levin, *The Stronghold* is a milestone, an adventure in form—a book that, following the conventions of the novel of hour-to-hour suspense, uses them to voice, with compressed and intensified power, the author's lifelong concern with the great issues of our time.

The Stronghold of the title is an ancient baronial castle—with moat and drawbridge, turrets and parapets outlined against snowy peaks—now a fortress deep in the Nazi redoubt. The time is the last day of World War II.

Inside the castle a dozen prisoners await liberation. These are no ordinary men. Political hostages—the ex-leaders of an Occupied Country—they include Cabinet members, an army marshal, bankers, a priest—and one woman, mistress of one of the ex-Premiers. On this last day, as the rescuing American army approaches, a final hostage arrives— the beloved elder statesman, Vered, ex. Prime Minister and a Jew—brou,